Chapter 1

Vidya Munasinghe sat on the floor, phone in hand, outside the bathroom in the cosy flat she shared with her sister and her best friend. Her younger sister, Udeni, was currently on the other side of the bathroom door, crying in little sniffling sobs.

'It'll be okay,' Vidya said. She didn't really think it would be, but this was more about being there for her sister than actually helping.

'What if it's positive?' came the slightly panicky voice from the other side of the door.

It would be positive. Even without the late period, Vidya had noticed the way her sister fell asleep watching *Strictly* and the way she rubbed her tummy with a puzzled expression at mealtimes. 'Let's wait and see,' she said.

How had this even happened? Since Udeni said she was three weeks late, the most likely time for her to have become pregnant was in February, when Udeni had been Vidya's plus one for the office party and pulled a random guy. For the last few months, Udeni had been working long hours at her new job in arts fund-raising. Going to the office party had been the one time she'd let her hair down and she'd gone overboard with the fun … so it *had* to be the guy from the office.

The timer beeped. 'Two minutes,' Vidya called out.

There was a moment of pained silence, then a little shriek. Yup. Positive. Vidya felt her heart grow heavier. She grabbed her phone and stood up.

If her little sister was pregnant, Vidya would support her. Whatever Udeni wanted to do. Vidya took a deep breath and reminded herself that Udeni was a twenty-five-year-old adult. She had to resist the urge to jump in and fix things, like she usually did. This time, big sister or not, she must not interfere. Only support.

Letting out her breath, Vidya knocked on the door. 'Nangi?'

The door opened and Udeni hurled herself into Vidya's arms. She sobbed, 'What am I going to do?'

All thoughts of recrimination vanished as Vidya tightened her arms around her sister's shaking shoulders. This was a major cataclysm in Udeni's life. There were no easy answers. Vidya rubbed her sister's back. 'It'll be okay, sweetheart, we'll work this out together. It'll be okay.'

A few hours and a lot of tissues later, Vidya made them both hot chocolates. She would have dearly loved a glass of wine about now, but it seemed rude when Udeni couldn't have any.

Her sister was sitting on the sofa, blanket tucked over her drawn-up knees, eyes puffy.

Thankfully, their housemate, Angie, was out this evening. Although maybe her presence might have helped.

The resemblance between the sisters was noticeable, but physically, they looked very different. Udeni was slim and willowy while Vidya was built for stability. Udeni had a pixie cut that made her features look exaggerated and elfin, while Vidya had similar facial features but with long black hair that came down her shoulders. Both had their father's big brown eyes and their mother's cupid's bow mouth.

'Here.' Vidya handed her sister the hot chocolate and sat down beside her. 'Can you drink that without feeling sick?'

Praise for Jeevani Charika

'Jeevani Charika has the perfect touch with character, story and sensitive subjects. I'm ready for her next book already.' **Sue Moorcroft**, *Sunday Times* bestselling author

'A love story as warm and comforting as a wearable blanket . . . So enjoyable and engaging it got me through a bout of Covid. (Are you allowed to put "Better than paracetamol" on a book jacket? Because this really worked.)' **K.J. Charles**, author of *The Secret Lives of Country Gentlemen*

'I totally loved this book . . . A beautiful tale of true love overcoming all obstacles.' **Kathleen McGurl**, author of *The Lost Child*

'A rollicking read with a fresh take on my favourite enemies-to-lovers trope. The perfect weekend read.' **Rebecca Raisin**, author of *Summer at the Santorini Bookshop*

Stephen Armishaw Photography

JEEVANI CHARIKA (pronounced 'Jeev-uh-nee') writes multi-cultural women's fiction and romantic comedies. She spent much of her childhood in Sri Lanka, with short forays to Nigeria and Micronesia, before returning to England to settle in Yorkshire. All of this, it turned out, was excellent preparation for becoming a novelist.

She also writes under the name Rhoda Baxter. Her books have been shortlisted for multiple awards.

A microbiologist by training, Jeevani loves all things science geeky. She also loves cake, crochet and playing with Lego. You can find out more about her (and get a free book) on her website www.jeevanicharika.com.

Also by Jeevani Charika

The Winner Bakes It All
Picture Perfect
Playing for Love
Knowing Me Knowing You

How Can I Resist You?

JEEVANI CHARIKA

ONE PLACE. MANY STORIES

HQ
An imprint of HarperCollins*Publishers* Ltd
1 London Bridge Street
London SE1 9GF

www.harpercollins.co.uk

HarperCollins*Publishers*
Macken House, 39/40 Mayor Street Upper,
Dublin 1 D01 C9W8
This edition 2025

1

First published in Great Britain by HQ,
an imprint of HarperCollins*Publishers* Ltd 2025

ISBN: 9780008745233

Printed and bound in the UK using 100% Renewable
Electricity by CPI Group (UK) Ltd

MIX
Paper | Supporting
responsible forestry
FSC™ C007454

This book contains FSC™ certified paper and other controlled sources
to ensure responsible forest management.

For more information visit: www.harpercollins.co.uk/green

To the awesome aunties

Udeni nodded. She untucked the blanket and held up one side, so that Vidya could slide in beside her. 'Thank you,' she said. 'What am I going to do?'

The way she looked at Vidya was as though she expected her to have a solution. This was always how it was. Vidya was the sensible one, who didn't take risks and didn't have adventures, but lived her life in her sensible groove. Udeni was the one who acted first, thought later. When they were children, Vidya often had to look out for her younger sister, who was too cute and too carefree to be left unsupervised. And this had carried through to adulthood. Vidya didn't meet her sister's eye for a moment, while she tamped down all the feelings she couldn't feel right now. 'Well,' she said, carefully, in case it prompted another flood of tears. 'What do you want to do?'

Udeni stared at the floor for a long while. Vidya waited. She would hate to have to make such a huge decision. Logically, the most sensible option would be to contact a clinic and ask about options to terminate. Udeni's career was just getting started and a baby really wouldn't fit into her life right now. But they'd been brought up in a Buddhist household. Neither of them was religious, but these influences ran deeper than one expected. If it were her, Vidya had no idea which option she would choose.

Udeni turned her head, eyes wet. 'I think,' she said. 'I think I'd be a good mum.' It sounded more like a question than a statement.

Vidya nodded. 'I agree.' She did, honestly. Udeni might be reckless at times, but there was no doubt that her baby would be loved to bits by Mum and Aunt. After a period of horror and bewilderment, Udeni's parents would adore their grandchild too.

'But it's a lot, isn't it?' her sister said, with unusual prescience.

'Yes. It will be. But you won't be alone,' Vidya said. 'I'll be here too.' She looked around the flat and mentally rearranged it. It had three bedrooms and was quite spacious by London standards; she and Udeni had the two double ones and Angie rented the single one. The open-plan living room and kitchen were tiny. The baby's cot would be in Udeni's room, obviously. If they swapped her bed for a single, there would be enough room in there for all the baby's stuff. They could get rid of some of the knickknacks and the cactus plants—

She was interrupted by Udeni throwing her arms around her and squeezing. 'Thank you. Thank you. You're the best big sister ever.'

Vidya smiled and hugged her back. 'I am, right?'

'This baby is going to be so loved.' Udeni let her go and sat back, eyes shining. She was clearly painting a rosy picture in her head.

Vidya blew on her hot chocolate and took a cautious sip. The baby was an abstract concept at the moment. Before that, there was a whole pregnancy to get through. She glanced sideways at her sister. Not to mention telling their parents. That was going to be the worst thing. Good Sri Lankan girls didn't get pregnant outside of marriage. And definitely not after a one-night stand. The worst part was that her parents would blame her as well, not just Udeni. She should have looked after her sister better. She was the one who took her to the party. Who 'let' her drink too much and go off with a stranger. Like she can stop Udeni when she decides to party. She shook her head and took another sip.

'What?'

She turned to find Udeni looking at her. The light in her expression dimmed. 'You're thinking about things. You're judging me, aren't you?'

She could have denied it, but … that wouldn't be true. 'I mean …' she said. 'It's not an ideal situation, is it?'

Udeni made a face. 'I didn't mean for this to happen.' She stared at a spot on the floor again. 'I'm pretty sure we used a condom.'

Vidya had to take a deep breath before she answered. 'Pretty sure?'

A shrug. 'Yeah. I always have one in my purse. It wasn't there the next day, so …'

This worried Vidya, more than a little. Someone that drunk shouldn't be able to give consent, surely. Except Udeni had been adamant that she'd really liked him and had no regrets.

'I guess it's too late to worry about it now,' Vidya said. They had more pressing things to think about. 'The main thing is to get you an appointment with the GP.'

'I'll call them first thing tomorrow,' Udeni said. 'And I'll order some books about pregnancy.'

This was good. She was taking the pregnancy seriously. At least she wasn't going into ostrich mode, which Udeni had been known to do. It had taken several overdue bills and a loan from Vidya for her to learn that ignoring credit card bills didn't make them go away.

Udeni was quiet for a few minutes. 'See. We have a plan.'

Vidya was about to point out that this was nowhere near a plan, when one of their phones started to ring. They both used a particular ringtone for WhatsApp calls from their parents. Vidya looked at her phone. It wasn't hers. She looked up to find Udeni staring at her ringing phone like it was a poisonous creature.

Their parents were away. They'd embraced early retirement and decided to travel to all the places they'd been putting off visiting. At the moment, they were in Central America on a tour.

'Shit. Shit. What do we do?' Udeni had gone grey. 'Do I tell them?'

Vidya's own heart rate increased. Her parents were going to go seven types of bananas when they found out. She rubbed her hands over her face. 'No. Let's wait a bit. It's still early days for you.'

'Yes. Good idea. Things can go wrong in the first twelve weeks.' Udeni was nodding but still holding her ringing phone like it was about to explode.

'And we should at least find out who the father is, before we tell them.' Vidya braced herself for a backlash.

'But why? I don't want to tell him—'

'Yes, but *you* at least need to know.'

'What for? I wouldn't want him to help.'

'You'll want him to contribute financially, though. Babies are expensive.' This was exactly what she'd feared would happen. Udeni would just hope that if she ignored things, the hard questions would just disappear. It took all her self-control not to shout. 'You need to have some options,' she said calmly. 'And most of them require knowing who the father is.'

'I suppose,' Udeni said, still staring at the phone. When it stopped ringing, they both breathed out. Udeni turned to Vidya. 'So, you reckon we get our shit together first and then tell them.'

'When they get back from their holiday, yes. That way we can always say we didn't tell them because we didn't want to worry them when they were away.'

The colour in Udeni's face was slowly returning to its normal light brown. 'That makes sense,' she said. 'You are really good at this.'

She really wasn't. The whole idea was huge and terrifying. Vidya jumped when her own phone started to ring. Her parents were trying to call her now. 'Let's tell them we couldn't find your phone,' she said. 'You do it.'

'Okay,' said Udeni. 'They'd see right through you.'

So, when Vidya hit accept and their parents appeared on the screen, it was Udeni who said brightly, 'Did you just try calling my phone? I couldn't find it in time. How are you?'

Vidya let Udeni do most of the talking, content to smile and nod, and add the odd comment when needed. She honestly didn't know how Udeni did this, pretending everything was fine, when it clearly wasn't.

It all went well until Udeni passed her the phone and said, 'I'm sorry. I really need a wee.'

Suddenly, Vidya was under her mother's scrutiny. 'What is wrong with your sister?'

'What?' How *did* she know things?

'Udeni looks tired. Her eyes are really puffy. She didn't say she was ill, so …' Amma's face moved closer. 'Have you let her go out drinking again?'

Vidya tried not to cringe. 'She's an adult. If she wants to go out, how can I stop her?'

'Aha. So, she has been going out drinking too much. You have to tell her to stop. You can really damage yourself by drinking too much, you know. And it can make you do really silly things. It's dangerous these days with everyone having cameras.'

Vidya managed not to say 'too late'. Vidya stared at a spot on the wall, and let her mother's voice wash over her. Conversations with her parents always ended up here. With her being held responsible for her sister's behaviour.

'The point is that you have to talk to your sister.'

'Amma. She's not a child. I can't tell her what to do. She doesn't listen to me anymore.' And she really needed to start working things out by herself. Especially now!

'Don't be silly, your sister worships you.'

Her father's face appeared at her mother's side. He seemed to be holding a doughnut. 'Are you well?' he asked her. 'Nothing worrying you?'

She really hoped her face didn't give anything away. 'I'm okay. Working hard, you know.'

'How is it going with the A … I?' He always paused between the letter A and I.

Work was safe territory. 'It's going well actually. I'm learning how to create queries that will do what we want it to do. It's a bit like learning a new dialect. It's really interesting.'

She chatted for a few minutes more, until Udeni came back and distracted them by talking about a new art exhibition she was involved in at work. Sometime in the middle of this, Angie came home and popped her head into the conversation to say, 'Hello, Aunty, hello, Uncle', before she ran off to change out of her work clothes.

The whole thing was making Vidya's head hurt. It was a huge relief when her parents finally hung up.

Udeni put the phone carefully down on the blanket. 'I think we got away with it.'

They sat together for a moment, Vidya finally drinking her hot chocolate. Angie came out, now in jeans and an oversized fleece. She stopped and stared at them. 'What's going on? Why are you both looking worried?'

Vidya let Udeni tell her the news. Angie was Vidya's best friend from school and was almost part of the family. She was the reason Vidya had applied for the job she had now. They worked in the same enormous open-plan office.

Angie sank onto the chair opposite. 'Oh, wow,' she said. 'I guess … congratulations?'

'Thanks,' said Udeni. 'I think.'

'Are you … um …?'

'I'm keeping it,' said Udeni.

'Neither of us will judge you if you wanted to—'

'I'm keeping it.'

Angie shot Vidya a glance. Vidya shrugged. If Udeni wanted to keep the baby, it was definitely her choice. But Vidya knew once the shock had subsided, she'd be relieved that her sister hadn't decided on the other option.

'Okay,' said Angie. 'Wow. How do you feel about this? Happy? Excited?'

Udeni chewed her lip. 'Terrified, mostly.' She turned to Vidya and said in a smaller voice, 'Akka. How do I handle this?'

'Are you asking me for advice?' That was a turn-up for the books. Usually, Udeni was shouting about how she didn't need Vidya's help, even though she always did.

'Don't be a cow,' said Udeni. 'I've never been in trouble like this before.'

This disarmed Vidya. Her sister was normally so sure of herself, even when she was wrong. If she was actually asking, she must really be scared.

Vidya set her hot chocolate down, put an arm around Udeni and gave her a hug. 'I'm here for you.'

Udeni sniffed and laid her head on Vidya's shoulder. Angie came and joined them, squeezing onto the sofa on the other side of Udeni. 'I'm here too.'

The idea that Vidya was going to be helping her sister raise a baby was too large a thing for her to comprehend. For now, she had to focus on the steps in front of her. Udeni needed support. Finding out who the baby's father was seemed like a good place to start.

Chapter 2

Leo Jones spotted an empty table and took two pints over to it. The pub was old and had beams low enough that he had to stoop to get under them. The walls were decorated with old theatre posters, giving the place a pleasant bohemian feel. The table he'd spotted was underneath a poster for *A Winter's Tale*. Leo carefully sat so that he had his back to it. His friend, Caleb, was late, but at least that gave Leo a few minutes to let what had happened at the meeting sink in. He wasn't the best at reading the room, but even he knew that things hadn't gone well. Leo tapped his fingers on the table and frowned.

Caleb arrived, his coat speckled with rain. He spotted Leo and hurried over. 'Sorry I'm late. That took longer than I expected.'

Leo gestured with his chin at the second pint glass in front of him. 'I ordered you a beer.' They had been friends long enough that he knew what Caleb liked. It had been an unexpected delight when Caleb joined him at Askew, Else and Thomas a few months ago. Now he got to share an office with someone who understood him well enough to not try to distract him with chit-chat when he was trying to work.

'Ah. Lovely.' Caleb draped his coat over the chair and sat down. His eyes drifted to the poster. 'Hah,' he said.

Leo rolled his eyes.

'So …' Caleb said, after a few minutes of companionable silence. 'The meeting with Charlie. Want to talk about it?'

He didn't want to talk about it, but he probably should. 'What was I supposed to do? He had missed a tranche of due diligence. If I'd kept quiet, and there'd been a problem, then the client would have lost money.'

'Yes, but you could have done it quietly: taken him aside and mentioned it; given him a chance to save face.' Caleb took a sip of his beer and shook his head. 'You have no sense of self-preservation. I just hope you don't take me out with you.'

Leo knew this was a joke, but the thought still bothered him. Caleb was more junior than he was. He would hate for Caleb's career at the law firm to be impacted by something he did. Or an enemy he had made. 'I'll do my best to make sure that doesn't happen,' he said, solemnly. 'My mistakes shouldn't affect you. If there is any fallout, I'll make sure everyone knows that it has nothing to do with you.'

Caleb stared at him for a moment then said, slowly, 'Leo. I don't think you need to worry about me. I didn't upset the boss. You did. It's not a case of the team being rubbish, is it? We're pretty good. It's just you being annoying. Just … don't antagonise Charlie any more than you have to, okay?'

Leo sighed. This was easier said than done. Charlie must have been a good lawyer at one time, but now, he was so concerned with high level things like efficiency and maximising income that he no longer cared about the details. Leo, on the other hand, loved details.

'I never had this sort of thing happen with Penny.' Penny's retirement had brought about many changes. The worst of which was her teams being reassigned to Charles Bexworth Huxley's area.

They drank in silence for a bit, then Caleb, who could never be down for long, said, 'Hey, at least we've got a bit of time away from the office in a few weeks. Did you manage to get Sarah for our administrator?'

Leo was grateful for the change of subject. 'I did. And you're right. Maybe a few weeks away from Charlie's sight will do us all some good.'

Caleb nodded, not smiling. 'But seriously, mate, watch your step around Charlie. You embarrassed him by showing up his mistake. There's no telling what he'll do to get his revenge.'

Vidya braced herself to ask the question that had been bothering her all night. It had been a few hours since the shock of the pregnancy test now and Udeni might be in a more responsive frame of mind. 'What about … what about the father? Of the baby, I mean …'

Udeni shook her head. 'I don't want to tell him.'

'So, you do know who he is?' Then, realising what that sounded like, she added, 'I mean, do you remember his name?'

Udeni looked up, her cheeks reddening under the brown. She shook her head. 'I was trying to think last night … but it was … you know … It was dark and we'd been drinking and there was the mask.'

Oh, dear. Vidya kept her voice as steady as she could. 'Okay, let's make working out who he is our priority. Why don't you tell us what you do remember?'

'Hang on, a mask?' said Angie. 'What?'

'At the office thirtieth anniversary party,' said Vidya. 'Fancy dress, remember?'

Angie's eyes grew huge. 'It was someone you met at the office party? Someone we work with? Oh my God.'

Udeni pursed her lips. 'Now you're definitely judging me.'

Vidya bit back the response she would have liked to make. 'He was wearing a suit and a rabbit mask, right?' She glanced over to corroborate; Udeni nodded.

'Oh. Oh,' said Angie. 'That narrows it down to Legal Team B.

Those were the guys who turned up late wearing identical rabbit masks and their work suits. They looked like something out of a gangster movie when they walked in. I remember.'

Vidya slipped out from under the blanket and returned with her laptop. She typed the company's web address and navigated to the staff pages. 'So, it's one of these guys.'

Team B had six members in it.

'We can rule out the two women, I assume,' said Vidya.

Udeni tilted her head and studied the pictures of the men. She chewed her lip. 'I don't think he was Black … No. He wasn't.'

That left three white guys about her age. Angie read their names, Piotr Kowalski, Leo Jones and Caleb Fotherill. 'Okay. Any other clues?'

'Like I said,' replied Udeni, 'it was dark. We didn't turn the light on in the room.'

Angie raised her eyebrows.

'There was quite a lot of light coming in through the windows … and, you know, we were in a hurry.'

Which was too much information to know about your little sister, really. 'Okay. Anything else you can remember that might help us narrow it down between these three guys?' Vidya said. 'But *nothing* a sister doesn't need to know, please.'

Udeni tipped her head back against the sofa. 'He was sexy and tall – I had to look up to kiss him.'

That wasn't helpful. Udeni was only five foot three.

'Okay.'

'He was funny and, you know, thoughtful, and he was a good dancer.'

Vidya shook her head. 'Still not helping us narrow it down here. Anything physical that might distinguish these three guys?'

They all looked at the colour photos. All three men were wearing suits and standing in the same pose, arms crossed, bodies angled slightly, looking at the camera. Leo had cropped brown hair and dark eyes, Piotr also had short dark hair and brown eyes, Caleb had dark curls and blue eyes. Only Caleb was smiling.

'Hair? Curly or straight?'

'Soft,' said Udeni. 'I don't remember if it was curly or not. Sorry.'

They might have different haircuts by now. These photos were probably a few years old.

'Eyes?'

Another shake of her head. 'Can't remember. They were nice eyes. Smiley.'

Vidya swallowed the urge to roll her eyes. 'You must remember *something* that identifies him.'

'He had a tattoo,' said Udeni.

'Oh, that'll help. Maybe Angie and I could see it on him in the office. Is it somewhere visible in workwear?'

Udeni shook her head. 'It was here.' She gestured to the front of her shoulder, just above her breast. 'It was something magical,' she said. 'Like a creature from Harry Potter or something. About this big.' She held her fingers about three inches apart.

'You can remember a three-inch tattoo on his chest but you can't remember his face well enough to pick him from a line-up of three?'

Udeni shrugged. 'It was dark. And we took turns with the mask. It was funny at the time.'

Ew. Ew. 'Too much information.'

Her sister shrugged again. 'You asked.'

Angie had been quietly typing on her phone for a while. She put it down. 'I think you can disqualify that guy.' She pointed.

'Leo Jones?' Vidya read off the website. 'Why?'

'He's a real miserable sod. I don't think he's even got a sense of humour, so he's not likely to be funny, and I think he'd rather gouge his own eyeballs out than dance.'

Both the sisters turned to look at her.

'Wow,' said Udeni. 'What did he do to you?'

'Me? Nothing. I just know a few people who have worked with

14

him. Apparently, he's difficult to work with and generally very cranky. I just double checked it was him.' She waved her phone. 'I didn't want to rule out the wrong guy.'

They all stared at the serious face in the photo of Leo Jones.

'Well,' said Udeni. 'My guy was definitely not cranky. He was funny and sweet.'

'So, we're down to two,' Angie said.

'Any goss on the other two?'

Angie tapped the picture of Piotr. 'I've worked with him. He's really nice and fun. He could be your guy.' She pointed to Caleb. 'I haven't worked with him – he's only been at the company for eight months or so. From what I've heard, he's nice too. He even gets on with grumpy Leo, but apart from that … I know nothing. Certainly, nothing that would rule him out as the baby daddy.'

Vidya sighed. 'Okay. So … they've both got dark hair, a good sense of humour and are potentially good dancers. That still doesn't help us distinguish between them.'

'And there's the tattoo.'

'Which is not in a place that we would be able to see at work and we don't even know what it is exactly.' She closed the laptop and rubbed her face. 'Oh, God.'

'It's a pity we can't just ask,' Angie said, gloomily.

Vidya rolled her eyes at Angie. 'At work? Can you imagine?'

Angie grinned. 'You'd be hauled into HR so fast.'

Udeni looked from one to the other. 'Wait, why?'

'We've had a lot of "appropriate behaviour in the workplace" discussions lately,' said Vidya. 'A lot.'

Angie leaned forward. 'One of the male managers got drunk at an event and asked people personal questions about their sex lives. It made everyone really uncomfortable, and it got reported. Then the company decided everyone should have training because they didn't want to be *that* sort of workplace.'

Udeni frowned. 'Isn't this a slightly different situation?'

'Not really,' said Vidya. 'Me rocking up and asking someone

15

if they'd slept with my sister, who was too drunk to remember who she slept with … that would have consequences. Especially if it's the wrong guy and they take it the wrong way.' She shook her head. 'We need to find out which one it is first, before we do anything else.'

'Or we could agree we're not going to tell the father,' said Udeni.

Vidya contemplated this for a minute, trying to be supportive, but it was too preposterous to get her head around. 'How can you not want to know?' she demanded. 'Apart from all the practical stuff, like money. This child …' she gestured to her sister's belly, '… this child is going to have half his characteristics. All you've got is tall, funny, sexy, good dancer. Don't you want to know *more*?'

Udeni was quiet for a moment. 'I suppose it would be good to know a bit more about him from that point of view.'

'So, we *need* to narrow it down between these two guys,' Vidya pressed. How was she the only one seeing the importance of this? 'And most children want to know about their parents, so when the child is old enough to ask, you should be able to tell them.' She looked at Angie for support, but she said nothing.

'I suppose it would be handy to know if there are any illnesses in the family,' Udeni said. She turned to their housemate. 'What do you think, Ange?'

Angie looked from one sister to the other. 'I think … I think it's your choice,' she said, carefully. 'But if it were me, I'd want to know. In case I change my mind about telling him.'

Udeni stared at the wall opposite for a moment. 'I don't think I would ever want to tell him,' she said. Her hand wrapped protectively around her still flat midriff. 'But yeah. I see your point that if the baby wants to know later on, I should at least be able to tell them.'

Vidya held her breath.

After a few more seconds, Udeni said, 'Okay. Let's find out which one it is. You can't tell him though.'

'Of course,' Vidya said. Thank goodness Udeni was seeing sense. Her little sister was impulsive and anything that helped keep her options open at this stage was a good thing. 'So, how do we do this?'

Angie typed into her phone. 'Apparently, Piotr's in the US at the moment,' she said. 'But I know enough people he's worked with; I can try and find out more.'

'Any chance you could get assigned as admin assistant for the team?'

Angie shook her head. 'Not for the next couple of months. I'm with Team A for the next six weeks. How about you?'

'I ... could try.' Normally, Vidya was part of the admin support team, but for the last year and a half, she'd been working with the IT team, first with digital archiving and now on a project to safely incorporate AI into their working practices. She hadn't worked as a paralegal administrator for a while. It was highly unlikely that she was going to be able to pick and choose which projects she got assigned. 'It would really help if I had more to go on, so that I can figure out which one of these two guys it is.'

'I'm sure you can work it out.' Udeni looked at her with an expression full of trust. 'I know you can.'

Vidya stared at her sister's big eyes and, as she always did, melted. 'Fine. I'll see what I can do,' she said.

Chapter 3

A week later, Vidya sat in the weekly team meeting. She had already given her update about the AI project and how they were slowly rolling it out. Making her stay for the whole meeting was just a ridiculous power play on her manager's part.

While Harry, her manager, droned on about other projects they were supporting, she ran through her plan. It had been a whole week and Udeni hadn't changed her mind about keeping the baby, so this was really happening. Which meant she had to make good on her promise to try to find out some information about the father of the child. Before she could do that, she had to confirm which one of the guys had a tattoo on his chest. Of some sort of magical creature. Udeni was so vague. It was so unhelpful. She looked down at her notepad, where she'd doodled a stick figure and a rudimentary sorting hat.

The words 'Legal Team B' caught her attention and caused her to startle. Her empty mug clattered to the floor, and Harry stopped talking to look at her. 'Everything okay, Vidya?'

'Yes. Sorry. Dropped my mug.' She retrieved it.

'As I was saying,' Harry continued, 'Legal Team B are being sent up to Waterloo Bay on the North East coast to do the due diligence on a hotel that the Somersby chain wants to take over.

They have requested admin support and specifically requested Sarah.'

Everyone nodded. Sarah, a pleasant Black woman in her fifties, said, 'I know about that. That's in four weeks' time. That'll be fine.'

'They want it done sooner,' said Harry. 'So, it's actually next week.'

'Oh … oh, no can do,' said Sarah. 'I'm on holiday for two weeks from next week.'

'But they asked for you specifically.'

Someone laughed. 'I expect that's because it's with Leo Jones. No one else wants to work with him.'

'That's right,' said Harry. 'Leo Jones and Caleb Fotherill. And we know you work well with them, Sarah.'

Vidya sat up straighter. Caleb was one of the potential candidates for operation baby daddy. Leo Jones was the one that Angie was certain they could disqualify.

'Except I won't be working with anyone for two weeks,' said Sarah, pointedly. 'Because I'm on holiday.'

'Oh. Right. Yes. Well, in that case we'll have to send someone else.' He looked around the table as a lot of people tried to make themselves as inconspicuous as possible. 'Clearly, you're all keen,' he said sarcastically. 'How about this – any volunteers?'

Vidya's heart sped up a notch. Here was a chance for her to work alongside two of the three guys and subtly find out more about them without resorting to weird and intrusive questions. This was an opportunity. She had to take it. 'I'll do it.'

Everyone turned to look at her.

'Vids, it's eight days. With Leo "are you sure you've done this right, check it again" Jones,' someone said.

'Sure.' She cast about for a good reason. 'Legal have had the AI assistant for a while and aren't using it. It would be good to find out why not. Besides, I … could do with a break. Er. Sea air.'

'You'll mostly be seeing the inside of the legal archive room.'

'I don't mind.'

'Well, that's excellent,' said Harry, writing something down. 'Come talk to me later about the details. Thanks, Vidya. Now, moving on to the next item.'

Vidya sat very still and stared at the doodle on her notepad. Okay. Step one was on its way.

'What do you mean, Sarah's not available?' Leo demanded down the phone. He was in the office he shared with Caleb. 'I spoke to her about this last week.'

'But the dates have changed.' Harry, the head of the administrators, sounded tired and apologetic on the other end of the line.

'They have?' Leo clicked on his emails. Had he missed one? He scrolled through the unread ones. As he scanned the screen, an email popped up. He swore.

He glanced over the half partition at Caleb, who was frowning quizzically at him. 'Did you know the dates for the Somersby hotel thing had changed?'

Caleb's eyes were focused on his computer. 'Just seen it. Oh, the timescales have shrunk too. We've got about eight days to get it done. Are we getting more people? That's not enough time otherwise.'

'Not that I've heard of.' Leo scanned the email again. 'This is an impossible task to do in that time.' He turned his attention back to the phone. 'Harry, can we have an extra administrator? There isn't enough time to get the work done with just three people. We'll have to come to some other—'

'I've spoken to Charlie and he says that you and Caleb were still the best people for the job. He's confident you can do it with only one other person on the team. I've found you an administrator who is free to come with you. At very short notice, I might add. You're just going to have to manage.' Harry's voice was clipped.

Charlie. If his boss had agreed on their behalf, there wasn't much he could do about it. 'Is there any chance we can have more time then?'

'Look, Leo. I don't think so. You'll have to talk to Charlie, but this is Somersby. You know what they're like.'

The Somersby chain of hotels were a big client. They had been acquiring a lot of smaller hotels lately. They were very relaxed about what they were billed for but expected huge amounts of flexibility from the team in return. Leo hated that.

He would try talking to Charlie, but he doubted he'd get anywhere.

'Okay, fine,' he said. 'Email me and Caleb the details. We have to be in Brussels on the fifteenth. So, we'll have to head back to London that morning at the latest.'

'Noted,' said Harry.

Leo remembered to say 'thank you' before he put the phone down.

When he'd hung up, Leo put his head in his hands. 'Aargh. Charlie. He did this on purpose, didn't he?'

Caleb wheeled his chair to the side, so that he could peer round the computer screen at Leo. 'Well, if you antagonise the boss in front of his friends …'

'But I was right.'

Leo re-read the email a third time. 'I had it all arranged with Sarah to do our admin support. Damn it all.'

'Is Sarah busy next week?'

'She's going on her cruise, remember.' He glanced over and saw Caleb quickly cover up his blank expression. Fair enough. Caleb didn't know Sarah as well as Leo did. 'She needs a break,' he said, quietly. 'It's the first holiday she's had since her aunt died. She's been spending most of her evenings and weekends sorting out her aunt's stuff.'

He liked Sarah. She was an extremely competent administrator. One of the few people that he could trust to get everything right without having to check her work. They had learned to work together when they'd been assigned to a project together a few years ago, and now they were friends. Sarah was always their administrator.

Caleb grinned. 'So, you're going to have to work with a new person? Oof. Am I going to need to pack body armour?'

Leo glared at his friend.

Caleb sobered up. 'Seriously though, I know what you're like. Don't give this new person a hard time.'

'I don't give people a hard time. I just like to be thorough.'

Caleb raised his eyebrows. Leo sighed. 'Fine. I will do my best to deal with the uncertainty without having to check their work. Okay?'

'Good. If there's something you want checked, why don't you send me in to do it?' Caleb's smile was back. 'I have people skills that you don't.'

Leo nodded. 'I'll bear that in mind.'

He opened the email again and re-read it, slowly this time, so that he could be sure he'd absorbed the information. He looked at the administrator's name. Vidya. He didn't think he knew her. He stared at the name for a moment and drummed his fingers. Then he called Sarah.

'I know, I know,' she said, without even saying hello. 'But I can't come to the north with you.'

'I wasn't going to ask you to. You're on holiday,' he said. 'I'm offended you think I'd forgotten. I put it in my work calendar. Specifically, so that I could avoid anything that required too much admin support during that time.'

Sarah gave a little laugh. 'I'm sorry, Leo.'

He grunted. 'Tell me about this Vidya person, then. Is she any good?'

'She's very good,' said Sarah, firmly. 'You have nothing to worry about. She's practical and thorough.'

That was reassuring, he supposed. Sarah's judgement on competence was probably sound. 'Hmm,' he said.

'She's nice,' said Sarah. 'I'll have a chat with her, if you like.'

'Could you? That would be good. Getting to know how people work, and all that, takes so long, and we really don't have much time.'

Another soft laugh. 'Caleb says you're freaking out,' said Sarah. 'Relax, Leo. It'll be fine.'

He would believe it when he saw it. He changed the subject. 'How did it go with your aunt's flat? All sorted?'

'I think so. It's empty now, so the estate agent can come and take photos. Thank you for your help at the weekend.'

'Oh, it was nothing.' He had spent some time helping Sarah pack and shift boxes to give to charity. He was glad that he had, because there was too much stuff for one person to deal with, and Sarah was clearly exhausted. He could still hear the tiredness in her voice. She needed this holiday.

'Ah, you're a good man, for all your funny ways,' said Sarah.

There wasn't much he could say to that, so he said, 'Well, enjoy your holiday. Come back refreshed.'

'I will.'

After Leo had hung up, Caleb peered around his computer monitor.

'Did you tell Sarah I was freaking out?' Leo demanded. 'I'm not freaking out. I'm having perfectly legitimate concerns over staffing and time frames for this project.'

Caleb rolled his eyes. 'You are freaking out. Just a little bit.'

They stared at each other for a moment. Aside from Sarah, Caleb was probably the only other person that he worked smoothly and in sync with. This project was going to be difficult, but he had Caleb with him. Maybe it would be okay.

'I'd best get this done, now that I'm suddenly much busier than I was,' Leo said. He threw another glare at Caleb. 'Stop gossiping with Sarah about me.'

Caleb grinned. 'Oh, but it's so much fun.'

Leo shook his head. He opened the folder he was working on.

A lot of the standard contracts were digital only now. He could work with them, but he did like to review things on paper. He smoothed the page down and started to read. There was something so reliable about paper.

Chapter 4

Leo got out of the car and stretched his arms. It was the following Monday. He and Caleb had taken turns driving up to the North East in a hire car. Waterloo Bay, it turned out, was hours and hours and hours away. At least they hadn't had to go across London to pick Vidya up. She was coming on the train later.

'I can smell the sea,' Caleb said, breathing in and thumping his chest like some sort of cave man.

'It's just on the other side of that building.' Leo gestured to the hotel. He wasn't as full of energy as his friend, but it was nice to glimpse the water. Something of that childlike excitement at seeing the sea never left you, no matter how old you got.

'When's the admin person joining us?' Caleb bounced on the balls of his feet, loosening up.

'Her name is Vidya. She should be here this evening,' Leo said. They may not know her well, but the least they could do was remember her name. 'We should check in and then go have a little walk around, maybe?'

Vidya paid the taxi driver and remembered to get a receipt. It was only then that she finally turned to look at the hotel she was going to be working and staying in for the next eight days. The

Waterloo Bay Hotel was much bigger than she was expecting it to be. It was four floors of Victorian curlicues and ironwork, all backed by a fetching shade of pastel yellow and white. It was impressive.

When she turned, she was looking down towards the beach. The hotel was set a little way back and halfway up a hill. The gardens sloped down, crisscrossed by a path that descended through the foliage and ended up by the road far below. Across the road was the promenade and then the beach. Beyond that was the sea. She breathed in and tasted the salt in the air. Seagulls wheeled and screamed above her, voices and the odd sound of a car floated up from below and, behind it all, she heard the steady beat and wash of the sea.

Realising that she was gaping like a tourist, Vidya closed her mouth, grabbed the handle of her case and set off towards the porticoed entrance. She wasn't here to enjoy the seaside; she was here to work. Besides, she had a mission. Udeni was still wavering about whether to include the baby daddy. Someone had to be sensible and find out – so that if Udeni decided to tell the father, they knew for certain which guy to talk to. And as usual, the sensible one had to be Vidya.

She'd had a quick chat with Sarah and now knew that Caleb was charming and laid back but sometimes needed to be reminded to meet deadlines, and Leo was intense and aloof but was fine if you were good at your job, which was a bit of a worry. It had been a while since she'd done actual admin work. She was confident it would all come back to her. Who knows, maybe her time working in digitisation and AI might actually help.

She was almost certain now that the guy she needed to get intel on was Caleb. Leo didn't fit the description of tall, kind, sexy and a good dancer. Most of her colleagues who had worked with him described him as 'uptight', 'nitpicky' or 'a pain in the arse'. The only one who seemed to like him was Sarah, who, it turned out, thought he was wonderful and considered him a friend.

26

Vidya had a lot of respect for Sarah, who was not a woman to suffer fools gladly. But being friends with Sarah didn't exclude Leo from also being uptight and picky.

She had tried to subtly ask Sarah if she knew if the guys had tattoos. It had earned her a stern glare, and Sarah replied how the hell was she supposed to know that. At which point Vidya had decided it was best to let it go.

Just as she reached the impressive front steps of the hotel something landed on her head. Oh, no. She raised her hand and touched something wet. Ugh. Yuck, yuck, yuck. Muttering curses, she tried to flick it off her hair. But it ran down her forehead and she clamped her eyes shut. 'Aaaargh.'

Someone came up to her and thrust a tissue into her hand. A male voice said, 'Here. This should help.' Then added, 'Do you … want some help getting it out?'

She wiped the descending goop off her forehead.

'Here.' The tissue was removed from her hand and replaced with another. She couldn't see her helper, but he had a quiet, calm voice.

'Thanks.' She used that one too and cautiously opened her eyes. She was looking straight at a man with dark eyes that seemed to radiate concern. When she took a step back, she recognised him as Leo. Oh, this was embarrassing. She was supposed to be giving off super competent vibes, which was hard to do when you were swearing about bird poo in your hair.

'I … er … have I got it all?' She wiped her hands on a fresh tissue.

He examined her hair solemnly, giving her a moment to study him in return. He was handsome, in a classical kind of way, and had an air of precision about him. Everything he was wearing was neat. Flawless suit, ironed shirt, straight tie, even his hair was tidy. It seemed that Angie's assessment was right. This guy definitely didn't seem the type to have a one-night stand.

'You've removed most of the … er … solid bits, yes. The rest should wash out.' His gaze dropped to her hands. 'Oh, I'd wash those very carefully. Seagulls carry a lot of germs.'

She rubbed at her hairline. Gesturing towards his hand, where he was gingerly holding the used tissues, she said, 'You too.'

'In some places they say it's lucky if a bird poos on you,' said another voice, laughter threaded through it.

Caleb. The man who might have got off with her sister. She tamped down the irritation at his amusement and said, 'You must be Leo and Caleb. Hi. I'm Vidya. I'm helping you with your due diligence work. I would offer to shake your hands, but …'

'Sarah's replacement,' Leo said, mournfully.

'Oh, right. Hi.' Caleb glanced at Leo and rolled his eyes. 'Ignore him,' he said. 'He doesn't deal very well with change. It's nice to meet you, Vidya.'

'I guess I should go check in and see if I can do something about … this.' She waved a hand to indicate her hair.

'There are some toilets on the left as you go in,' said Leo. 'We'll bring your bag in for you.' Leo, still not smiling, took the handle. 'Come on.'

Vidya walked into the hotel with Caleb in front of her and Leo behind. She couldn't help feeling the situation had got away from her a bit.

Leo could still feel the bird poo on his hands from touching those tissues. He'd washed them already, but they still didn't feel clean. Spotting a hand sanitiser bottle at the reception desk, he took a detour to sanitise his hands before he went over to where Caleb was sitting, slumped back on one of the plush chairs, Vidya's suitcase standing next to him.

The hotel had once been grand but now felt faded. The atrium they were sitting in had a reception desk at one end and a wide-open space with tired-looking chairs clustered in groups. An enormous chandelier and a grand piano tucked away in the corner suggested that this room was sometimes used for events. Right now, it had an old-fashioned air of gentility about it.

He took the chair next to Caleb. 'I guess she's not come out yet?'

Caleb shrugged. 'Probably trying to wash the stuff out of her hair and then dry it under the hand dryer. That would take a bit of time, I guess.'

Leo imagined it would. She'd had her black hair in a plait over her shoulder. If she had to unplait it to clean it, it would take a very long time. His sisters usually took hours to do their hair. 'I suppose we have to wait and mind her luggage,' he said.

His friend gave him a sidelong glance. 'We're not on the clock yet.'

That was true. It was Monday evening. They didn't officially start the project until tomorrow. Tonight was meant to be about getting here, settling in and meeting the liaison from the hotel. Leo's leg twitched. He needed a walk. He had been sitting still or driving for far too long today and he needed to burn off some nervous energy. A brisk walk would have been ideal. Instead, they were sitting here waiting.

Caleb smiled. 'Be nice,' he said. 'She's not used to you like Sarah is. You have to put your human face on.'

What Caleb called his 'human face' was when Leo had to pad out his usual bluntness with meaningless phrases. He didn't see the point of it. He was still conveying the same information. Okay, maybe when imparting bad news or pointing out a flaw … but otherwise, what was the point? That said, it did seem to make a difference in a professional setting, so he did his best. It reminded him of his parents. *Emote, darling! Show more emotion. Not like that. More convincingly. Widen your eyes. That's better.*

'Vidya seems nice,' Caleb said. There was laughter in his voice again.

Leo tensed a little, sensing he was being teased. 'Hard to tell from the few minutes we spent with her.' Although, he realised now that he had met her before. He was pretty sure she was the woman who had been wearing that odd Zorro costume at the work anniversary party a couple of months ago.

'Pretty,' said Caleb.

Well, yes. He had spotted that. It was hard not to. Everything about her was generous – curves, lips, eyes. Such beautiful big eyes. He looked away. 'That's not exactly appropriate. She's a work colleague.'

'Just pointing it out, in case you hadn't noticed.'

He knew better than to respond to that. No matter what he said, Caleb would make a big deal of it and tease him. Caleb noticing a woman wasn't news, but he himself rarely did.

'She reminds me of someone,' Caleb said. 'Like, off the telly or something.'

Leo had no idea who that might be, so he just shook his head.

'From what I gather, she's single.' Caleb was still watching him. 'Caleb.'

'Right. Right. Work colleague,' said Caleb, grinning. 'Sarah says she's very efficient.' He looked down at his phone. 'She says, "please remind Leo that people are motivated by praise".' He tilted the phone to show him, where it did indeed say that.

Leo flicked a piece of lint off his leg. 'Yes. She told me that last week.'

He liked Sarah. She was a ruthlessly efficient administrator. They'd got to a point now where they barely needed to talk to each other at the start of a job. She did her bit, seamlessly making sure everything was in place for Leo and Caleb to do theirs. It was going to be hard having to train someone else to that level of efficiency. There was bound to be a lot of lag time where they were sitting around when they could have been working. Like they were doing right now.

'I miss Sarah,' Leo said, with feeling.

Caleb gave him a sympathetic nod. 'Maybe it'll be good for you to work with someone different. You know, see other people …'

Sarah had called Leo again to reassure him that Vidya was sensible and efficient. Rather worryingly, she'd also said, 'She's very good at automating systems and doing AI things. From what I heard of this project, you're going to need some of that to get you through the workload in time.'

This worried him more than he liked to let on. While he had no objection to AI-derived automation in principle, he didn't want to be the one to test it. He should probably tell Caleb what Sarah had said.

A smartly dressed woman with red hair came up to them. 'Excuse me, gentlemen, are you from the Somersby legal team?'

'Yes, we are.' Leo rose to his feet.

'I'm Stella. I'm your liaison person. Welcome to the Grand.' She had an East Yorkshire accent, which was a little different from what he'd come to expect as 'Northern'.

They shook hands. Stella looked around. 'I was expecting three of you.'

'Our colleague, Vidya, will be joining us,' Leo said. 'She had an encounter with a seagull, so she's just in the bathroom …'

'Oh, no,' said Stella. 'That's awful.'

He caught sight of Vidya walking across the room towards them, her hair had been scraped back into a low ponytail and looked damp. 'Here she comes now.'

Stella turned away from him to talk to Vidya. 'I heard you encountered the seagulls already. I'm so sorry. They are such a pain. They don't work for us, unfortunately, so we can't fire them.'

He watched as Vidya's serious expression was replaced with a smile. Caleb was right. She was pretty.

'I think I've washed most of it off,' Vidya said.

'Did it get on your clothes? We have a laundry service …'

'It's okay,' said Vidya. 'Luckily, I caught most of it in my hair, it seems.' She reached for her suitcase.

'Do you need a few moments to find your room?' said Stella. 'I was going to show you where you'll be working.'

Vidya glanced from Leo to Caleb and said, 'Just let me check in and then we'll stick to the plan.'

31

Efficient. That was good. Leo would happily drag her suitcase around for her if it meant getting this done on time. His legs were complaining; that walk was getting quite urgent. He reached for the bag, just as she did.

She looked up. 'It's okay,' she said. 'I've got it.'

Feeling slightly chastened, he followed them to the reception desk.

Chapter 5

Vidya felt a lot better once she'd finally had a shower. She dried her hair and put some clean clothes on. She debated whether to wear the pair of jeans she'd brought with her. The guys had both been in suits, but it was after hours now. After some dithering, she decided smart casual was the way to go and put on a dress with a cardigan over it.

Her hotel room was near the top of the building, which meant she had a wonderful view of the sea. The room itself was small, with just enough space for a desk, which doubled as a dressing table. Vidya opened the sliding door and stepped out onto the tiny balcony with its iron fretwork railings. There was only enough room to stand, but the view was spectacular. The late March sun shone weakly on the sea, casting it in a shifting, gleaming gunmetal grey. She was high enough up that the seagulls were mostly below her, annoying the tourists, although she noticed, warily, that they could fly higher. The breeze blew her hair back, reminding her that it was still damp. She had arranged to meet the two men at seven at the hotel restaurant. There was still plenty of time.

Vidya looked down at the promenade far below. They had said they were going for a walk. She got a definite vibe that they were a team already and she was an interloper. The first impression she'd made, covered in seagull poop and stressing, was not what she'd hoped for. Sarah had said all she had to do was show them she was confident and professional, and she had completely failed to do that.

Ah, well. Tomorrow. Tomorrow she would do better. In the meantime, she had three missed calls from Udeni. She stepped back inside and called her sister.

'Are you there? Did you see him?'

'Hello to you too,' Vidya said. 'And yes, I am here. I met him, very briefly.' She outlined what happened. It took a full minute for Udeni to stop laughing. Looking back, it probably was quite funny. It had been mortifying at the time. And the guys had been … pretty nice about it. One of them had given her tissues and they'd both sat with her luggage while she got the worst of the goop out of her hair.

'So, what do you think?' said Udeni, cautiously. 'Did you learn anything useful?'

'I think Angie was probably right about discounting Leo from the candidates,' she said. It had been clear that of the two men, Caleb was the chatty one. Leo had been quiet and aloof, standing back with a slightly judgy expression on his face. He had seemed fidgety and impatient as Stella showed them the meeting room they would be working in and sorted out their guest passes so that they could get into the non-guest areas of the hotel. She couldn't imagine Leo being described as kind, funny or sexy. Caleb, on the other hand, had been charming. He was exactly the sort of guy Udeni would hook up with.

'Angie's finding out more about Piotr,' said Udeni.

'You know, it would be so much easier if you could just meet them. I'm sure you'd work it out in a second.'

'Look, I don't even want to work it out. You're the one who's convinced we need to know stuff about the father,' Udeni said.

Vidya pinched the bridge of her nose. 'You might want to

know at some point.' She knew this was all part of Udeni being in denial. She tried a different angle. 'It's for the baby too. They'll want to know when they're old enough. And it would be useful to have as much information as we can about the biological father – from a genetic point of view.'

Udeni sighed. 'Yes, yes. Fine. But you are not allowed to tell him. Only I get to decide about that.'

Which was fair. It was Udeni's body. Her baby. Her choice.

'I think Caleb could potentially be our guy. But I don't know for sure. I'll keep working on it,' Vidya said. 'Hopefully, we'll be able to eliminate him or Piotr soon.'

'All you need to do is check if he has a tattoo on his shoulder,' said Udeni, with infuriating calm.

'I can't very well go up to a work colleague and ask to see his tattoos, can I?'

'Why not?'

'For the same reason I can't ask them outright if they had a one-night stand. I'd get reported to HR for inappropriate conduct. Especially if it turns out to be the wrong guy.'

'Oh, yeah, okay, maybe not. But maybe you could guide the conversation towards it …'

Vidya sighed. 'All this is so awkward. The things I do for you.'

'You know I love you, though, right?' Udeni's voice was more upbeat than it had been in days. That was good.

Vidya honestly didn't understand her sister at times. Quite apart from the one-night stand thing – where Udeni seemed blithely unconcerned about the fact that she couldn't remember what the guy looked like – she genuinely seemed to think that she didn't need the baby's father in her life. Not even financially. There was a real chance that Vidya would do all the detective work, find out everything about Caleb, and Udeni would still decide she wasn't going to tell him anyway. Vidya had to respect her sister's wishes though. All she could do was make sure Udeni had the option to tell him – if and when she wanted to. Vidya checked the time. 'I should go downstairs. I'm meeting the guys for dinner.'

'You're eating out on the company account. Make sure you have something lovely.'

She rolled her eyes. 'I suppose.'

'Aw, come on. You're having dinner with two hot guys,' said Udeni. 'And someone else is paying. That sounds like the best dinner plan ever. I'd have so much fun with that.'

That was the difference between them. Udeni saw everything as fun. She never thought of the consequences – which happened, obviously. But then again, she didn't have to, because Vidya could worry enough for the both of them.

Leo wished he could just go to his room. They had chosen to have dinner in the hotel restaurant that evening. It was an unremarkable place, with unremarkable food. Everything felt terribly awkward. He was never really comfortable socialising but today seemed to be extra hard. He didn't know what was wrong with him. Whenever there was a chance to contribute to the conversation, he would look at Vidya and his brain would go blank. Thankfully, Caleb could chat enough for three. So, Leo sat at the dinner table, eating his salmon quietly, while Caleb made small talk with Vidya.

When the meal finished, Caleb said, 'We should go to the bar and grab a drink before we head our separate ways.'

Leo really didn't want to. 'It's been a long day—'

'Oh, come on. We're going to be working together, quite closely, for the next few days. We should get to know each other. Break the ice, as it were.' Caleb turned to Vidya. 'What do you say?'

Leo hoped she'd say no. They were all professionals here. They didn't need to be friends to work together.

Vidya's luminous eyes moved from Caleb to Leo and back again. 'Just one,' she said.

Leo gave up. 'Sure.' He paid up and they walked down to the

bar. The hotel wasn't exactly busy, but there were people in the bar. They found a table in the corner and got a round of drinks. Vidya opted for a gin and tonic. The two men got the craft beer.

Vidya leaned forward. 'You guys were at the anniversary party, right? You came in wearing suits and rabbit masks.'

'Oh, yes. That was fun.' Caleb laughed. 'We weren't intending to go to it, but we'd just wrapped up quite a big project and it seemed only right to go celebrate. Just as well I'd ordered the masks the night before.'

'You were Zorro,' Leo blurted out, surprising everyone, including himself.

Vidya blinked at him. 'I ... I was. Yes.' She gave him a small smile. 'I'm amazed you remembered.'

'You had a Z on your chest,' he said. This had bothered him at the time, which was probably why he'd noticed her in the first place. 'Why would Zorro carve a Z into his own chest?'

Her lips contracted, making a moue, like she was about to blow him a kiss. But she was frowning. He had the sinking feeling that he wasn't doing very well at this ice-breaking thing.

'I just noticed,' Leo said. 'That's all.' Then, because that didn't seem enough and he didn't want her to think he was being weird, he added, 'It was a very nice Zorro costume. You looked very ... Zorro-like.'

Her lips curved back into a small smile. 'Thank you. I think so.' She blinked, as though working out what to say next, then seemed to give up and turned to Caleb. 'Did you have a fun time at the event? Since you came in late.'

Leo knew he'd messed up that conversation somehow.

Caleb was chatting as though nothing was wrong. 'We'd been for a drink beforehand, so that we weren't totally behind everyone else.' He smiled at her. 'How about you? Did you have a nice time?'

'I did, yes,' Vidya said. 'My sister—'

She was interrupted by Caleb's phone ringing. He pulled it out and looked at the screen. 'I'm so sorry,' he said. 'I have to get this.' He stood up and headed out of the bar, leaving Leo, Vidya and an awkward silence.

Leo cast about for something to talk about. 'So,' he said. 'You're vegetarian?'

'Pescatarian,' she said. 'Yes.'

'Me too.'

They both nodded. Leo took a gulp of his drink. The awkwardness stretched.

Vidya looked around and seemed to come to a conclusion. 'Do you think we'll be able to get this review done in the time we have?' she asked.

Ah, work. They were on firmer ground now. 'I think it'll be a challenge,' he said. 'There are a lot of contracts to check.'

'That's what I thought too, from what Stella said.'

'Well.' He felt his shoulders unclench a fraction. It was always safe to talk about work. He didn't need to think quite so hard about that. 'We'll have to see the extent of it when we get hold of the files tomorrow.'

'There's absolutely no way we'll get through all those hanging files we saw today.'

'No. I think you're right there.'

They both sipped their drinks. This seemed okay. Whatever it was that had made his social skills desert him must be wearing off. The silence between them didn't seem so strained anymore.

Vidya seemed to be thinking. Suddenly, she said, 'Do you think your boss sent only a team of three out here for such a big job on purpose?'

'Charlie?' Of course he did it on purpose. He was trying to make the team fail so that he could nudge them out. Could he say that out loud though? 'I don't know,' he said. 'You'd have to ask him.'

She gave him a look that said she already knew. 'I've been out of the general admin pool for a while,' she said. 'But I see that fee-earner politics hasn't changed.'

This amused him. 'No. I guess it never does.'

Vidya didn't know what to make of Leo. He seemed so ... inscrutable. The only thing he seemed comfortable talking about was work. Caleb was cheerful and charming – she could see how Udeni would have fallen for that, especially after a few drinks. When Caleb was around, Leo seemed more relaxed too. He didn't contribute much to the conversation, apart from the odd comment, but she could tell that he was paying attention.

A lot of people at work had said he was difficult to work with. Did they say that because he wasn't very sociable? Or was there more to it? She stirred her drink, making the ice clink against the glass. Leo was looking at the paintings on the walls, sipping his drink.

Now that he'd mentioned it, she remembered meeting him at the office party. She had left the main room, in search of the toilet and he had been standing in the hallway, rabbit mask pushed up onto the top of his head, checking his phone. He was still there when she came back. He studied her as she walked up to him.

'Are you dressed as Zorro?'

She thought it was pretty obvious. She had the mask and hat and everything. 'Yes.'

'It's ... good. Well done.'

This was clearly not what he had meant to say. She gestured to the rubber mask that was scrunched up on top of his head. 'Nice rabbit mask.'

He pulled it off and looked at it with distaste. 'It was a last-minute choice. To enter the spirit of the thing. You know.'

She nodded, her thoughts already drifting back to finding where her sister had disappeared to. 'Catch you later.'

He had given her a nod and set off as well, walking away from the hall.

Back in the present, Vidya considered what this meant. He hadn't seemed very drunk when she saw him and it looked like he had left early. So, Angie's assertion that Leo was definitely not the man they were looking for checked out. They could safely remove him from the list of potential candidates. Which meant she could focus on Caleb.

She needed to think of a way of verifying whether Caleb was the father, maybe by verifying whether he had that tattoo. While she figured out how to do that, she could find out more about him as a person. She threw another glance at Leo, who was still pretending to be looking at the artwork. Thank goodness it wasn't that guy. He was so very awkward and closed off. Finding information about him would be a nightmare. At least Caleb was chatty. If she asked enough questions, under the guise of being friendly, he was bound to tell her useful things. It wouldn't be hard to do, because she genuinely was interested.

When Caleb finally came back, he looked a little worried.

Leo said, 'Everything okay?' His expression barely moved, but she somehow sensed that he was genuinely concerned about Caleb. How strange? They must be friends, more than mere colleagues.

'Ah … yes. Just family stuff.' He slid back into his seat.

Vidya watched as Caleb seemed to shrug off his worry and switch back into sociable mode. 'So, what did I miss?'

Leo flicked his eyes up to the ceiling. Wait, was he rolling his eyes? Was he making fun of himself? But he wasn't even cracking a smile.

'Oh, right.' Caleb grinned and gave Leo a gentle punch on the shoulder. 'I forgot it was you. So, I didn't miss much then.'

So, Leo *was* laughing at himself. Interesting. She hadn't expected him to have much of a sense of humour, but it turned out she was wrong. She watched him finish his drink. What a strange man. And then there was Caleb, who seemed to be very fond of him. What was he like? She had a few days to find out.

Vidya took a good sip of her gin and tonic. This was going to be a challenging eight days.

Chapter 6

They started work at nine the next day. Vidya had been down to breakfast early and gone back up to her room, so she hadn't seen the men until she met them in the meeting room that they were using as an office.

The room was locked, but Stella had given them all key fobs last night. It was empty when Vidya arrived, so she plugged her laptop in and took a look around. This was clearly a room that the hotel rented out to business clients. The conference table in the middle was made up of several tables put together. She got the impression that the room was used for events as well as meetings.

It had windows along one wall that looked out onto the car park a floor below. But if you looked further out, you could see the other side of the bay.

Today the sea was a shifting mass of blue-green with white frills. She really should go and have a look at the beach. It would be a shame not to.

Since it was still only a quarter to nine, she checked the WhatsApp group that she had with Udeni and Angie. They usually discussed household-related things on there, but lately, there had been pregnancy-related chat too.

This morning's conversation was mostly suggestions about

how Vidya might get a glimpse of Caleb's chest to verify the tattoo. Angie seemed to have interpreted the brief as 'how to get a man to take his shirt off' and was coming up with increasingly ludicrous ideas. Udeni wasn't helping either.

Vidya: *Cut it out you two. I'm at work. Not in a low-budget porno.*

Angie: *It would have been easier if you'd been in a porno.*

Vidya: *I have to work with these men!*

Udeni: *Make sure you find out if he has any allergies. I think those are hereditary.*

Angie: *Maybe check mannerisms too. My brother and my dad have a lot of the same mannerisms.*

Vidya: *That might be nurture not nature.*

Udeni: *Maybe you should get some videos, just in case.*

Vidya: *Yeah, like THAT wouldn't get me into trouble with HR at all!*

Udeni: *I'm sure you'll find a way to make it work.*

Vidya: *I might be too busy working. You know, doing my job.*

Angie: *Speaking of which, we have a sweepstake going in the office on how long you last before you get sick of Leo and want to quit.*

Udeni: *What time slot did you choose? Angie's been telling me the gossip about him. He sounds like a real charmer to work with.*

The door to the meeting room opened. Vidya hurriedly exited the app. Leo and Caleb walked in, both dressed in suits. Once again, Leo's suit looked crisp. Caleb, although still smart, looked less polished.

Leo gave her a nod and said, 'Good morning.'

This was in contrast to Caleb's big smile and cheery, 'Morning, Vidya.' He put his laptop on the table and came to stand next to her and look out of the window. 'This is some view. It's almost a shame we'll be too busy to enjoy it.'

Vidya smiled. 'It's nice to be able to rest your eyes from time to time. You're supposed to look into the distance.'

'The horizon is pretty distant here,' Caleb said, agreeably.

'Although … isn't it always the same distance away?' He turned. 'Leo?'

'Depends how high you are off the ground.' Leo didn't even look up. 'We're on top of a hill and on the second floor.'

'Hah, so I was right. Pretty distant.' Caleb looked pleased.

Vidya added 'smug when right' to her mental list of observations about him. But then, he did check his facts with his friend. That made him less smug.

'Are you ready for this?' Caleb asked Vidya, indicating the laptops.

'We can only do our best,' she said.

Leo looked at the clock on the wall. It was a few minutes past nine. 'I thought Stella was meeting us here at nine?'

'It's only five minutes, mate. Give her a moment,' Caleb said.

Leo's glare suggested that he didn't think much of people who were late. Woah. Grumpy.

She watched him as he opened his laptop, presumably checking his emails. The weak sunlight caught him and highlighted the deep browns in his hair and the sharpness of his features. In the cold light of day, he was very good looking. His expression was fixed on stern, though. No, she decided, it wasn't so much stern as solemn. He was a very serious guy. He didn't like it when people were late and he didn't like incompetence. He also didn't smile much. What a waste of that face!

'We have paper copies of the agreements in here.' Stella unlocked the door using her key fob and opened it. The file room had no windows. It was a wall of rolling shelves that were currently all pushed to one side. The aisle in front of the file stacks was barely wide enough for two people to pass, a couple of feet wide.

Vidya smiled. She liked these sorts of rolling cabinets.

Stella explained the filing system and showed her the legends on the ends of the shelves, that showed which files were in which rolling stack. Stella glanced at Vidya and said, 'We have a kick stool.' She pointed to it, tucked away underneath the small desk, which was the only other piece of furniture in the room. 'In case you're not tall enough to reach the top files.'

'Thank you.' She would definitely be using that.

'It's all in hardcopy?' This was Leo, who was standing in the doorway, looking serious.

'We made a start digitising it,' said Stella. 'Got all the signed agreements scanned and put into a big folder, but we didn't get around to setting up a database or anything, so we pretty much rely on the paper files.'

Vidya's heart sank. Reviewing all of this to work out what they needed to worry about was going to be an absolute nightmare. A glance at Leo's expression told her that he was thinking the same thing.

'How do you find what you need?' she said. 'For example, if you needed to find all the agreements that were about … say, catering supplies, for example.'

Stella looked uncomfortable. 'We used to have a line manager, who knew where everything was. She had spreadsheets that she used, but she went off sick and then left without ever coming back and there was no handover, so we don't know where the spreadsheets are. Nowadays, I have to look through the file index and work it out.'

This was going to take forever. They only had six working days – eight days, if they worked the weekend. Doing this the old-fashioned way – manually looking through all the files – simply wasn't feasible. An idea stirred.

'But you have all the originals scanned as PDFs?' Vidya asked.

Stella nodded. 'All of them. Even the new ones. They're just not organised. We have a big folder with them all in. Saved by file number.'

'That includes any addendums?'

'Yes. We literally attach them together in the paper copy, so they got scanned together.'

Vidya knew Leo was watching her. His face was impassive, but his eyes were narrowed slightly, as though he was wondering what she was up to.

'I have an idea,' she told him. 'I think I can make some sense of all of this. It'll take … a day or so to set up.'

He raised his eyebrows like he didn't believe her.

'Do you have a list of the documents relating to property?' he asked Stella. 'Leases, deeds, that sort of thing?'

'I can get that for you.'

'We'll start there. If you get us a list and help us pull the paper files, that would be very helpful.' He didn't smile, but his tone was pleasant.

Back in the meeting room, they each set up their laptops.

'This is not looking good, is it? I've had a look through their folders to see if I can find this spreadsheet that has the detailed information on it, but it's not obvious,' said Caleb. 'There's a lot to review and no sense of order to it. How on earth did they function?'

This was pretty much what Vidya had been thinking. There had to be some order to the madness. She just needed to work it out. A bit of time talking to Stella, without Leo glaring at them, would help. Probably.

'Maybe we should call Sarah,' said Leo. 'She might have some ideas.'

Wait, what? 'Excuse me,' Vidya said. 'I have some ideas on how to deal with it.'

He glanced over at her, brows furrowed. 'Yes?'

Rude, rude man.

'I was going to see if I can run a query through the AI and get it to pull out a table of information for us. They must use the same template for their agreements. I can use that as a basis.'

There was a moment of chilly silence. Caleb groaned and closed his eyes.

'You're going to use AI?' said Leo. 'To review serious

documents?'

'Yes. We've been training the AI to read and recognise key phrases. I just haven't tested the query in the real world yet.' She had been working on this for weeks.

'Wait. You want to let an AI loose on some company's legal documents? Are you mad? The security implications—'

She stood up. 'I've already run this query past IT security—'

Leo snorted.

'And I checked with compliance,' she said, louder. 'And in our testing phase, we used expired agreements which were not flagged as sensitive, just in case of leaks. I do know what I'm doing, Leo.'

'But the AI is a blunt instrument.'

'It's still an instrument. A tool. You give it clear instructions and it carries them out. Just like any other tool. This isn't generative AI. I'm not asking it to make stuff up or draw conclusions. I'm asking it to extract information that's already there. There's a difference.'

Leo opened his mouth, but Caleb interrupted.

'Okay, okay, guys. Let's not turn this into a debate on the merits of AI.' He held up his hands, palms outward. 'We,' he gestured to himself and Leo, 'are naturally a bit cautious. But … as you say, this situation is a mess, and we'll never get it done in time without some sort of intervention.' He paused to glare meaningfully at Leo, who crossed his arms and gave a grudging nod.

'And Vidya, you're sure this is safe?' Caleb said. He was looking at her now, but one hand was still pointing at Leo, as though holding him at bay.

'As far as I can tell. I have emails from IT assuring me that if we run this type of query within our own systems, nothing will leak. We have NDAs in place and provision to move the information onto and out of our servers.' She was still standing.

'Well, then?' Now Caleb was looking at Leo.

Leo uncrossed his arms and picked up his pen. 'Fine. Fine, let's try it,' he said, with very bad grace. He gave Vidya a suspicious glare. 'If you're sure it'll work.'

'It'll work,' she said, with more confidence than she felt. 'I'll go talk to Stella.' Vidya marched out. The company had bought access to an AI service that came with secure storage. She had been part of the first group that was trained in how to use it to write prompts telling the AI what to do. The results were only as good as the instructions you put in. She had been working on this one for a while now and she was pretty sure it would work. It had certainly done well in the trial data set.

She would have explained all this to Leo if he'd taken a minute to listen, but no. He was not inclined to do that. Sarah had seemed fond of him. Vidya couldn't for the life of her imagine why.

Leo braced himself. Sure enough, the minute Vidya left the room, Caleb turned on him.

'Did you have to be so … you?' Caleb said. 'It's our first day working with her. You could try being nice.'

'We don't have time for that, Caleb.' He opened his laptop with the template to drop his notes into. 'Besides, AI? Seriously?'

Caleb chewed the inside of his cheek. 'It is a tool …'

'But the results are only as good as the instructions and we don't know anything about how good Vidya is at preparing them. It's not like she's someone who specialises in working with AI. She's someone who happens to have taken a few hours training on it.' He shook his head. 'What if it goes wrong?'

The sheer size of the job was stressing him out. Adding another unknown into the mix wasn't helping.

'I have nothing against Vidya,' he added, just in case that wasn't clear. She did weird things to his insides, but he wasn't about to let that get in the way of work. 'I'm only concerned about getting this done properly.'

'You might want to let her know that,' said Caleb. 'Because from that last exchange you just sounded suspicious of her ability to do her job.'

To be fair, he always started from that position with people he didn't know. Ever since the time a new administrator had managed to miss three deadlines in the same week, he was wary of new people on his teams. He had been wary of Sarah too, until she'd been with them for a couple of projects without any mishaps. Now, he would trust her with his life.

'I know she's not Sarah,' Caleb said. 'But you can't assume she's the same as that idiot Rupert either. I mean, she's clearly not here because her uncle pulled some strings.'

This was a good point. One of the reasons Rupert was so bad at his job was because he didn't pay attention. Vidya presumably did.

'Did I insult her?' Leo didn't think he had. He had merely disagreed with the use of AI. Sometimes people misunderstood and took things the wrong way. The sudden discomfort that Vidya might think ill of him was unexpected. Since when did he care what people thought of him when he was doing his job?

'Well, you weren't pleasant, put it that way,' said Caleb.

Caleb could read people much better than he could, so he trusted his observation. 'Okay. When I get a chance, I'll apologise.'

His friend nodded. 'You shouldn't worry so much,' Caleb said. 'Who knows, the AI thing might work out. Why not take a punt?'

Leo didn't bother replying. They had had this discussion before. Actions had consequences. He knew that better than most.

Leo hadn't done a stint in a file room for a very long time. He put the printout of the list on the table and faced the enormous rolling shelves. It took a minute or two to work out which files would be on which shelf. The shelves had been set so that the end one was visible. He grabbed the list, found the files that were in the visible shelves and put them on the file trolley. That was the easy part.

Now he had to move the end shelf away from the one next to it, so that he could reach the files inside. The heavy metal shelves were on runners. Each row had a wheel at the end. You had to unlock the wheel and turn it, so that the shelves moved apart and an aisle opened up between them. It was a great way to fit more shelves into a room, but he always worried about someone getting squashed between the heavy stacks.

He was the only person in the room, but just in case he said out loud, 'I'm moving the stacks now.' Feeling a bit silly, he paused for a second, then unlocked the stacks and turned the wheel. The end stack moved with satisfying smoothness, making a new aisle. He locked it into place and pushed the kick stool into it. He didn't need the kick stool to reach the highest files, but it was reassuring having something solid as a buffer. He liked to think that if the stacks moved, the kick stool would buy him some time to get out before the stacks squashed him.

The door opened. 'Oh. Hi.'

Vidya stood there with a piece of paper in her hand. 'I ... er ... need to get some files too. I'm running a test on a small batch first, to check if the prompt works.'

Leo gestured towards the open stack. 'Feel free.'

She entered the room fully and stood still, her eyes flicking between the paper in her hand and the labels on the side of the stacks while she worked out where things were.

Leo thought about what Caleb had said. If Leo had upset her or got her back up, this was probably as good a time as any to put things right.

He cleared his throat. 'I ... I can be a bit blunt, at times. I gather I came across as doubting your ability earlier. I'm sorry. That wasn't my intention.'

Vidya looked at him, her face neutral, and didn't reply. Such a serious gaze. It shouldn't be making him feel things in his chest.

'I am, I admit, a little bit apprehensive about the use of AI in general,' he said. 'But I do trust you to do a good job.'

Her mouth moved a little, as though she was working out what to say. Then she said, 'Thank you. I appreciate that.'

There was one more thing he needed to say. 'Since I'm the

team lead, I have to be sure I'm comfortable with what we do as a team, because I'm responsible for the decisions,' he said. 'Now that we've agreed to try the AI method to sort the agreements, if something goes wrong, know that I'll have your back. I'll take the flak.'

'I'll do my best to make sure nothing goes wrong,' she said. 'That's why I'm running a test on a bunch of agreements that are about to expire.' She shook the paper.

'That's a good idea.' Leo gestured again for her to go and get the files she needed. When she returned with a couple of files, he went in and got the ones he was looking for.

They worked in silence, which he appreciated. There wasn't that much to say and silence didn't always need filling. He moved the next set of stacks and they took turns again. When he reached to unlock the wheel for the next stack, she said, 'Can I do this one?'

'Sure.' He stepped back.

Vidya took her place in front of him. Since she was much shorter than him, he found himself looking down. He could see down her top. He quickly looked up at the wall and took a step back. He suddenly felt like he was boiling. The image of the soft curve of her breast seemed to have burned itself into his brain. He stared at the ceiling light in an effort to dislodge it.

Thankfully, she didn't notice anything, she was too busy peering down the aisle between the racks. 'I don't know why I'm checking. I can see that we're both out here.'

'I always check too,' Leo said, risking looking down again, now that she was a safe distance from him. 'And I usually say, "I'm moving the stacks now", just in case. It's better than getting it wrong.'

Vidya hooked the kick stool out with her foot. 'I'm moving the stacks now,' she said, with a sidelong glance at him. He suppressed a smile. The shared joke gave him an unexpected hum of warmth.

She unlocked and rotated the wheel. The wall of files moved slower than when he was doing it. It clanged into the next stack and she locked the wheel into place.

'That was so satisfying.' For a second, a fleeting grin illuminated her face. Delight seemed to radiate off her. It transformed her, making her look young and luminous. Leo felt a flutter in his chest. This was worrying. Maybe he should leave?

She disappeared into the files. 'I love moving stacks,' she said.

He pulled himself together. He was an adult. Surely, he was capable of working alongside an attractive female colleague. He might not be able to banter, like Caleb could, but he could manage small talk. A little, anyway. 'Really? I find the nagging worry about being squashed to death between the shelves takes the edge off the experience.'

A laugh floated out. 'It reminds me of being a kid. When we were little, my sister was a bit obsessed with *The Pirates of the Caribbean*, especially the ships. So, my dad found a big steering wheel from somewhere and fixed it to the wall in the garden so that it rotated. We used to spend hours playing with it, pretending we were steering a ship through a storm.'

Leo thought of the way she stood, feet planted firmly apart, and spun the handles. Yes. He could see that. 'That's a much better thing to think about. Much less anxiety provoking.'

Vidya emerged with a couple of files and they swapped places. In the shaded aisle surrounded by files, he took a minute to peer back out at her. She was leaning against the table, looking down the rows of spin handles, a soft smile on her face. He felt the sudden urge to smile back.

The file in his hand slipped and he tightened his grip. He needed to focus. Staring at this pretty woman was not focusing. Hitching the file up more firmly, he consulted his sheet and found the next file he needed to get.

Chapter 7

Vidya set her prompt to run and looked up. Caleb and Leo had a stack of files each and they were reading through them, making notes. Interestingly, both were making their notes on paper first before typing them up.

She needed to find out more about Caleb. She studied him. With dark hair, he was handsome in a classical sort of way – chestnut curls, square jaw, broad shoulders. Then there was the ready smile. She could see how Udeni would be drawn to him.

How on earth was she, Vidya, going to check his shoulder for a tattoo? Even if he had one, was it the right sort? She didn't know exactly what she was looking for. It was just too hard.

Her gaze drifted across towards Leo. Unlike Caleb, he was prickly and awkward. He seemed inscrutable most of the time. The only expression she'd really seen on him was a frown. Angie's gossip about him suggested that he was a strange guy – supercilious and pedantic. According to Angie, he had made more than one of the secretaries cry with his criticism.

Vidya thought about her encounter with him in the file room. An apology was the last thing she'd expected. Leo seemed like a proud guy. It must have taken a lot to apologise for slighting her. In fact, now she thought about it, had he actually said he doubted her? He had queried her methods, which was fair enough. Perhaps she had been a little overwrought too. Once they'd cleared the air, he had seemed a lot nicer. He was handsome in a different way. Slim, angular and sharp featured. Striking. She wondered if he ever smiled.

She was still staring at him when he looked up and met her gaze. Vidya jumped, feeling like a guilty student caught by the teacher. Leo's brows came together and he gave her a quizzical look.

'I ... er ... was thinking about lunch,' she said. 'When did you guys want to break for food?'

Caleb sat back and stretched his arms above his head. She wondered again how on earth she was going to see his chest to check if he had a tattoo.

'I could eat now,' Caleb said.

Leo looked down at his work. 'Give me five minutes,' he said.

Caleb nodded and stood up, twisting into a different stretch. 'Shall we wait for him outside, Vidya? Get some fresh air.'

'Sure.'

Outside the meeting room there was a foyer with a few seats dotted around. Patio doors led out onto a large balcony with a few tables and sunshades scattered around. Vidya and Caleb went out there. Although the sky was overcast, it was still lovely to look out at the sea. There seemed to be people on the beach, despite the chill.

'The view on this job is next level,' said Caleb.

Vidya had to agree. She glanced at him. It wasn't often she got to talk to him alone. Now would be a good time to ask him something. How to do that naturally though?

'Do you like the seaside?'

He nodded, with a little smile. 'We used to go to the seaside on holiday when I was kid. I have fond memories. You?'

She had been with her family too. 'Just for the day, usually.

But when we went to Sri Lanka on holiday, we went more often. The beach there is different.'

'I bet.' He laughed. 'Our beaches must look really lame to you.'

'Yeah. Especially when it's windy and cold and everyone sits there huddled against the weather, because you've come to the seaside and you're going to enjoy it, dammit.' It was the sort of thing her father would say. Her mother would put up with it for a bit and then suggest that it was possibly not good for Udeni to be outside in the cold like this and they would end up inside a coffee shop. 'We spent a lot of time in coffee shops, which … let's face it, are just the same as coffee shops everywhere else, just with more sand on the floor.'

They stood side by side, looking out to sea for a moment. What else could she ask him? The main thing she needed was to find out about the tattoo.

'There's something about the seaside that makes you want to do something whacky though,' she said, carefully. 'Like eat fish and chips or get a tattoo.'

'What's whacky about fish and chips?' He looked genuinely puzzled.

Oh, great, he'd focused on that and not the tattoo part. 'Um. Nothing, I suppose. I don't know why I … said that.' Damn. Damn. Now he was going to think she was weird. She looked up at him, worried.

'What are you two discussing so seriously?' Leo came to join them.

'It seems that Vidya fancies fish and chips,' said Caleb.

Leo faced the breeze and did up a button on his suit jacket. 'Why not? We're by the sea. Let's do that. Maybe Stella can recommend a place.'

Stella suggested a van that was parked at the end of the promenade. They got a cone of chips each. Vidya wrapped her hands around the warm cone and breathed in the smell of freshly fried chips.

'Salt? Vinegar?' said Caleb.

'Just salt please.' She held it out for him to shake salt into. Leo did the same.

'You're sure you don't want vinegar?' Caleb swapped the salt for the vinegar container.

'I don't know why you'd ruin perfectly good chips with vinegar,' she said.

'Exactly,' said Leo. 'Why mess with perfection.'

Caleb shook his head. 'So unadventurous.'

They started walking back. Vidya popped a chip into her mouth. It was hot and salty. The potato inside was the perfect texture of floury. She closed her eyes and gave a little sigh. 'These are so good.'

She licked the salt off her lower lip and opened her eyes to find Leo staring at her. He looked away. What? Had she embarrassed herself? She had, hadn't she? Argh. She popped another chip into her mouth and looked determinedly ahead.

'So, Vidya,' said Caleb. 'Have you been at the company long?'

'A few years. You?' Good. This was information gathering.

'Eight months-ish.' He looked at Leo, as though seeking confirmation.

'Around that,' said Leo. 'But we've known each other much longer than that.'

'Oh? How come?'

Caleb said, 'We were trainees together, when we first started out. Used to share an office a long, long time ago. Then this guy climbed up the ladder and moved out of private practice into industry. It was nice to meet up again, really.'

Vidya looked from one man to the other and got the distinct impression there was more to the story than that. Interesting. Did she need to know more? Was this going to be relevant to the baby? Probably not, she guessed. 'It's nice that you get to work together again,' she said.

She was eating her cone of chips, as they carried on walking, when suddenly a seagull appeared in front of her face. She screamed. It screamed back at her. Then the bird attacked the paper cone. She pulled it away. The paper ripped and her chips scattered in an arc above her. The gull snapped one up and flew off triumphant.

Vidya swore. In an instant, she was pounced on by what felt like a hundred gulls. She shrieked and threw her hands up to protect her face. Her lovely, lovely chips were devoured in a storm of wings, feathers and noise.

Someone gently pulled her away by the arm.

'My chips,' she said, not sure if she was annoyed, scared or both.

Leo stepped in front of her, shielding her from the gulls. 'Are you okay?'

She shook herself, rubbing the feeling of the gull attack off her arms. 'I'm fine. Those evil creatures though. Bastards.'

The corners of Leo's eyes creased at the edges and his mouth twitched upwards, as though he was trying not to laugh. 'What is it with you and seagulls?'

'They hate me, clearly.' It probably did look quite funny to someone watching. She should have remembered about the wicked gulls.

Not far away from the teeming mass of birds, Caleb was laughing. She noticed that he had shielded his chips with his scarf. Leo had covered his with his coat. She was the only idiot who had been walking about with her food on display.

'Do you want to go back and get another cone of chips?' Leo said.

Even though she hadn't eaten enough, she couldn't face going back to the chip van. She shook her head. 'I have a packet of crisps back in my room,' she said. That would have to do.

'Shall we … head back to the hotel?' Leo said. She nodded and started to walk, one man on either side of her.

'You're welcome to share mine, if you like,' Leo said. He moved his arm to allow her access to his chips. 'No vinegar.'

'I … er …' She was hungry. There was a time and a place for pride. 'Thank you.' It meant that she had to reach into his coat, where he was holding the chips in a hollow, close to his chest. It felt like an intimate thing to do. Leo noticed her hesitation and moved the cone of chips out a bit, making sure they were still shielded with his other hand.

Vidya reached into the warm space and snagged a couple. 'Thanks,' she said, again.

'You have to guard your food from seagulls,' said Leo, solemnly.

'I clearly haven't developed the same chip-guarding skills that you have,' she retorted. 'You guys must have experience from coming here with your parents.'

'Parent,' said Caleb.

'Pardon?'

'Parent. It was just me and my mum. The sperm donor doesn't get to be a part of my childhood.' This was unusually stern for Caleb, who seemed to live life lightly.

'Oh. I see.' She filed that fact away to tell Udeni later. Raised by his mum. 'I'm sorry. I didn't mean to assume.'

Caleb shrugged, the smile returning. 'It's fine. Most people assume. I just … prefer to make it clear. It's important to me.' He nodded towards Leo. 'He thinks it's weird that I tell people all the time.'

Leo offered Vidya another chip. 'It's not really necessary to define yourself by your parents,' he said, mildly.

'Just because you don't,' said Caleb.

Wait, what was going on? She felt like she'd stumbled halfway into a different conversation; one that was ongoing between these two. She often felt like that with them. They seemed to be very good friends who had been around each other so long that they communicated in some sort of shorthand. She looked from one to the other. 'Have I touched on an old argument or something?'

'Sorry,' said Leo. 'Yes. Something like that.'

'No wonder people think you're a couple,' she said.

Caleb laughed. 'Oh, no. It's not serious. He's just my work husband.'

'Just?' said Leo. 'I'm wounded.'

Vidya stared at him, not sure if he was joking or not.

His eyes crinkled at the edges. 'More chips?'

'I'm eating so many of them,' she said but took a couple anyway. 'It's your lunch.'

'I'm not big on lunch,' he said. 'I find it hard to concentrate in the afternoon if I have too big a meal.' They walked up the slope towards the main entrance of the hotel. 'Here,' he passed her the last of the chips. 'Don't let the gulls have them. I'll see you back in the office.' He nodded towards Caleb and set off at a jog, coat flapping around him.

She stared after him. He was so odd. She looked down at the chips and shielded them with her arm. Odd, but kind.

'You get used to him,' Caleb said.

'I can never tell when he's joking.'

'It's usually safe to assume he's always being serious,' said Caleb. 'He's a very serious person.'

She studied Caleb, who was the opposite. Smiling seemed to be his default. He was happy and charming and entirely not serious, which reminded her of Udeni. With two parents the same, the baby would also be smiley and charming. That was a good thing.

'And you're not? Serious, I mean?'

He wrinkled his nose and shook his head. 'Life's too short for that,' he said. 'Don't get me wrong. I'm very good at my job. Leo wouldn't have me on his team if I weren't. But I think there's a lot to be said for not letting life get you down.' He grinned, sunnily, at her.

Oh, God. How had Udeni found someone who was so like her?

What if the baby was all sunshine and smiles and no common sense? She glanced sideways at Caleb as they walked the final stretch to the hotel. Well, it was a good job she was going to be around for this baby. She would provide the common sense when needed.

Leo got back to the meeting room and sank into his chair. He needed to pull himself together. He had to stop noticing Vidya. It was unprofessional and distracting. He closed his eyes and saw her sigh with satisfaction at the perfect chip. His eyes flew open again. Stop.

Oh, and offering her his chips. Really? The sentiment was fine, but he could feel the neediness in him. He wanted her to like him. It all made him feel like a teenager. Hopefully, she hadn't noticed and she just thought he was cool and generous or something. Cool, like Caleb was.

He tipped his head back and pressed the heels of his hands into his brows. He was here to *work*. So was Vidya. She hadn't shown even the slightest hint of being attracted to him. He was just being weird. He needed to get it together.

The door opening made him jump. He snapped upright and pulled a file towards him.

It was only Caleb. Leo relaxed a fraction.

Caleb shut the door carefully and stood with his hands on his hips. 'So,' he said. 'What was that earlier?'

'What?' Damn. Caleb had noticed. Leo didn't know why he was surprised. Caleb was an observant kind of guy and he knew him very well, so would probably realise …

'"I don't eat much for lunch?"' said Caleb. 'Since when?'

'I– It's a new thing. I'm trying to stay more awake after lunch.'

Caleb leaned on the desk. 'You like her, don't you?'

Leo opened the file, not looking up. 'Who?'

'Vidya. I saw your face when you looked at her. You like her.'

He shook his head. He couldn't look at his friend because his face was burning.

'You do.' Caleb chuckled. 'It's so cute.'

'Caleb, I don't have time for this.'

His friend leaned further forward. 'Leo? Leo, look at me.'

Finally Leo looked up and Caleb said, 'It's the first time in years that I've seen you look at someone like that. I know you're scared, but—'

'She's a work colleague,' Leo said. He knew better than most how badly that could go. The last time had nearly destroyed him.

'She's only working with us for this project. She works on a completely different floor to us. There's enough distance between you if things go wrong.'

'No. It's not worth it,' he said firmly and pointed at himself. 'For me, it's not worth it.' It was fine for Caleb. He flirted with everyone; for him hooking up and moving on were as easy as breathing.

Caleb shook his head. 'I think you're just using that as an excuse because you're scared. You know what, you should feel the fear and do it anyway. Do we know if she's single? Shall I find out for you?'

Leo groaned. 'Please don't. We have a job to do. Can you just let me get on with my work?'

'Oh, but come on—'

The door opened and they both looked over. Vidya came in and paused, giving them a suspicious look.

Caleb straightened up and smiled at her. 'Back to work, I guess,' he said, cheerfully.

Leo rolled his eyes and turned his attention back to the document in front of him.

Vidya: *Here's what I've learned today:*

Caleb likes salt and vinegar on his chips.

He was brought up by his mother (no dad). He seems angry with his father. He is an only child.

He laughs when other people are attacked by seagulls.

He laughs a lot actually. Generally, very cheerful.

Udeni: *Cheerful is good. I like cheerful.*

Angie: *I haven't got anything to report on Piotr, I'm afraid. He's still out of the country. Apparently, he's back in the office sometime this week though. The gossip mill thinks he's single.*

Vidya: *Keep trying. I'll do the same.*

Chapter 8

By mid-afternoon, Vidya was exhausted. She had tested her query, checked the results, fixed a problem, run it again and now things were looking good. She would leave the AI running overnight to complete the same query on the full collection of contracts by the morning. Then she would have to check a selected cross section of them to make sure they were right.

Leo telling her that he would take the flak if anything went wrong made her more anxious rather than less. She was fine with taking responsibility. The idea that any mistakes she made would reflect on him made her feel … odd. Although he was gruff, she was fast getting the feeling that he was one of the good guys. She didn't want someone like that getting into trouble because of her.

She glanced at him. He was leaning over his file, with his forehead propped up on the fingertips of one hand, while he scribbled away with the other. You could feel the concentration radiating off him.

At the other side of the table, Caleb had spread his papers out and was slumped in his chair, reading. He certainly had a different style of working, compared to Leo. Her first instinct was to think that Caleb wasn't working as hard and just wasn't as good. But as he himself had pointed out, Leo wouldn't have dead weight on his team. So, Caleb must be good at his job. Was the laid-back persona an act? Or was he so clever that he made hard work seem effortless.

She looked at the stacks of contracts the men were working through. Leo's file was dwindling a lot faster than Caleb's. Maybe not then.

Udeni was very bright, if a little unfocused, and all evidence suggested she was talented at arts fundraising. Unfortunately, when it came to real life, she was impulsive and did stupid things. Caleb seemed less impulsive, but very relaxed. Perhaps that was a good thing? Maybe the baby would be a relaxed kind of child. Heaven knows the last thing their house needed was another highly strung Munasinghe.

She checked herself. She was falling into the trap of thinking Caleb was definitely the guy. Piotr was still a possibility. Angie hadn't discovered anything definitive to rule him out yet.

Vidya still had to confirm the tattoo. Even if she didn't know what the tattoo was, if he had one in the right place, it would make it much more likely that Caleb was the right person. Whenever she saw him, he was wearing a suit. It would even help if he would just take off his jacket. There had to be a way.

She secretly opened her phone and checked her messages. She had a notification from Angie.

Angie: *So, have you got him to take his shirt off yet?*

Vidya: *No. It's not a thing you can do easily with work colleagues!*

Angie: *Does he wear thick shirts? If not, could you drop a glass of water on his shoulder to make it see-through?*

Vidya: *That's an option … except it's not that warm, so he's rarely just in his shirt.*

Angie: *You're just going to have to challenge him to strip poker then. LOL*

Vidya: *You're really not helping.*

Angie: *I mean, I totally would. Caleb is hot.*

Vidya: *Ew. He slept with my sister …*

Angie: *Oh, yeah. Sorry. Forgot about that for a second. I guess that renders Caleb's hotness moot as far as you're concerned. It's a shame Mr Grumpy is so uptight. He would be hot too if he had a better personality.*

Vidya: *It was interesting today … I got attacked by seagulls and lost my chips. Leo shared his chips with me.*

Angie: *That was kind of him.*

She thought about the strange intimacy of it. A quick glance across the room showed her that Leo was still working, concentrating fiercely as he flipped through the file in front of him. He was uptight, as Angie said, but he was also quite nice. He had helped her when that blasted bird had pooed on her. Nothing showy, just solid, practical help when she needed it. There was something real about that.

Vidya: *He is quite kind, actually. Still serious though, he's very serious about everything. I think that's why he comes across as grumpy.*

Angie: *I don't think I've ever seen him smile.*

Vidya: *No. Me neither.*

Angie: *We (the girls and one guy in the admin pool) think that he's simply not capable of smiling.*

That made Vidya feel sorry for him. Yes, he was aloof and particular, but it was weird to think people talked about him like that.

Vidya: *Come on, he's not so bad. He must smile sometimes. Maybe he's a completely different person outside of work. Caleb seems genuinely fond of him. He wouldn't be if Leo was miserable all the time.*

Angie: *Do you think he wears a nicely pressed suit all the time? I can't imagine him mooching around in jeans and a T-shirt, can you?*

Vidya sneaked a glance at Leo; his dark head was still bent over his work. No. She couldn't imagine him wearing jeans and a T-shirt. Or joggers. She could barely picture him wearing a dishevelled suit. He looked like the sort of person who could walk through a hurricane and come out immaculate.

Another message popped up from Angie: *Although, he's quite tall and broad shouldered …*

Vidya shook her head. She wasn't even going to go there. Her initial dislike for Leo was draining away, but he was still just the project leader for this piece of work.

She looked at the other side of the room, where Caleb was slouching over the file he was reading. He was her other project. Maybe she was being too subtle. While she didn't want to draw attention with her questioning, she did need to find out more. She must make progress on that.

Leo finished his notes, put a few sticky tabs in the relevant places, and looked up to see Vidya staring at Caleb with a small smile on her face. The stab of jealousy he felt was as intense as it was unexpected. He didn't know why he was surprised. Women always liked Caleb. It just had never bothered him before.

It shouldn't be bothering him now. He hated that it did. He couldn't get involved with a work colleague. Especially one that liked Caleb, his closest friend.

Vidya read something on her screen and her smile brightened. Was she working? Or talking to someone about Caleb?

Leo closed his file with a slap. It rang out in the quiet room. Oh, no. They were both looking at him now. Think of something to say. Quick.

He cleared his throat. 'How is your experiment coming along, Vidya?'

'Not bad, actually,' she said. 'I ran some of the scanned contracts through and the query put it all into a spreadsheet correctly.' She called it up on her screen and turned it around.

He leaned forward to look at it. 'What am I looking at?'

'We have agreement number, agreement title, signing parties, third parties, if they're named, signature date, expiry date, type of agreement, term.'

That was pretty impressive, considering all she'd had to start with was a jumbled mess of PDFs. But he had reservations about using an AI to do work that normally required a pair of human eyes. A machine couldn't spot nuance, could it?

'That's great for when they use a template and just plug in names and dates,' he said.

Vidya's eyes narrowed and she gave him a tight smile. 'If there are extra clauses compared to the template agreement or if clauses have been taken out, they get flagged in this column.' She reached over the top of the screen and gestured with her pen. 'I have to review those individually to see what's changed. If it's anything substantial, I'll pass it over to one of you.'

Which made complete sense. But … 'How sure are you that it's all correct?'

She took a deep breath. 'I'm currently checking every fiftieth entry. If I find anything wrong, I'll go to every twenty-fifth one. If not, I'll assume that there aren't any errors.'

'What if they didn't use the in-house template at all? They could have used the other party's—'

'If they used a different template,' she said, before he had finished speaking. 'Then the system flags that as non-standard and we … *I* have to review that manually.'

Damn. She was good. She had anticipated what he was going to ask.

'Extensions?'

'I have a separate table from Stella of extensions and agreements. I'll incorporate that into the spreadsheet if it's not an issue.'

Leo stared at the screen for a few seconds more, trying to think if there was something she'd forgotten. There was nothing. Then he said, 'Good work.'

This time the smile was genuine. 'Thank you,' Vidya said. She pushed herself away from the desk. 'I think I'll take a comfort break for a few minutes. Go stretch my legs.'

When she left the room, her step was jaunty, as though she

was very pleased with herself.

Leo tried not to watch her leave, but he couldn't help himself. She was capable as well as pretty. That was so unfair. How was he supposed to ignore her now?

When the door clicked shut behind Vidya, Caleb said, 'Oooh.'

Stay calm. Don't respond. Don't respond. Leo let out a slow sigh. 'What?'

'She's good, isn't she?' said Caleb in a childish singsong voice. 'Really competent. You looove competent.'

'Yes. That's a good thing. We need competent people.' Leo moved the file he'd just read to the 'concerning' pile and reached for another one. He didn't meet his friend's eye.

'You already like her and it turns out that she's good at her job … and she's not scared of you. You really are in trouble now.'

'I don't know what you're getting at.' He could feel the heat rising from his collar.

Caleb laughed. 'You don't fool me, my dude. Admit it. You're a little bit turned on by that.'

'For heaven's sake, Caleb, what are you? Ten?' He didn't look up because Caleb was right. He *had* found the intensity of that exchange really hot. The more he got to know Vidya, the more he liked her. But he knew better than anyone not to get involved with a work colleague. Anyway, she didn't feel anything towards him. He cast a quick glance at Caleb, who was still grinning at him. Knowing his luck, Vidya would fall for Caleb.

Leo sighed and opened the next file.

His life was a tragedy.

While she was outside, Vidya took the opportunity to call her sister. 'How're you feeling?' she asked and braced herself.

There was a pause before Udeni took a deep breath and said, 'Okay, I think. I'm not crying randomly anymore. Well, I cried when I saw an advert for nappies, but … that's pretty normal, right?'

Vidya nodded. 'I imagine it is. How's the nausea?'

'Oh, that's still terrible,' Udeni said. 'But I worked out that if I eat between eleven and three, I can eat a proper meal. So, I'm having breakfast at eleven and lunch at three and then having toast for supper. That seems to work.'

Vidya worried about nutrients. 'You're taking the vitamin supplements I got you, right?'

'Yes, Akka, I am. Stop nagging. I'm reading the same book you read. I know just as much as you do. A bit more, in fact, because I'm the one that's actually pregnant.'

Ouch. 'Cheek,' she said. But Udeni had a point.

'So … what have you found out about him?'

Vidya gave her an update.

'So, you're no closer to being sure he's our guy.' Udeni sounded disappointed.

'No, but I'm going to find out as much about him as I can,' said Vidya. 'Just in case he is.'

'What if he's the wrong one?'

'Then I'll know quite a lot about a work colleague,' she said. Aside from Angie, Vidya didn't have that many friends at work and from what she'd seen, Caleb was pleasant. It would be good to have him as a friend. 'Has Angie had any luck finding information about Piotr?'

'Don't think so,' said Udeni. 'He's back from the US now, so she's trying to get herself invited to the pub with that group, after work on Friday.'

'That's a good idea.'

Udeni laughed. 'This is quite fun!'

'For you, maybe. Not for me and Angie.'

Chapter 9

Vidya grabbed her coat and scarf and hurried out to meet the guys. They had decided that they would all go for a quick walk as part of their afternoon break. Rather than wait for the lifts, she used the stairs. When she appeared on the first-floor landing, she saw Leo crossing the floor below. He was frowning at his phone as he walked, so she could observe him safely. He was wearing his suit and had added a scarf, but no coat.

She thought of Angie's comment that she couldn't imagine him wearing anything other than a suit. Leo did look great in a suit though. Wait. Where had that thought come from?

Vidya blinked and paused to watch him approach the stairs. He had come to a halt because two elderly ladies were standing at the foot of the stairs with their wheely bags. He looked at them, his frown smoothing out.

Without the habitual crease on his forehead, his natural good looks shone through. She thought of him as angry looking, but as she got to know him better, she realised it was an expression of worry. He wasn't perpetually angry; he was just permanently stressed.

'Oh, good,' the smaller of the two ladies said. 'I was wondering where all the staff had disappeared to. Young man, will you carry the bags up for us, please?'

Leo shook his head. 'I don't work here—'

'We need to get these to our room,' said the other lady, as though he hadn't said anything. 'And these bags are far too heavy for us to carry up the steps.'

'There's a lift—' He pointed.

'Oh, I don't like lifts,' said the smaller one. 'There's only one little box I'm going into and I'm not coming out of that one. Come on.' She gestured at the stairs with her chin.

Leo hesitated, then looked at the ladies again and smiled. It transformed his face. 'Sure,' he said. He bent his knees and picked up a bag in each hand and started up the stairs.

'Oh, my, aren't you strong,' said one of the ladies, slowly climbing the stairs behind him. They nudged each other and smiled. One of them was clearly checking out Leo's bum.

Vidya leaned against the railing and watched, amused.

'Have you worked here long?' one of the ladies asked him. 'Will you be here next year?'

They reached the top of the steps and Leo tried, once again, to explain that he didn't work there. The ladies weren't paying the slightest bit of attention.

One of them pressed a note into his hand. 'Here's a tip, young man. Thank you.'

He took a step back, holding up his hands. 'Oh. No, no. That's—'

'Please take it,' said the woman. 'Buy an ice cream for you and your girlfriend.'

'I can't imagine that a handsome young man like you doesn't have a girlfriend.'

Leo took another step back, looking so flustered that Vidya giggled from her vantage point.

'I must insist.' The old lady reached out, grabbed his hand and pressed the note into it. 'You've been very helpful.' She looked back down at the deserted concierge desk. 'You couldn't request some more milk for our room, could you?'

Leo shook his head. 'I'm so sorry. I can't.'

'Probably not trained on the system,' said the other lady, sagely.

'Something like that,' Leo said. He wasn't smiling, but there was a definite air of amusement about him. 'I'd better get on. It was lovely to meet you.'

As he started to go back down the stairs, another guest, a man this time, approached the bottom of the stairs and said, 'Ah. About time we saw a member of staff. I need some fresh towels. I'm in room—'

'I don't work here,' said Leo. The frown returned to his face. 'I'm a guest.'

'Nonsense,' the man said. 'I saw you helping those women.'

Vidya decided to take pity on him and hurried to the stairs. 'I'm so sorry I'm late,' she said, when she reached Leo. She looped her arm through his. 'Ready?'

The surprise on Leo's face lasted only a second before it was swiftly replaced with his usual neutral expression. 'Of course. Let's go.'

When they got outside, Caleb was on his phone. When he saw their linked arms, his eyebrows shot up. Vidya quickly removed her arm.

'Thanks.' Leo stepped away and didn't meet her eye.

'I thought you needed rescuing.'

'I did,' he said.

Caleb finished his call and came up to them. 'What's going on?'

Leo glanced over his shoulder. 'Let's walk, please? Before someone else asks me to restock their room.'

Vidya explained and Caleb started laughing. 'You're useless, you know that. They walk all over you,' he said to Leo.

'They needed help with their bags,' Leo protested. 'And they didn't like lifts.'

'He can never resist helping an old lady in distress. They seem to sense it and home in on him. The number of times we've been

71

late for social things because some little old lady wanted directions or help with bags …' Caleb shook his head. 'They sense weakness, I tell you, and pounce on it. Like sharks with blood.'

Leo rolled his eyes. Vidya tried to work out if Caleb's teasing was upsetting him or not.

'It's like walking around with a granny magnet.'

'Stop,' Leo said. 'You make me sound like a pervert.'

Vidya glanced up at him. His expression was still neutral, but he had gone a bit red. Poor guy. He must be really embarrassed. She should rescue him. Again.

'I thought it was nice,' she said. 'You made a pair of older ladies very happy.' She paused and added, because she simply couldn't help but tease him a little. 'One of them was definitely checking you out though.'

Leo's lips were pressed into a line. 'That's it,' he said. 'No ice cream for you.'

Caleb perked up. 'Ice cream? What ice cream?'

'The ladies gave him some money to buy ice cream for his friends,' she said.

'Well, it would be rude not to,' said Caleb. 'I'll have a 99 Flake, thanks.'

At the bottom of the sloping drive, they crossed the road and walked along the promenade, parallel to the sea, where there was an ice cream van, not too far along.

'Fine,' said Leo. 'Ice cream it is. What'll you have, Vidya?'

'I …' She squinted at the big sign next to the van. She eyed the birds flying around. They'd probably nick whatever she got. 'I'll have a Magnum, please.'

Leo nodded and joined the queue, leaving her standing next to the sea wall with Caleb.

'I'm not making it up,' Caleb said. 'Grannies do seem to know to ask him for help. Like they know he'll be nice to them. Which is weird, because he doesn't give off helpful vibes, does he?'

She watched Leo standing in the queue, shoulders raised,

phone in hand. He looked so uncomfortable wherever he went. Then she thought of the moment of decision, when he smiled at the old women and picked up their bags. For that minute he had been a different person.

'I think it's because he was so close to his gran,' Caleb said.

Vidya was still watching Leo. The sunlight caught the rims of his glasses and tips of his hair. When he looked down, the shadows made his eyelashes look long and his cheekbones dramatic. Wait. Why was she noticing this?

'I know he doesn't look it,' said Caleb. 'But our friend is a bit of a soft touch. He's very kind. So, if you ask him for help, you'll almost certainly get it.'

It was interesting that Caleb was telling her this, because she had noticed that too. But, why *was* Caleb telling her things about Leo? She hadn't asked. Besides, her mission was to find out more about Caleb.

'What about you?' she said. 'Are you the sort of guy who people come to for help?'

He seemed taken aback. 'Me? I … don't think so. As in, they don't approach me the way they do with Leo.'

Vidya wondered why that was. They made an odd pair as friends. Caleb was charismatic, with conventional good looks and easy-going charm. Leo, on the other hand, walked around glowering. What was it that made people go to him for help, rather than Caleb? She looked up at Caleb, who was staring out to sea now. It was something about Leo's eyes, she decided. Whatever his face was doing, you could always get what he was thinking from his eyes. He even smiled with his eyes first.

There she was, thinking about Leo again, when she should be finding out about Caleb. Focus. She needed to know what kind of person Caleb was. Nature versus nurture was all very well, but the baby could inherit his personality traits.

'But if someone asks, you help, right?' she said.

He was still staring at the sea, but frowning, uncharacteristically serious. He didn't reply. It was almost as though he hadn't even heard her. 'Caleb?' she said. 'Is everything okay?'

He twitched. 'Hmm? Oh. Yes. I'm fine, thanks.'

Leo returned with the ice creams, hunching over them a little to keep them safe from marauding seagulls. 'A 99 Flake and a Festival. They didn't have Magnums.' He handed them out. He had chosen a strawberry split, which seemed at odds with his well-buttoned-up suit.

Caleb took the 99 without a word. Vidya watched as Leo raised a questioning eyebrow and Caleb returned his look with a minute shake of the head. It was the sort of nonverbal conversation she had with her sister. These two really did know each other very well.

'Would you like me to leave you alone for a bit, so you can catch up?' she said.

Caleb stared at her for a moment, then shrugged. 'No. It's fine. My mum's split up with her boyfriend, and I'm worried about her, that's all.'

'Oh,' she said. 'I thought you were arguing with your girlfriend.'

Caleb gave a mirthless little laugh. 'No. I don't have a girl-friend right now.'

Vidya tried to tamp down the feeling of relief. It wouldn't matter whether he was single. Udeni didn't need him to be there for the baby, but as the protective big sister the idea he was with someone else made something inside her growl. 'Is your mum very upset?'

'Yes. Surprisingly so,' said Caleb. 'She was only with him for about a year, but the breakup seems to have hit her hard. I guess she really liked him.'

'Poor Sandra,' said Leo. He frowned. 'Do you … need to take some time off and go see her?'

'I'm tempted,' Caleb said.

That was nice. He clearly cared for his mother. Oh, goodness. That could be the baby's grandmother.

'But it'll be fine. She's always like this. Big drama and then she gets over it. She'll have met someone new in no time. She's impulsive, is my mum,' Caleb said to Vidya smiling.

Huh. So was Udeni. This poor baby was going to need some serious supervision to make sure it didn't embrace spontaneity at the cost of common sense. Vidya nibbled at the chocolate shell of her lolly.

'My sister's like that,' she told Caleb.

He nodded. 'It's a good way to be,' he said. 'Like I say, she's never down for long. She'll bounce back. But …' He ate some ice cream and shook his head. 'Well, I guess I worry about her a bit too much. You know how it is.'

She did know how that was. 'I understand,' she said.

For a moment, they were all quiet. Vidya kept a wary eye on the seagulls. Were they congregating?

Beside her, Leo bit another chunk of his lolly. He was staring intently out to sea. She glanced up at him and watched his jaw move as he sucked the lump of ice cream in his mouth. The cold had made his lips go red.

He was softer and kinder than she'd expected him to be. 'How about you, Leo? Do you have brothers or sisters?'

'Two sisters,' he said. 'I'm in the middle.'

'What do they do?'

'The older one is a teacher. The younger one followed my parents and took to the stage.'

'Your parents are actors?' She had not expected that. If anything, she'd imagined that he came from a long line of lawyers. She glanced between them. She was beginning to see why the two of them had found each other.

Leo rolled his eyes. 'Yes. Theatre actors. Very keen ones. My sisters and I mostly grew up with my grandmother.'

'Is that why you're so helpful to old ladies?'

He glanced at her, his eyes creasing at the edges and the corners of his mouth lifting. 'I guess it must be. My grandfather married his sister's best friend, so I saw a lot of my great aunt too. They taught me to never underestimate old ladies.' He nodded. 'Always be nice to them. You never know what they're capable of.'

This made Vidya laugh. She thought of some of her own elderly aunts. Of course, she had been taught to respect her elders anyway, but some of her aunts were formidable women. One of them, a retired judge, was actually terrifying. 'I know some women like that. My dad has sisters with big personalities.'

'You'll know what I mean then.' Leo checked his watch. 'We should head back.'

'Yes, boss,' said Caleb.

The smile faded from Leo's eyes, replaced by worry. 'We have a lot to get through. I'd hate to run out of time,' he said. 'Even with Vidya's cunning AI solution, there are too many interconnected contracts to unravel in the time we've got.'

'We can but try,' said Caleb.

They walked back. Leo had finished his lolly, but Caleb and Vidya were still eating theirs.

A seagull dive-bombed Vidya. She shrieked and ducked, protecting what was left of her lolly. 'Get away from me, you bastard bird.'

Caleb had covered his ice cream with his free hand. 'The gulls really are aggressive here,' he said. 'Bloody hell.'

'Do you think it's the same one as yesterday?' said Vidya.

She didn't expect them to take her comment as seriously as they did.

'Hard to tell,' said Leo, thoughtfully. 'You'd have to tag them to know for sure.'

'Bet it is though,' said Caleb. 'A particular seagull who's taken against Vidya.'

She looked from one to the other. They were discussing this with all the gravitas of a real problem. Peering at Leo's face, she could see the amusement in his eyes. Okay, fine. She could do this kind of silliness too. 'We should give him a name,' Vidya said.

'Charlie,' Leo said, promptly.

She frowned. 'Like … your manager?'

Caleb sniggered. 'It would suit,' he said.

Leo nodded. 'Swoops in, makes a lot of noise …'

'Shits on people and then swoops out again,' Caleb finished. 'Definite seagull.' He finished off his ice cream and looked up at the birds wheeling in the sky. 'I wonder why Charlie the seagull hates Vidya.'

'Why does a Charlie take against anyone?' said Leo. 'It's one of life's mysteries.'

They reached the hotel again and Vidya felt her shoulders tense up. 'Back to work,' she said.

Caleb sighed. 'Guess so. Assuming Leo can reach the meeting room without getting waylaid by old ladies.'

Chapter 10

The rest of the afternoon passed slowly. Leo had read so many contracts that his head was starting to hurt. It wasn't so much that things were complicated – he had an idea of what was going on now – it was that the work was so repetitive. He had to focus because he couldn't make a mistake. He could tell from their body language that both Caleb and Vidya were struggling to concentrate too, so he called an end to the working day. It was already past six p.m. No one could accuse them of slacking off.

Twenty minutes later, they were in a local pub that Stella had recommended. Leo ordered a veggie burger and chips and a pint of the local draft beer because, dear God, he needed a drink now.

The beer helped him relax, so that he wasn't quite as much of a social disaster as he had been the night before. He was still puzzled about what had happened to him. He had met attractive women before. Why did she have this effect on him?

The work had bonded them, so once they'd eaten, the conversation flowed a bit more easily. He sat back with his second pint and listened as Caleb regaled them with a story about a time he'd got lost in Copenhagen.

The pub was a low-slung building, decorated with fishing-related memorabilia. Netting hung from the ceiling, with little lights threaded through. He would have thought it was all fake if it hadn't been for the photos of boats and fishermen on the walls. This was once a fishermen's pub. Vidya fiddled with her glass of wine as she listened, everything about her radiating amusement. She seemed to show emotion with her whole body. His parents used to say it was how you were supposed to portray emotion when you were acting, except Vidya wasn't acting. She just seemed like a very open person. He envied that.

When Caleb finished, she asked, 'Do you travel a lot for work?'

For example, Leo thought sourly, she's transparently interested in Caleb. She's trying to be subtle, but it's so clear to anyone who is paying even an ounce of attention.

Caleb looked across to Leo. 'A bit, would you say?'

Leo nodded. 'Two or three times a month, give or take.'

Vidya seemed to note this. 'Do you enjoy the travelling?'

Caleb considered this. 'It's okay. Depends on the company, right, Leo?'

'Yes. Definitely.' Why was Caleb dragging him into the conversation? Vidya had turned her attention to Leo now, so he felt he had to say more. 'I used to try and fit in some sightseeing, but I don't really bother now,' he said. 'How about you?'

'Ah, no. I don't often travel for work,' she said. 'This, coming out here, was a bit of excitement.'

'Is that why you joined us?' Leo asked. 'Sarah said you'd volunteered.' He was aware that he had a reputation. People didn't normally volunteer to work with him. He hadn't had the same admin support person twice for years until Sarah came along.

Vidya didn't meet his eye. 'It ... seemed like a challenge. A good chance to put the AI query training to use,' she said.

It wasn't a very convincing reason. An awkward silence followed. Hmm. There was only one reason that would make someone volunteer to work with them. It must be that she had a crush on Caleb. She must have wanted a chance to get closer to him. Leo tried to ignore the stab of disappointment. He wasn't surprised. After all, people liked Caleb more than they liked him; it was a fact and he was used to it. It was only that he felt some sort of attraction to her first. But that didn't mean that she had to like him back.

Vidya took a big sip of her wine and asked, 'So, what do you do for fun, Caleb? Do you have any hobbies?'

Yes. She definitely liked him. Her attempts to get to know him better were almost comically transparent. Leo looked away. If Vidya liked Caleb, then there wasn't anything he could do about it. He would simply have to get his own feelings in check and remain professional. He usually had no problem with that.

Vidya smiled at Caleb and Leo's heart burned. He excused himself and went to the toilet.

Vidya looked towards Leo as he left the table. She hoped it wasn't obvious that she was fishing for information about Caleb. She should probably try and make it less blatant by asking about Leo too. Caleb seemed not to have noticed anything amiss. He was watching Leo make his way across the pub, with a thoughtful expression on his face.

'How long have you guys been friends?' she asked. 'You seem close.'

'Oh, seven or eight years now,' said Caleb. 'I love that guy. He's the brother I never had.'

'Oh, yes. You said you were an only child. How did you find that? Was that lonely?'

'Not at all,' said Caleb. 'I had friends. And Mum, obviously. It wasn't lonely. I just … would have liked a sibling, you know, someone I could trust to be there if I needed them. I never knew what it was like to have that until I met Leo.'

'Wow. That sounds like a pretty intense friendship.' He was clearly loyal to his friend. Loyalty was a good thing. She hoped that was one of the traits the baby would get.

Caleb took a sip of his beer and used his lower lip to suck the beer froth off his top lip. 'Hmm,' he said. 'Leo is genuinely one of the nicest people I've ever met. I know he comes across a little cranky, but he's a really great guy when you get to know him.'

Vidya thought about what she knew of Leo. He did have a sense of humour. It was quite dry and easy to miss. 'I'm not sure he is all that cranky,' she said. 'He just seems quite stressed a lot of the time.'

'He is. He has trouble showing emotions.' Caleb waved a hand to indicate his own face.

'It's not like he doesn't show emotions,' Vidya said. 'The expressions are only there briefly.'

Caleb looked delighted. 'You noticed!' he said. 'Yes. It's like … what do you call them? Micro-expressions? You can see them, if you're looking for them, but then he covers them up. Honestly, I don't think he even realises he's doing it. When he gets drunk, he forgets to do it and he becomes so much more normal. That's fun.' Caleb laughed. 'If Leo drinks too much, he's tremendous fun and does all sorts of things … some of which he regrets in the morning, if you know what I mean.'

That was an interesting piece of information. She wondered what a drunk Leo would be like. Less inhibited might be a good thing. She took another sip of wine. Speaking of people drinking too much and doing regrettable things, she was supposed to be getting information about Caleb, not Leo. Jeez. Focus, Vidya.

'What about you?' she said. 'Do you do things you regret when you're drunk?'

Caleb grinned. 'Life is for living, I reckon. I don't think I regret anything I've done,' he said. 'Drunk or sober.'

If only that were true. Vidya gave him a second glance. Maybe it *was* true. Maybe he would take the news in his stride and accept the baby as part of his future? It wasn't her choice to make though, was it?

'Leo, though,' said Caleb. 'He does regret things sometimes. He doesn't often drink much and it's really hard to persuade him to do social things. Like the office thirtieth anniversary do, for example. I had to get a couple of drinks down him before he would even agree to pop into it.'

Oh, excellent. This was what she needed to talk about. 'How was the anniversary party? Did you stay long? Who did you talk to?'

'I don't think I talked to you, did I?' he said. 'Leo did though. He said you were dressed as Zorro. Did he flirt with you? He loosens up quite a bit once he's had a few drinks.'

This wasn't going the way she wanted it to. Caleb kept deflecting her questions. It was very annoying. 'Why,' she asked, 'do you keep talking about Leo? I want to know about you.'

There was movement at the other side of the table as Leo quietly sat back down and picked up his drink. Had he heard? Did he think she was rude?

Caleb seemed taken aback by her comment. 'Oh, I'm not that interesting,' he said.

'I think you are,' Vidya said, with complete honesty. Oh, wait, that sounded like she was coming on to him. She shot a glance at Leo. She didn't want either of them to think she was interested in Caleb. That would make things very awkward later, if it turned out that he was the father of Udeni's child. 'I mean, we're working together,' she said, quickly. 'It makes sense to get to know each other better, right?'

The two men exchanged a glance, then Caleb smiled and said, 'Yes. I agree. It's always better to work with friends.' He raised his glass and she clinked hers against it.

Caleb leaned forward and said in a ridiculous stage-whisper, 'I'm not sure Leo agrees though.'

Leo, his face impassive, said, 'I work with you, don't I?'

Later, they walked back to the hotel through the quiet streets. Vidya wished she'd remembered to bring a hat. The air was biting cold.

'I imagine it's much busier here in the summer,' said Caleb.

'Yes, Stella said the population pretty much doubles,' Vidya supplied.

They rounded a corner and saw the sea at the bottom of the hill. Vidya huddled further into her coat and tugged her scarf up so that it covered the bottom of her face.

'Are you cold?' Leo said. He had his hands stuffed into his pockets.

'Yeah. But the walking will keep me warm.'

They were approaching the hotel from the opposite direction to the way they normally came, which meant going downhill. In places, the going was steep. Bundled up as she was, Vidya slipped and fell backwards. Leo caught her.

She was suddenly surrounded by warmth. Her back was against his chest and his hands were on her elbows.

'Steady,' Leo said, as he supported her back to standing. 'There's a handrail. It might help to hold that.'

Vidya glanced up at him, her heart racing, only partly from the shock of slipping. She grasped the handrail. 'Thanks for catching me.'

He shrugged. 'We can't have one of our number out of work because they've fallen and hurt themselves.'

'Always about the job,' she said, smiling.

'Is there any other way?'

Caleb, who had stopped a couple of steps away, suddenly yawned. 'I don't know about you,' he said, 'but I'm going straight to bed.'

She had to call Udeni before she could do the same. The yawn was contagious and she yawned too.

'Come on,' said Leo. 'Let's get back to the warm.'

They set off again, all single file with Caleb at the front.

'I might go for a run tomorrow,' Caleb said.

'I was thinking the same,' Leo said, from behind her. 'We should go together.'

'Oh,' said Vidya. 'What time are you going?' This might be useful.

'Are you going to join us?' Leo asked.

'Oh, God no. I was just wondering, so I could plan …' *Quick, Vidya, think.* '… when to come down for breakfast.'

'If we go at seven, we can run, get changed, have breakfast and be at work by about half eight,' said Leo, thoughtfully.

'Sounds like a plan,' said Caleb.

'So, I need to be at work by eight-thirty as well,' said Vidya. 'That's great.'

They walked along the side of the hotel and into the main entrance. The atrium seemed less tired than it did in the daytime. The enormous chandelier was lit up, drawing the eye upwards. The brass on the stair rails gleamed. Vidya stopped to soak it in properly. 'I think this looks so much better than the big corporate hotels,' she said.

Leo stopped and gave her a strange look. 'How so?'

'Everything looks more … real.'

Caleb looked puzzled too.

'It's grand, but it's not impossibly sleek. It looks like something you can imagine being made … not something from the future. It's a bit less uncanny valley.' She looked from one man to the other. 'I've lost you, haven't I?'

'No,' said Leo. 'You mean it's like the difference between special effects at the cinema and special effects at the theatre. The second one feels more impressive because you know it's done with levers and pulleys, and smoke and mirrors. Given enough time and a good explanation, you could work out how it was done.'

'Exactly,' said Vidya. 'It's more real.'

'Oh, I don't think much about theatre is real,' Leo said. 'But I take your point.'

'Oh, my,' said a voice. 'There's two of them.'

They all turned to find the two elderly ladies from before standing together.

'Oh, hello,' said Leo, his manner softening fractionally.

'Are you off duty now?' said one of the ladies.

Vidya laughed. 'He really doesn't work here,' she said.

'I really don't,' said Leo. 'We – all three of us – are here for our work. We're staying at the hotel as guests.'

The women both nodded, then one asked, 'Is this your young lady?'

Leo spluttered. Caleb laughed.

'No,' said Vidya. 'I'm a colleague.' She smiled. 'I'm Vidya, by the way. You've already met Leo, and this is Caleb.'

'It's nice to meet you,' said one of the ladies. 'I'm Jill and this is Linda. We're guests too.'

Leo seemed to have recovered himself. 'Are you ladies on holiday?'

'Yes,' said Jill. 'We are. We've just been to see a play. It was really good.'

'And now we're heading to the bar,' said Linda.

'We've just got back from dinner and I, for one, am going to turn in,' said Caleb. 'It was lovely to meet you both. Was it you that gave Leo money for ice cream?'

'Oh, yes! That was us.'

'Well, thank you. He did buy us ice cream with it.' Caleb grinned at them. 'Right. I'll see you tomorrow for our run,' he said to Leo. 'Good night, all.'

'I'm going to turn in as well,' said Leo. 'It was nice to meet you properly, Jill and Linda. I'll see you tomorrow, Vidya.'

Caleb and Leo headed up the main stairs.

'Are you going running too?' Linda asked Vidya.

'No.' Vidya laughed. 'But I know they're meeting out there at seven tomorrow morning, if you want to join them.'

Both the ladies laughed.

'I'd better let you get to the bar before last orders,' Vidya said. 'Good night.'

As she walked away, she heard one of them say, 'Ah, that's a pity. I could have sworn there was romance in the air.'

Vidya tried not to laugh. No. There was no romance. Not here.

Chapter 11

Angie: *Why are you up so early? You only have to go downstairs to get to work.*

Vidya: *The boys said they were going out for a run this morning. I thought I'd make it so that I was outside when they came back.*

Angie: *What? You think they'll run with their shirts off?*

Vidya: *No! I was thinking if Caleb's wearing something light, I might be able to see if there's something that looks like a tattoo on his upper chest*

Angie: *Ooh. Maybe they'll do that thing where they lift the hems on their T-shirts to wipe the sweat off their brows.*

Vidya: *That's not going to be much help, unless he's trying to wipe the back of his head. He's not going to lift the T-shirt up past his shoulder, is he?*

Angie: *No, but you'd see abs …*

Vidya: *That's not relevant to my interests at this point.*

Angie: *Fun though.*

<Vidya is typing …>

Angie: *Do you think Leo has nice abs?*

Vidya stopped typing. This thought had crossed her mind too, in the middle of the night. She wasn't going to admit that to Angie though. She would only get the wrong end of the stick.

Viyda: *Who cares?*

Angie: *Do you think Leo goes jogging in a suit?*

Vidya grinned at her phone. Angie had a point. She couldn't imagine Leo in anything other than a suit either. Then again, he wore a suit so well. He was always so immaculate. She hit the laughing emoji.

Vidya: *I'll report back about what he wears when running.*

Angie: *You have the most fun assignments. I just get to try to be invited to team drinks with the legal gang. Piotr is back in the office now, so I'm trying very hard to find out more about him.*

Vidya: *Good luck.*

Angie: *Have fun ogling lawyers in their running gear. I hope you get lucky and Caleb takes his shirt off.*

Vidya: *That would be so helpful. I need to think of ways to see his chest. I tried asking about the anniversary party but didn't get very far with that either. I'm not anywhere close to confirming he is the guy.*

Angie: *50 percent chance that he is, though.*

Vidya: *50 percent chance that he's not too. I wouldn't want to spring the pregnancy news on the wrong guy. Listen, I'd better get outside. I'm going to call Udeni.*

Angie: *I don't think she's up yet.*

Vidya: *She'll be late for work! Bang on her door and wake her!*

Angie: *On it.*

Leo was regretting this run with Caleb.

'I saw you sneaking glances at her,' Caleb said.

His friend was far too observant. 'I did not.' He had. With every passing hour, he seemed to think of Vidya more and more often. It was really annoying. 'I can't get distracted,' he said. 'We have to get this done and I'm not sure we have time. A week is just not long enough.'

'I wonder why Charlie insisted that we couldn't have anyone

else. I know the others were already on projects, but he could have allocated more admin support. I'm sure of it.'

They split apart to go around a man walking his dog and joined up after they'd run past.

'I think he wants us ... me, in particular, to fail to get it done. Or mess up because we're rushing. I told him how many personnel hours we'd need.' Leo sniffed. 'I don't know why he's got it in for me.'

Caleb made a noise that might have been a scoff, if he weren't so out of breath. 'You did publicly question his decisions a few weeks ago.'

'Because he made a stupid decision. And I was right.'

'Yes, but he's not going to like that, is he? I'm just pointing out why he doesn't like you.'

Leo grunted. If he hadn't spoken up, they would have missed a vital part of the company's liabilities and there would have been hell to pay when it came out. What was he supposed to do? Keep schtum?

'Tell you who does like you though,' said Caleb, his voice rising a little. It always did that when he was trying to be funny. Leo braced himself.

'Vidya,' said Caleb. 'It wasn't just you sneaking glances at her, she was looking at you too. I felt like a proper gooseberry yesterday. The tension in the room was ... wow.'

No. He wasn't going to rise to this. 'We were both working. You should have been working too.'

Caleb side-eyed him. 'Stop deflecting. I know you like this woman. You're showing all the signs. Including this excessive denial thing that you do.' Caleb shook his head. 'You know I'm right. Just admit it.'

Leo didn't reply for a few minutes. They reached the end of the promenade, turned round and started back. He listened to the rhythmic thud, thud, thud of his feet on the pavement. This run wasn't particularly challenging. He should speed up.

'It's been a while,' Caleb said, suddenly. 'I understand if you're nervous.'

Nervous? Hah. That wasn't the half of it. He wasn't nervous. There was so much wrong with what Caleb was saying, it was hard to know where to begin.

'I know you're worried about seeing someone from work again after what happened before. But, mate, that was years ago. Everyone has forgotten about it.'

'I haven't.' It came out more like a growl than the calm statement of fact that he'd intended.

'You should. It's time to move on. No one is thinking about it, apart from you. And just because one relationship went wrong, doesn't mean you should run away from the next one.'

Leo picked up speed. 'First of all, I don't avoid relationships. I just avoid getting involved with people from work. Secondly, she's not interested.'

'What do you mean she's not interested? What gave you that idea?' Caleb was sounding a little short of breath now.

Leo knew she wasn't interested because she only wanted to talk about Caleb. He had seen her staring thoughtfully at Caleb in the pub the night before. Even when they went for ice cream, she'd been too busy asking Caleb about his family to talk to Leo. It was so obvious; it seemed impossible that Caleb hadn't noticed. Caleb, who could spot female interest from a mile away.

Leo increased his speed again. Caleb sped up to keep pace. Now the run was starting to hurt. He leaned into the pain. Thud, thud, thud.

They reached the bottom of the hill that led up to the hotel. 'Race?' Caleb said, and shot off with an increased turn of speed.

Sod that. Leo drew on the last of his reserves for a final uphill sprint. He gave it his all, legs and arms pumping, heart and lungs burning. He passed Caleb and carried on until he got to the portico. When he finally stopped, he leaned over, resting his hands on his thighs, gasping for breath.

It was only when he finally caught his breath, that he looked up. Vidya was standing in front of him, staring, her mouth slightly open.

Leo was too winded to speak. What must he look like right now? A sweaty, out-of-breath lump. He tried to take in a bigger breath, but he was still panting too much.

Vidya closed her mouth and smiled. 'Hi.'

Leo nodded. He was about to have another go at speaking when her attention abruptly switched to something behind him. Still leaning over, he turned and looked back to see that Caleb had slumped against the wall and pulled his T-shirt up to wipe his face. A quick glance confirmed that yes, that was indeed what Vidya was looking at. Leo shut his eyes. Proof, if proof were needed, that she was interested in Caleb. She might be trying to use Leo to get closer to Caleb. That must be what Caleb had mistaken for interest.

The stab and twist of jealousy in his gut was almost painful. Leo straightened up and drank some water.

Vidya watched as Caleb dropped his T-shirt back down and bent over double. There was no way she was going to get a glimpse of his shoulder through that dark T-shirt. Which was probably just as well because she was standing next to Leo and it was really hard to stay focused.

It turned out that Leo did not go running in a suit. He ran in T-shirt and shorts, just like everyone else, which was only semi unexpected. What was really unexpected was that he had amazing legs.

She had watched him run up the hill, muscles moving rhythmically under his skin, his face set with concentration as he raced his friend to the top of the hill. He had been too focused on his destination to notice her, so when he finally stopped right in front of her, she'd had plenty of opportunity to observe the way his T-shirt stretched across his chest and shoulders, the way his torso tapered down to his waist. And those legs. Those thighs. For a moment, every single thought fled from her head. Then he'd looked up and caught her ogling. Right now, she wanted to die of embarrassment.

He had staggered off to find a wall to lean an arm against, so that he could stretch. The muscles in his arms stood out as he leaned. She dragged her eyes up to meet his face. 'Er … good run?'

'Not bad,' Leo said. He seemed to be talking to a spot just to the left of her head. 'The sprint up the hill was a killer though.'

'Tomorrow,' Caleb wheezed, 'I'm going to beat you.'

Leo looked over his shoulder, his face unreadable. 'You can try.' He switched legs. 'Were you enjoying the morning air?' he asked Vidya. 'Or did you need us for something?'

His voice was terse. Vidya frowned. Had she annoyed him? Had he somehow guessed why she was loitering here? 'Er … no. No. I don't need you for anything. I just … just had a phone call and needed a bit of space.'

Leo nodded. 'Everything okay?' Now, there was genuine concern. Cranky but kind. Why was that combo so attractive? Oh, no, she was staring at his legs again. She quickly raised her gaze to his face. Which was glowing a little and shiny from the exertion. She fought back the desire to touch his skin, to see if it was as warm as it looked.

'Um. Yes. Fine. I'd better—' She pointed to the interior of the hotel. 'I'll see you at work.' She gave them both what she hoped was a carefree smile and practically ran inside. When she turned to look at them again, Leo was braced against the wall, stretching his hamstrings. She walked back to her room, fighting the urge to fan herself.

Leo ironed his shirt in his underwear. He liked ironing. There was something soothing about the process of pressing crumpled fabric until it was smooth, like he was creating order from chaos. The little travel iron hissed. The sound always reminded him of his grandmother. She and his great aunt used to split the chores between them and Grandma always did the ironing while watching TV. He missed her.

He carefully repositioned the shirt. Wearing a properly ironed shirt was important to him. Despite his disdain for his parents' chosen profession, the one thing he had learned from them was the power of costume. He saw how both parents could step into different versions of themselves, but the thing that cemented the change into a character was putting on the costume. That's what his suits were to him.

In a suit, he was Leo the lawyer. He wasn't socially awkward; he was focused and detail oriented. He wasn't odd; he was clever. They were different names for the same things, but he liked the 'in a suit' version much better. Besides, his sisters told him he looked good in a suit. All at once, he was swamped by the memory of walking into the living room in his interview suit for the first time and the way his grandmother's face had lit up, just as her eyes welled with tears. The weakness had lasted only a second or two, before she fussed about finding him a tie, but he had seen it and it meant something … No. It meant *everything*. No one had seen him the way Grandma had.

He wondered what she'd say about his current predicament. He switched the iron off and held the shirt up. Crisp. It was still warm when he slipped his arms into the sleeves.

As he buttoned it up, he gave himself a stern talking to. Okay, he fancied Vidya. That happened. He was only human, and she was very attractive … and good at what she did … and curiously vulnerable, in a way that made him want to jump in and do things for her, which was probably completely at odds with what she wanted. And okay, it had been a long time since he'd felt that way about anyone. But the fact remained that she was clearly more interested in Caleb than him.

She was nice enough to try and include him in the conversation, but she was always on the lookout for Caleb. Like this morning, he had reached her first and she had clearly been about to talk to him, but when Caleb made it to the top of the hill, all her attention had instantly been drawn to him. Jealousy stabbed Leo in the gut again. He sighed and did up his belt.

He should be used to this, he thought, as he knotted his tie. Caleb always commanded more attention than he did. That was how it worked. It was only in the office that everyone took Leo more seriously than they did Caleb. In all other scenarios, Caleb won. The only difference this time was that Leo cared.

He pulled on his jacket. None of this was Caleb's fault. If anything, Caleb was doing his level best to push him and Vidya together. His excuses to leave them alone with each other were becoming increasingly thin. He couldn't blame Vidya either. She was a grown woman and allowed to like whomever she chose.

No. The problem lay entirely with himself. He had to pull himself together and keep a lid on these feelings. Workplace romances were a terrible idea. He suppressed a little shudder as he remembered the awful embarrassment of the last time. When he and Jessica had got together, he had done his very best to remain professional at work, even if Jessica occasionally teased him about being uptight. He had thought everything was going well between them, until she got drunk at a work social and snogged some other guy. It was only then he'd realised she'd been cheating on him all along. It seemed like he was the only one who hadn't known. The embarrassment had made it very difficult for him to remain in that job. He still didn't understand why Jessica hadn't simply broken up with him. Why try to keep two relationships going if you were unhappy? He came to the conclusion that he would never understand it. He also decided that office relationships were a risk to your career.

Leo buttoned up his jacket – all but the last button. No. Romance wasn't his strong point and another office romance was definitely out of the question.

Looking in the mirror, he checked his tie was straight. Now his costume was complete.

Caleb was his friend and Vidya was his colleague. He just had to go out there and act accordingly.

Vidya was in the file room. She wasn't hiding. She really wasn't. The files had to be taken out and she needed to be in there to get them. She had a list and everything.

It wasn't taxing work, which meant her mind could wander. Unfortunately, that meant it could wander in the direction of Leo. Ever since she'd seen them come back from their run that morning, she couldn't get him out of her head. Her plan to try to spot Caleb's tattoo had backfired. If only Caleb had won the sprint up the hill, she would have been able to focus a bit more on him without being distracted by Leo.

She really didn't want to be attracted to Leo. It was all so awkward. She had to work with him. Time was tight and it really wasn't helpful when she had to re-read things over and over because her eyes and her mind kept drifting across the room. It was so damned inconvenient. Leo clearly wasn't the type to entertain any sort of romantic shenanigans in the office. If only he'd remained the cold, aloof guy she'd initially thought he was.

But nooo. She had to find out that he helped old ladies with suitcases and got flustered when his friends teased him. That he had a dry sense of humour. That he stood up for his team when something went wrong. That he went out of his way to make sure he looked after people. That he smiled with his eyes, before the rest of his face. That he liked his chips without vinegar just like she did … and he shared them. That his legs looked amazing in running shorts.

Vidya rested her head on one of the uprights in the filing rack and groaned. She had a job to do. This was no time to fall in lust.

The door opening made her jump. She quickly held up the

list and stared at it. Files. She was searching for a file. Yes, it was somewhere here. She hurriedly studied the rack in front of her.

'Oh. Hello,' Leo said.

'Hi.' She gestured with her list. 'I'm just getting the files for today.'

Durr. Obviously, she was. She was in a file room, standing in between two racks of files. What else would she be doing? She really *had* to pull herself together.

'Handily, you've opened the rack I need.' He came down the narrow aisle. He read out the file number. 'Can you get that for me?'

It was right at the top. She stretched but couldn't reach. She would have to get the kick stool.

'It's okay, I'll get it,' Leo said. There was barely room for two people. 'I'll just—' He reached past her and up to the top rack. This meant that he was partly behind her.

Vidya could feel the warmth coming off him and smell his aftershave. If she leaned back or even to the side by a centimetre, she would be leaning against him. Her skin was screaming at the proximity of him. She glanced up and had a close view of the column of his neck, the sharp jawline. Suddenly her heartbeat was louder.

Leo got his file and looked down. Their eyes met and, for a second, she saw something that felt like want in them. He swallowed. She watched his throat move. Her heartbeat was deafening now.

Leo moved back, slightly. 'I … er … got it.' He reversed out of the file stack, clutching the large file. 'I'll see you back in the … erm … the room.' He backed out, then practically fled.

Vidya let out a long breath and slumped against the rack, making the file hangers rattle.

Oh. God. She needed to get herself together. They were here for a week and it was only day two. She couldn't keep doing this.

Outside the file room, Leo checked both ways, then leaned against the wall and pressed his hand against his racing heart. That was close.

He was supposed to be getting over these awkward feelings. Vidya was interested in Caleb, not him. He needed to shut this attraction down. Instead, the last few minutes had just made it worse.

He pushed himself away from the wall.

Note to self: Never go into the file room if you know Vidya is in there.

Chapter 12

They worked hard through the next two days, but there was still too much to do. On Friday, Leo told Vidya that he and Caleb would be working through the weekend to get through more of the backlog. He presented it to her as an option, with time off in lieu the week after, but she didn't have to. Since she wasn't going home, she agreed to work the overtime.

Over the past four days, they had settled into a pattern of eating sandwiches for lunch, sometimes on the hotel balcony or, if the weather permitted, in the town itself. In the evenings, they ate at a pub. Vidya was no closer to finding out if Caleb was the guy Udeni had slept with, but she was getting to know both guys pretty well. She had reached a level of companionship with them where she was relaxed while still remaining professional. This helped, because the work was tiring.

She glanced at Leo. Since that moment in the file room, she made sure she was never alone with him. While she still found him attractive, it would be awkward in the extreme to let herself feel anything more. Even though they'd eliminated Leo from the list of possibilities as the father of Udeni's child, he was still Caleb's best friend. If it turned out Caleb was the one and Udeni decided not to inform him, being close to Leo would make things very difficult for Vidya.

If they discovered that Piotr was the father … then … Vidya closed her eyes and shook her head. Then what? She could allow herself to fancy Leo? Ask him out? She was pretty sure he would turn her down. So far, he had given no indication he might want them to become more than colleagues. Even the moment in the file room had probably just been her overheated imagination.

Vidya sighed. It was nearly noon and she needed a break. She volunteered to go and buy a round of sandwiches from the shop they'd found the day before. As she left, Leo reminded her to get a receipt.

The sandwich shop was in the opposite direction to the beach, which meant walking uphill. The steep climb made her thighs burn. She stopped halfway to catch her breath and turned to look back at the spectacular view.

The sea was a shifting mass of blue, sparkling under a lighter blue of the cloud-brushed sky. A few boats bobbed in the distance. Those blasted gulls were, of course, everywhere. She took in a deep breath and smelled the saltiness in the air. This would be such a nice place to come on holiday.

Except, she reminded herself, she wasn't on holiday right now, was she? She was working … overtime, no less, and she was on a secret mission to find out about the guy who may be the father of her sister's child. She was still working on the assumption that it was Caleb, even though she still hadn't confirmed he had the tattoo. Maybe this weekend would provide her with an opportunity. Vidya turned and continued her march up the hill.

She had to be more careful. Leo was suspicious, she was sure of it. Yesterday, when she'd asked Caleb about his time at uni, she could sense Leo's interest. He had been watching her, his face inscrutable. When she turned to him, he'd looked down at his drink. She needed a cover story for her questions.

Leo was quicker on the uptake than Caleb, she decided. Even though everyone thought Leo was socially awkward and unable to read a room, she felt he got the measure of people fairly quickly and she was worried about what he thought of her.

At the sandwich shop, she took a welcome rest, sitting next to a couple of other customers on a low window ledge while her sandwiches were being made. On the way back down the hill, she decided to call Udeni and catch up.

'I think Leo is getting suspicious,' Vidya said, once she'd checked that her sister was okay and was still managing to eat, despite the morning sickness. 'I need a cover story.'

'Couldn't you just tell him you're a very nosy person?'

'I could, but I'm not sure that's going to be good enough.'

'Angie is here. Hang on, I'll put you on speakerphone.'

Angie came straight in with, 'It's the weekend. There must be more opportunities to get Caleb to take his shirt off.'

Vidya shook her head. 'I don't think so.'

'Oh, come on, you need to be more positive than that. You're at the seaside. You could go to the beach. Prime shirt-removing territory!'

'It's March!' Vidya glanced at the sky – it was almost sunny today. The weather was improving. So, maybe it wasn't a completely mad idea. Her thoughts drifted towards Leo. For a second, she tried to imagine him in swimming trunks and her brain short-circuited. No. He would never agree to that. 'I'm pretty sure Leo would object. He's a very serious guy.'

'Serious, huh?' said Angie. 'Sounds very much like your kind of person.'

Vidya reached a particularly steep bit and shifted the phone to her other hand, so that she could hold the handrail. It meant the bag of sandwiches was hanging uncomfortably from under the crook of her elbow. 'Oh, shut up.'

'Wait, wait. What's going on? Have I missed some Vidya gossip?' Udeni asked.

'Well,' said Angie, theatrically. 'While Vidya was doing all this research for you about your man … she's developed a crush on the wing man.'

Udeni squealed. 'You have? Why didn't you tell me?'

'I didn't want you to think I was slacking on my assignment.'

'That's so stupid.'

'Is it though?' A gull swooped overhead and Vidya instinctively clutched the sandwiches to her chest. She carried on, with a cautious eye on the birds. 'What if you decided you don't want to have anything to do with the father of your child … assuming it *is* Caleb, which I haven't confirmed yet.'

'Assuming it is,' said Udeni.

'Okay. Well, Leo's his best friend. Even if the best-case scenario happens and he likes me back, how is that going to work? You don't want Caleb to know about the baby, and I'm terrible at lying. I can't go out with Leo and still keep your secret. That's just a disaster waiting to happen.'

'Oh.' Udeni's voice was quiet.

'No,' said Angie. 'I don't think you should hold back from flirting with a guy you like just because it *might* get awkward.'

'You think I should just jump in and hope nothing goes wrong? Like that worked so well for Udeni.' It came out snappier than Vidya had intended.

There was a sharp intake of breath from both the other women on the other end of the line.

'I'm … I'm sorry. I didn't mean it like that,' Vidya said.

'Except you did,' said Udeni. There was a tremor in her voice. 'You think I'm being incredibly stupid for keeping this baby. And you're judging me because I made a mistake and got pregnant.'

'I'm not—'

'Because you'd never do that, would you? Sensible, sensible Vidya who never does anything wrong.'

'Udeni—' Angie said.

'No. It's always like this. I can't do anything right, and Vidya judges my choices every single time. Just because she doesn't understand spontaneity and joy. She wouldn't understand an

101

opportunity if it came and bit her in the face.' Udeni sounded like she was crying.

Vidya rolled her eyes. This again. If Udeni didn't want people to judge her thoughtlessness, maybe she should stop doing things without thinking about them. This argument happened every so often. Now was not the time. Vidya simply didn't have the energy for it. 'Nangi,' she said, patiently. 'I'm not judging you. I'm trying to help.'

'You absolutely are judging me. Oh, you don't say anything, but I can sense it. And then you go around with your holier-than-thou attitude. My sister has screwed up again and I have to fix it. Poor old me. Like you're such a martyr.'

A martyr? Seriously? Vidya stopped walking and glared out at the shifting sea. Here she was, trying to help, and this was the thanks she got?

'Ladies, please—' Angie tried again to keep the peace.

Both sisters said 'shut up' simultaneously.

'Just because you're too afraid to go and get something that you want,' said Udeni, 'you don't need to judge me when I do.'

Then Udeni hung up.

'Ude—? Hello?' Vidya stood very still, her heart pounding. How dare Udeni? After all she was doing.

The phone buzzed in her hand. It was a message from Angie: *She's hormonal and overwhelmed. I'll deal with it. I'm sure she didn't mean it.*

Vidya didn't bother to reply, just pocketed her phone and resumed her journey back to the hotel. By the time she got to the entrance, her anger at her sister had reduced to a low simmer. After all, Udeni was pregnant and overwhelmed as Angie had said. Hell, Udeni's emotions were close to the surface at the best of times. And she had no self-control. That's how she got herself into these situations. That's why, as the big sister, Vidya had to keep digging her out of them. It had started with small things – like forgotten lunches, so that Vidya had to share. Or that time

Udeni slept through her alarm and nearly missed her A-level exam. Or when she left it too late to work out how to get to an interview and Vidya had to pay for a taxi. That interview had led to the job she had now, for heaven's sake. She didn't mind doing it, but Udeni didn't seem to appreciate it, or even notice.

It sometimes felt like Udeni floated through life, not taking responsibility for any of it. Sure, she paid rent towards the mortgage on the flat, but Vidya did all the organising. She was the one who made sure the bills were paid, the plumbing got fixed when it went wrong. She even made sure the bins went out on the right day. And what thanks did she get?

She pushed the door to the meeting room with a harder shove than she'd intended. The door banged as she entered, and Leo and Caleb looked up. She put the bag of sandwiches on the table.

'Vidya?' Leo said.

She snapped out of her angry contemplation back into the here and now. Both the men were staring at her, Leo's brow furrowed, Caleb's eyes wide.

'Um. Sorry. I was … miles away.'

'Are you okay?' Leo sounded genuinely worried.

Vidya realised she was still scowling and tried to relax her face a bit. 'Yes. Yes, I'm fine. I just had an … awkward phone call with my sister. It's fine. Nothing to worry about.'

Leo's eyes narrowed briefly, then he nodded. 'Let's stop for lunch then.' He closed the file with a slap and pushed himself up to standing. 'Shall we eat on the terrace? I'm sick of this room.'

She was pretty sick of it too. She took the bag of sandwiches and followed Leo out.

Chapter 13

Vidya yawned. It was nearly five p.m. on the Saturday and they were still working. She couldn't really focus anymore. She checked her phone again. There was a message from Angie to say Piotr hadn't gone to the pub last night after all so she had no news. Still nothing from Udeni. Vidya had sent a message with a brief apology, which her sister had read and clearly ignored. According to Angie, Udeni had cried a bit, shouted a bit and then shut herself in her room. Even Angie had to admit that there was probably more to it than hormones.

Vidya ran a thumbnail over her teeth as she stared at her phone. This was not good. She and Udeni had argued before, but this time felt different, probably because Udeni was extra delicate right now. Vidya understood that pregnancy could make you more tired and emotional. The few days before your period were hellish enough, she couldn't even begin to imagine what pregnancy might do to your mood and self-esteem. She should have been more sympathetic. Vidya sighed.

Out of the corner of her eye, she saw Leo's head rise. Oh. Right. She was probably distracting him. She pushed her chair back wearily and stood up. May as well take a break and see if Udeni would talk to her.

The terrace was busy this evening, with people wrapped up against the chill. She would go down into the garden below the entrance and call Udeni from there.

The 'garden' was a multilayered terrace that broke up the steep incline down to the seashore. Vidya trudged down two levels before she found an empty bench. She sat and stared out at the clouds. The sun was behind there somewhere, slowly sinking. Much like her mood right now.

She breathed in a lungful of sea air and let it out. Time to try her sister again.

To her amazement Udeni answered. 'What?'

'I ... I thought we should talk.'

'I'm only answering the phone to tell you that Amma and Thatha called. They were pretty annoyed with your bosses for making you work this weekend.'

'I'll get time off in lieu next week. It's fine.' Vidya shook her head. 'I explained all this to them.'

'Whatever. That's all I had to tell you—'

'Wait. Don't hang up.'

'Why not? Is that being stupid too?' There was a real bite to Udeni's voice. It grated on Vidya's nerves.

'I don't think you're stupid, okay? We all make mistakes. I'm here for you—'

'I don't need you to be,' Udeni snapped. 'I know you think I'm an idiot for wanting to keep this baby and for wanting to do it alone.'

Vidya gave an exasperated 'ugh!' and said, 'If I genuinely thought that I wouldn't be helping you, would I? I'm only working on this project so that I can snoop out some information for you.'

'I didn't ask you to do that!' Udeni screeched down the phone. 'I told you. I don't want to tell him. Or have anything to do with him. You're the one who thought we needed information on the father. I don't want to owe a stranger anything.'

'Caleb's not a stranger—'

105

'Yes, he is. He was a one-night stand. That's all. I have no connection with him whatsoever. But you – you do now, don't you? You're the one who's complicated things by making friends with the random stranger. If this turns into something awkward, it's all your fault.'

That was so preposterous, Vidya was speechless for a second. 'I am trying to help! This was an accident and I'm trying to make things better for you. It's not like you have a plan!'

'Of course I don't have a plan, but I recognise a gift when I'm given it. You wouldn't, of course. You'd need to plan everything to the nth degree before you even consider doing anything. That's why you've been single for a million years.'

Anger rose in Vidya, hot and bitter. 'How dare you!'

'How dare *you*?' Udeni shot back. 'Stop interfering with my life and judging my choices, Vidya. We can't all be perfect and organised like you.'

'I thought that made me a lonely old spinster.'

'If the shoe fits.'

'I don't know why I bother talking to you.'

'Neither do I.'

This time, it was Vidya who hung up.

She closed her eyes and tipped her head back. This was too hard. What on earth had made her think volunteering for this project was a good idea?

The work was detailed, but also repetitive, which made it exhausting. She liked Leo and Caleb, but the pressure of having to keep Udeni's secret made things difficult. Going home would have been nice, but her argument with Udeni meant even that was now awkward. Why couldn't life be easy?

Tears rose under Vidya's eyelids. It wasn't fair. She was doing her best to help and Udeni was being so ungrateful. Ever since that accident in the playground, she'd done her best to look after her sister better. What started off as being a bit protective when she was a child had persisted into adulthood. It was just a fact of life. It was as natural as breathing.

Normally, Udeni was quite happy to lean on her. She almost expected Vidya's support. So why was Udeni being like this now? Over something so important?

Vidya wiped her eyes. It was so frustrating. Of course, she had wanted to work out who the father of the baby was. How could you not? A baby wasn't a trivial thing – it was a *person* Udeni was bringing into their family. How could you not want to be prepared? It made no sense.

Vidya hadn't made things complicated. She *hadn't*. If Udeni hadn't insisted on keeping the pregnancy a secret, they could have approached Caleb openly. Or arranged for Udeni to meet him and see if they recognised each other. Instead, Vidya was stuck looking like a nosy colleague and trying to work out whether he had a tattoo. Meanwhile Leo who was the one she really wanted to get to know better, was getting suspicious of why she kept asking questions. It was all such a mess. She was trying so hard to do what was right for her sister, and Udeni didn't even appreciate it.

Maybe she should just let Udeni stew in her own mess for once. Vidya dashed the tears from the corners of her eyes. That's what she should do. Leave Udeni to it. She didn't want help, after all. It would serve her right if Vidya stopped trying. Let Udeni handle telling Amma and Thatha alone. See how she liked that. They were going to be a nightmare when they found out.

She raised her head and looked at the darkening horizon. The colour had drained out of the sky and the temperature had dropped even more. At the bottom of the hill, a band of street-lights shone over the promenade, with the shifting darkness of the sea beyond. The gulls seemed to have quietened down. She shivered and wished she'd thought to bring her coat.

Her phone buzzed. She checked it hesitantly, half hoping, half dreading that it was Udeni. It was Caleb. He and Leo were calling it a day. They were going for a walk to stretch their legs and would meet her in the foyer at seven to go to one of the pubs for dinner. She stared at the message for a moment, then turned the phone facedown.

Udeni was right about one thing. Caleb had become a friend. So had Leo. If Udeni insisted on not telling Caleb about the baby, then Vidya would have to be very careful when she spoke to either of the guys.

Realistically, she could finish this project and not have anything further to do with them apart from the odd friendly nod if they met in the lift. She thought about Leo and his elusive smile and Caleb with his easy sense of humour. What a shame it would be to lose touch.

She rubbed the last of her angry tears from her cheeks. 'Dammit, Udeni. Why did you have to drag me into all this?'

When Leo got down to the foyer at seven, Caleb was there waiting for him.

'Where's Vidya?'

Caleb looked up from his phone. 'She messaged to say that she'd grab something from the bar menu and take it up to her room. I guess she wants a bit of alone time.'

It was silly to feel disappointed. They had been working so hard, in the same room most of the day. Small wonder she wanted a bit of space. 'Fair enough,' he said.

'So, it's just us then,' said Caleb. 'Which pub shall we go to?'

'I honestly don't care.' Leo stretched his neck from side to side. 'Somewhere that's a bit of a walk would be good. I still feel the need to move.'

'Let's go to the one at the top of the hill, then.' Caleb put his phone away.

They set off at a brisk pace.

'It's much quicker walking places without Vidya,' Caleb observed. 'Not that I mind slowing down for her, obviously.'

Leo said nothing. Vidya had been quiet all afternoon. Maybe it was because they were working the weekend. Or maybe it was something else. Come to think of it, she'd been distracted ever since she did the sandwich run at lunchtime. 'I hope she's okay,' he said, out loud.

Caleb rolled his eyes. 'She's a grown woman. She'll be fine in the hotel. She probably just needs a break from your moody face.'

'Huh?' He hadn't been particularly moody, had he? He'd been working. Busy wasn't the same as moody.

'You've been so tense around her; you practically squeak. I don't know why you don't just ask her out, honestly.'

'It's not that simple—'

'What if it *is* that simple?' said Caleb. 'You like her. Just get a couple of drinks down you and muster up the courage to ask her out.' He shook his head. 'How on earth did you and Jessica get together back in the day?'

There was that familiar twist of embarrassment every time someone mentioned her name. 'Um … office drinks. A group of us went to a bar after we finished a project and … things sort of went from there.'

'See. You liked her. You went for drinks. Bam.'

'Bam!' pretty much described the effect that Jessica had on Leo.

Especially eight months later when he found her at the Christmas party with her tongue down the throat of some guy from HR. He shuddered. 'Yes, well. I don't want a repeat of my relationship with Jessica, thanks.'

'She was an opportunistic witch,' said Caleb. 'But Vidya's not. You guys have so much in common. You're both serious. You're both obsessed with proper file keeping. You're both a little bit awkward.'

'She's not awkward, is she?' Was she? He hadn't noticed.

'She asks a lot of questions. I think it's her way of keeping the conversation going,' said Caleb.

'Or … she wants to know everything about you.' *Why do you keep talking about Leo? I want to know about you.* It couldn't have been any clearer. 'I appreciate your efforts to try and set me up,

Caleb, but I honestly don't think she's interested in me.'

Caleb frowned. 'See, that's the weird part. You're right. She does ask me a lot of questions and she does seem keen to know the answers, but I don't get the feeling that she's in any way attracted to me. Honestly, I think I'd know. The way she looks at you, on the other hand ... woah.'

Leo said nothing. He didn't believe a word of that, but he did know that he'd been extra tense around Vidya lately. 'Is it really noticeable that I'm ... attracted to her?'

'Yes.'

'Do you think I make her feel uncomfortable? That would be bad. We have to work together.'

'I ... No,' said Caleb. 'I noticed, but I know you really well, remember? She's only just met you. I doubt she'll be able to tell. Your poker face is still more or less intact, don't worry.'

A gust of wind brought with it the sound of laughter from a group walking down towards the seafront. Leo tugged his scarf up around his chin.

'I'd hate to think I was part of the problem,' he said. 'Whatever I think about her, it shouldn't affect her place of work.'

They walked up the steep hill, looking down at their feet, not talking.

When they got to the top, Caleb said, 'Listen, mate. You're overthinking it. You're right. You don't want to make things awkward, but ... people get together through work all the time. Think about it. How many other places are there to meet people at our age?'

'You manage,' said Leo.

Caleb made a noncommittal noise. Come to think of it, it had been a few months since Caleb had mentioned a woman, which was a while for him. 'Has something changed?' Leo asked.

His friend looked up at the sky. 'Not really,' he said. 'My heart's just not in it right now.'

Leo raised his eyebrows. It was much better to talk about this

110

than to dissect his own disastrous prospects. 'What's happened to your heart?'

'Nothing. I just feel … like, why bother, you know? You meet people, you hook up, maybe you date for a while … and then it just ends. It all seems so pointless.'

This was most unlike Caleb, who normally grabbed life with both hands and squeezed. Leo turned to look at him, which meant he was walking backwards. 'What's brought this on?' He thought back to what had happened in the past week. 'Is it your mum breaking up with her boyfriend?'

'Partly,' said Caleb. 'How many times does it have to happen before she gives up? Every guy, she's convinced he's the one, and then she's devastated when he isn't.'

Leo didn't know what to say, so he fell into step with Caleb again. 'But what happens when she gives up?' Leo said. 'She'll be alone. Won't that be worse?'

Caleb nodded. His normal cheeriness had fallen away. This was the Caleb the world didn't often see. The one who worried about his mother, who burned with anger at his father, who thought too hard, too long about the people he loved. Leo slung a companionable arm around Caleb's shoulder.

'But every time she's so optimistic she's met "The One",' said Caleb. 'I wish she really would. The last guy was so nice and he was really smitten with her that I thought maybe he was …'

'What happened?'

Caleb sighed. 'Mum said they just drifted apart. She said breaking up was the right thing to do, even if it hurts in the short term … and then she cried a lot. I wish … I wish there was something I could do.'

Leo tightened his arm, giving his friend a hug. 'All you can do is be there for her. Which you are. She knows that no matter what happens with the other men in her life, you will always love her. And she will always love you.'

They reached the pub and stopped outside. Leo removed his

arm. He watched as Caleb pulled himself together and put his mask of cheerfulness back on.

'You know what?' said Caleb. 'I really fancy a drink.'

'Sounds like a plan.'

Maybe it was just as well that Vidya hadn't joined them.

Chapter 14

They started work a bit later the next day. Partly because it was Sunday, partly because both Leo and Caleb had drunk a little too much at the pub. Leo hadn't drunk enough to do anything wildly out of character but enough to feel it in the morning.

Vidya had made a few amused comments, but mostly, she was quiet. They'd sat in different corners in the meeting room, silently working. Between them they had drunk a huge amount of coffee.

This time Leo volunteered to go and get sandwiches for lunch. He needed the walk to stretch his legs. On his way back to the hotel, he'd had to protect the bag of food from the gulls, which made him think of Vidya. Of course, everything made him think of Vidya these days.

The sun had come out and, when you were in the sunshine, it was pleasantly warm. Along the road Leo noticed there were buds on the plants in the gardens he passed. The sap was rising and there was a feeling of hope starting to grow. Overnight, the earth had decided it was springtime.

It was a shame they were stuck working in this beautiful place. It was a really nice day to take a break, if they had the chance. Could they? The deadline was tight, but maybe they could slack off for a few hours. All three of them had been working hard since Tuesday, and it was Sunday now. The long hours of focus were starting to take a toll. Maybe a rest was just the thing they all needed.

When Leo got back to the meeting room, he found Caleb sitting next to Vidya, sharing her computer screen. She was pointing something out to him and he was leaning across, concentrating. The stab of jealousy Leo felt was entirely unfounded. He shut the door behind him with a quiet click and told himself to pull it together. Caleb had said he wasn't interested in Vidya, so the poor woman was heading towards disappointment. If anything, Leo should feel sad for her. Or feel nothing at all, because it wasn't any of his damn business. If only his heart would listen to his head.

Leo put the bag of sandwiches and crisps down on the table with a thump. They both looked up.

'Oh, lunch,' said Caleb. He glanced at Vidya. 'Have we covered everything here?'

She frowned briefly and said, 'I think so. I'll pull out a report and send it to you so that you can show me how you cross-referenced it.'

Caleb wheeled his chair back to where he normally sat. Anyone else would look ungainly, but somehow he made it look laid back and fun. Since it was the weekend, Caleb was dressed casually and wore jeans. So did Vidya. Leo wasn't sure he approved.

'Vidya was showing me what she got the AI to do. It's quite impressive actually,' Caleb said.

Leo nodded. 'I know.' He had to agree that it was impressive. He still had some reservations about trusting the outputs completely, but Vidya was being careful. The results did seem to be accurate, so he was slowly coming round to trusting it.

'I was reading about the possible use of AI in contract drafting.' Leo unpacked the bag, sorting the sandwiches with the relevant can of drink.

'It'd be fine for standard ones, I should think.' Vidya sounded distracted. Her fingers were still flying over the keyboard – she must be compiling whatever it was Caleb had asked her to find.

Leo stood and studied her for a moment. She looked tired. She had bags under her eyes and her mouth was pulled down at the corners. It couldn't just be that she had been working nonstop. She'd said she'd gone to bed early last night. There must be something else.

Vidya hit a key on her laptop with a flourish. 'There,' she said. 'It's done and on its way to you, Caleb.'

'Thanks, Vid.'

Oh. They'd progressed to nicknames now, had they? Leo took a deep breath and let it out. It was none of his business. How his colleagues chose to speak to each other was between them, so long as no one was offended. 'Shall we break for lunch?'

'Yes. Exactly what I was thinking,' said Caleb.

Vidya checked her phone and frowned. The brief flash of vibrance seemed to disappear, and she looked like she was going to cry.

'Shall we go sit outside? The sun is out.' When she didn't reply, he said, 'Vidya?' He picked up her sandwich and showed it to her.

'Oh. Right. Yes. Sure.'

The sun wasn't strong – it was still too early in the year. It was pleasant but they still needed coats. There were more people than usual out on the terrace. Leo spotted an empty table with an umbrella and made a beeline for it. He expected Vidya to take a seat in the sun, but she chose the seat with the most shade.

Caleb sat fully in the sunlight and tipped his head back. 'Aaah. This is nice.'

Leo had to admit it was nice out there. He tilted his head from side to side to get rid of the stiffness that had set in.

Leo distributed the lunches. They ate in silence for a while. Sneaking a glance at Vidya, he could see that she was still

115

preoccupied. He guessed that her discussion with her sister had definitely affected her.

What could he do to help? Vidya hadn't asked for help or support, so it would be weird to offer it. Leo sighed and looked out at the pale sunlight. It was the nicest day they'd had so far. They had already done one and a half days of overtime this weekend, perhaps it would do them all good to get out a bit.

Caleb sat up. 'How come,' he said, squinting at Vidya, 'you're sitting in the shade?'

Leo had wondered that too but hadn't felt comfortable asking. He knew that Sarah sat in the shade too. When he'd asked her, she'd said it was because only mad dogs and Englishmen went out in the noon-day sun, and laughed.

Vidya chewed her mouthful and swallowed. 'Because I have a lot more melanin than you do and if I spend any time at all in the sun, I get even browner.' She put her sandwich down. 'Here. Let me show you.' She pushed up her sleeve. Leo tried not to stare. Her arm was brown and plump. There was a clear demarcation where her sleeve ended. The exposed part of her arm was clearly browner. 'That's mostly just from yesterday's walk up the hill, and it wasn't even that hot yesterday,' she said. 'You should see my legs in the summer. I'm stripey depending on the length of trousers I wear.'

Leo couldn't stop the mental image. She probably had delightful legs. Maybe knees with cute little dimples at the back. No. No. He looked up at the sky in an effort not to think about his colleague's legs.

A gull flapped down. Leo threw out a hand to cover Vidya's sandwich. She did the same. His hand landed on top of hers, instinctively curling over to grip it. He felt the thrill of contact race up his arm. Her eyes met his. For a second, he had an awful feeling that she could see what he was thinking. He snatched his hand away and flapped it in the direction of the bird. 'Dammit, Charlie, get your own lunch.'

He was rewarded with a small smile from Vidya. That was better.

Once they'd finished lunch, no one seemed keen to move. Vidya was still preoccupied. Caleb announced he was going to the loo and disappeared, leaving Leo alone with her.

He leaned forward. 'Are you sure everything is okay? You seem … sad.'

'I do?' Suddenly, she looked even sadder. 'I had an argument with my sister, that's all. It's … I'll get over it.'

Oh yes, that would do it. He knew all about sisters and arguments. 'Older sister or younger?'

'Younger,' she said, morosely.

'I have one of those. My little sister is the most pig-headed, impulsive and annoying creature.' He thought of Cordelia fondly.

Surprise flashed across Vidya's face. 'Mine too,' she said. Her eyes lost focus again as she sank back into her thoughts. 'I'm trying to help her and she—' Her expression lowered again. 'She's not …'

'Not grateful?' Leo said. He understood that all too well. 'Did she ask you for help?'

Vidya's frown deepened. 'Yes. I mean … she needed it and … no, she definitely *did* ask me to help. She did.'

'Well, that's just rude of her not to appreciate it then,' said Leo.

Vidya sniffed. 'Sometimes I wonder why I even bother doing stuff for her.' She was staring at her hands, but he could bet she wasn't actually seeing them.

'But,' he said, cautiously, 'maybe she will, later. You know, when she's had time to think about it.'

Vidya looked at him through narrowed eyes. She didn't say anything, but she nodded, ever so slightly.

And Leo knew exactly what he needed to do.

Caleb returned. 'Back to it?' he said.

'Actually,' said Leo. 'This is the first nice day we've had since we got here. And it's Sunday. I think we should leave the files

117

for a bit and go explore.'

Caleb put his hands on his hips. 'Who are you and what have you done with Leo?'

'I mean it,' Leo said. 'I'm just as fed up with those documents as you are. We've already worked overtime. Vidya's excellent intervention with AI has bought us a bit of time. Let's just take a half-day off.'

He turned to Vidya, conscious that she hadn't asked him for help. 'You don't have to come with us, obviously, but you're welcome to join.'

She looked from him to Caleb and back again. 'Okay,' she said. 'I'm in.'

Caleb rubbed his hands together. 'Great. We'll meet downstairs in … twenty minutes. It'll give you time to change, Leo.'

Leo looked down. 'Why do I need to change?' He was wearing suit trousers, a shirt and a pullover. Since it was the weekend, he'd been going for smart casual. Caleb and Vidya were both in jeans.

'You look like a lawyer.'

'I am a lawyer.' Leo got up anyway and followed Caleb out. A quick glance over his shoulder showed Vidya shaking her head as she watched them leave. At least she wasn't looking quite so down as she had been.

Vidya didn't bother changing, she was already in jeans, but she swapped her cardigan for the thicker fleece she'd worn on the way down. When she looked in the mirror, she could see evidence of her sleepless night in the deep shadows under her eyes. Her face looked as worn out as she felt. Great. She wasn't exactly in the mood for sightseeing, but she was in even less of a mood for work. Spending some time outside with Leo had its attractions. Besides, it was a good opportunity to find out more about Caleb.

Did she want to, though? She was only doing it for Udeni, who was being a bit of a cowbag right now. Maybe she should stop and just chill.

Yes, Vidya decided as she locked her door, today she would simply enjoy whatever sights the town had to offer.

When she got downstairs, she saw that Leo had swapped the suit trousers for chinos. He still managed to look formal, like he was play-acting at relaxing. It was quite sweet really.

'What is there to see around here?' Caleb stood by the stand which held all manner of leaflets.

Vidya joined him. He passed her the leaflets as he read them.

'Ornamental gardens,' Vidya said. 'The seafront, which we've seen already, the beach. That's pretty much it for here.' She looked up and saw that, for once, the concierge was at the desk. 'We could ask an expert.'

'Let me.' Caleb thrust the rest of the leaflets into her hands and went over to the reception desk, leaving her standing with Leo.

'Are you sure about this?' she said. 'We could just push through and do more work.'

'We're all losing focus now,' said Leo. 'It's best that we have a proper break. Get some air and all that sort of thing. Then we can come back refreshed tomorrow.'

He was standing a respectful distance away from her. He looked faintly concerned. Wonderful. Now the guy she liked was looking at her with pity. Thanks, Udeni.

Caleb came back. 'If we head to the next town over, which has some nice shops in the old part of town, there's a funfair. She said it's open on Sunday until four.'

'Let's see …' Leo frowned at his phone, thoughtfully. 'Ah, yes. Funfair, old shops, tea and cake … arcade.'

'Ooh, arcade!' said Caleb. 'I haven't been to one of those in years.' His eyes lit up. In some ways, he reminded her a lot of Udeni. Was that a good thing? Or not?

Leo raised his eyes and met Vidya's gaze. 'Is there anything you'd particularly like to do?'

She had to stick with them whatever they did. Even without Udeni's needs, Vidya genuinely did want to know more about this baby's father. Besides, she liked their company. When they weren't at work, Caleb and Leo were easy people to be around. She couldn't believe she had once thought that Leo was uptight and annoying. He was tense, sure, but he was also easy to like.

Leo was still waiting for an answer, his expression serious. His gaze was fixed on her face, brow creased slightly as though he was worried about her. He was handsome in a serious and intense kind of way. She wanted to know more about him too. She said, 'Let's explore the next town. I haven't been to a funfair in ages.'

'Well, that's settled then.' Caleb clapped his palms and rubbed them together. 'This is going to be fun.'

Leo nodded. 'It'll definitely do us all good to put some distance between us and the files.' He dug a set of car keys out of his jacket pocket. 'Come on then.'

Chapter 15

Leo drove. He was glad to have something to focus on to avoid making conversation. Caleb was far better at chit-chat than he was. Vidya had somehow got him on to the subject of childhood illnesses, and he was yakking on about the time he got chickenpox. Vidya either fancied Caleb like mad, if she was willing to listen to random stuff like that, or she was a very inquisitive person. Or possibly both.

It was most inconvenient to have developed feelings for this woman, who wasn't interested in him. Worse, who was interested in Caleb. Like he could compete!

But why couldn't it be him, just once?

Leo glanced in the rearview mirror. Vidya was staring out of the window, she wasn't actually listening to Caleb. Oh. She must still be thinking about her argument with her sister. The fact she wasn't all that interested in what Caleb was saying cheered Leo up immensely. He focused on the road. Was it petty of him? Well, yes, but he didn't care.

Hopefully, there would be enough at the next town to take her mind off her troubles. He glanced in the rearview mirror again. She was looking straight at him. He nodded to her. She gave him a tiny smile in return and warmth blossomed in his chest.

There was a pier, a low line of arcades and something that, if you were generous, you could call a funfair. They had unanimously agreed to look at the funfair first. It was noisy and busy. There was a funny mix of hand-painted wooden signage and LED screens. Most of the rides were nothing dramatic, but Leo was pleased to see that there was a roller coaster.

'I guess the nice weather has brought everyone out to the beach,' Caleb said.

It did seem like it. There were a lot of families with kids, all wearing odd combinations of summer and winter clothes. Leo paused to help someone lift their pushchair up a couple of steps. Caleb and Vidya held a gate open for them.

'So, boss? Are the tokens going on the company card?' Caleb asked him.

'I don't think I can get away with that,' Leo said. 'And don't call me boss.' Caleb only did it to annoy him.

They each bought a handful of tokens.

'What shall we do first?' Leo asked, looking at Vidya.

'Let's see. I need three tokens for the roller coaster …' She picked three out and put them in her pocket. Scanning the rides, she said, 'I fancy the helter-skelter. You?'

Caleb nodded. 'That's about as much of a thrill as I can cope with. Let's go. You coming, Leo?'

The helter-skelter was a red-white-and-purple-striped cone sticking up between food stalls. A slide wound around it. People zipped down sitting on mats and slid to a halt on the bottom. There was something timeless and real about it. Unlike some of the other rides, there were no moving parts, and you could imagine it being used exactly in the same way a hundred years ago.

They handed over their tokens and were shown the steps that wound around the inside. The climb up was chilly and steep, and quite dark. Small windows running up the side of the structure let in a meagre amount of light. The structure trembled as people went down the slide. Leo wasn't entirely convinced it was stable, but once you started climbing the stairs, a queue formed behind and you had to keep going. There was no time to change your mind. When they reached the top, the light felt very bright. He shielded his eyes with one hand while a bored-looking kid shoved a coir mat into his other. Caleb had already gone down. Vidya sat on her mat, pushed off and vanished round the slide.

Leo sat on the prickly mat and drew his knees together.

When the kid said, 'Go', Leo pushed himself off. The slide down was surprisingly fast. The salty wind blew in his hair. The view of the small fairground switched repeatedly with the view of the sea as he corkscrewed down. All too soon, he shot out of the end of the slide and slowed to a halt. Caleb gave him a hand up.

When he looked at Vidya, Leo knew immediately that a visit to the fairground had been the right decision. The cloud of gloom that had hung over her had disappeared. She still wasn't her usual sparkly self, but this was progress.

He handed the mat back. 'That was fun. Next?'

Caleb chose hook-a-duck, which all three of them were hilariously bad at. Eventually, Caleb won a small teddy, which he stuffed into his jacket pocket.

After a few more rides, they came to the roller coaster. It wasn't huge, in the grand scheme of roller coasters, but it still dwarfed everything else around it.

Caleb shook his head. 'I'm going to sit here on the nice, safe ground and have an ice cream.'

Vidya raised her eyebrows. 'You don't like heights?'

'It's not the heights,' said Caleb. 'It's being thrown around at high speeds in a small tin can. You two go ahead, though. Take your life – and your lunch – in your hands.'

'Can I leave my handbag with you?' Vidya was already removing it from where it was slung across her body.

'Sure. Do you want me to hold your glasses as well?'

She hesitated. 'I can't see very well without them.' She undid her ponytail and refastened it tightly at the nape of her neck.

'There. Hopefully, my hair should hold the arms of the glasses more securely.'

Since he didn't have long hair, or a spare pair, Leo handed his glasses to Caleb and followed Vidya.

'How well can you see without your glasses?' she asked him.

'I can get by,' Leo said. 'Just don't ask me to read anything.'

They got in next to each other. The bar lowered onto their laps.

When he looked across at her, she gave him the most dazzling grin. Even without his glasses he could see the excitement on her face. It gave him a warm feeling in his chest. He wished he could reach over and touch her. She was so close, but in the back of his mind, he heard the people from HR talking about boundaries. They'd been so firm on the matter of inappropriate conversations at work, he could only imagine how much worse it would be if Vidya reported unwanted touching.

The ride was cranked up to the top of a slope, going higher and higher. Somehow going slowly was worse than plummeting at speed. Leo's heart rate increased. A glance showed him that Vidya's eyes were huge and she was tightly gripping the bar in front of her tightly.

They reached the top of the ascent and the moment before they tipped downwards seemed to last forever. Just when he felt he couldn't take it anymore, the carriage plummeted. The air whipped out of his lungs. Vidya screamed. Her hand clutched at his. He was too preoccupied with hurtling down the slope to respond.

The roller coaster had a loop-the-loop, and after more twists and turns they were returned back to the starting stage.

Leo's heart was loud in his ears and his nerves were singing. Vidya laughed, then turned and grinned at him, eyes shining, and he thought he'd never seen anything so joyful in his life. Her eyes met his. If he'd been a different sort of bloke, he would have swooped in and kissed her right there. Her smile faded, but her eyes didn't leave his. Her hand was still on top of his. It would take only the smallest movement to kiss her.

The restraining bar lifted, forcing them to move apart. She removed her hand from his and the loss of contact felt like a tragedy. Still, probably for the best. She was a work colleague after all. As such, she should be off limits.

He stood and offered his hand to help her out. She took it without hesitation. Something inside him vibrated with pleasure. Although he wasn't holding her hand particularly tightly, he noticed she didn't let go for a few seconds after she was out of the carriage.

At the exit, Caleb was standing by the gate, finishing off a 99 cone.

'Good ride?' His tone suggested that he had seen the bit with the hand holding. Leo was too happy to care.

'It really was,' Vidya said. She bounced in place for a second. 'I'm buzzing now.'

'Well, in that case, it's probably the perfect time to hit the arcades,' said Caleb, as he held out their stuff.

Vidya took her handbag and slung it over her shoulder. 'Let's do it.'

Leo put his glasses back on and walked alongside her. His hand felt empty without hers, so he stuffed it in his coat pocket.

Vidya hadn't been in an arcade in years. After the bright sunlight, it was dark inside, but it was noisy and chaotic. Lights from the machines flashed in different colours, and there was a cacophony of beeps and bings and trills. For a few seconds it was overwhelming. She followed Leo and Caleb towards the machines and slowly acclimatised to the lighting and the sounds.

Leo leaned towards her and said, 'What do you fancy trying?'

She looked around. This wasn't the sort of thing she did. 'I ... don't know,' she said. 'What requires the least hand–eye coordination?'

But then there was an 'oooh' and Caleb bounded off and put

his money in a vintage game machine. Vidya and Leo shrugged to each other and went to watch.

The game involved Caleb using a joystick to shoot things. It wasn't interesting to watch, but she was distracted in any case. Leo was standing next to her. When she had first got into the roller coaster, she hadn't appreciated how close they would be. Sitting so they were thigh to thigh had felt … almost as though she was trespassing on his space. It would have been fine if she didn't fancy him, but since she did, it had felt like the most insistent call on her attention. She hadn't dared look at him in case he'd notice.

When the ride had started, she had put her hand on his in a moment of adrenaline-fuelled panic. He hadn't objected. Not even after the ride had slowed to a halt. At the end of the ride, still buzzing from the high, she had turned to look at him and for a wild second, she'd thought he was going to kiss her. Part of her really wished he had.

Now, Leo was standing next to her, following Caleb's game, egging him on. Her skin prickled with the awareness of him. Glancing sideways, she watched his face. The fast-changing lights reflected off his glasses and made it hard to see his eyes, but the frown that was always present during the working day had gone. He wasn't smiling or laughing, but his features were relaxed. Unguarded.

Leo's expressions were always guarded. His emotions appeared on his face in brief flashes, before he regained control. Caleb had said Leo didn't even realise he was doing it. It must be so exhausting having to school your face to be neutral all the time. No wonder Leo was so tense.

Leo leaned towards Caleb to say something. She watched his lips move. Such an attractive face. She should look away. There were so many reasons not to let herself be drawn any closer. He clearly wasn't looking for a relationship right now. Or ever, possibly. Besides, Leo was technically her line manager while she was on this project. Hankering after him was stupid at best and inappropriate at worst. She had to get a grip.

Caleb lost his game with a score that wasn't anywhere near the highest score.

'Hmm,' said Leo. 'Maybe I should have a go at that.'

'You think you can do better?' A challenge flashed in Caleb's eyes.

Vidya automatically made a mental note that Caleb had a competitive streak. Her attention switched to Leo and she saw the smile in his eyes. He was winding his friend up. Caleb's expression suggested he knew that. 'I mean, you're welcome to try …' he said as he stepped aside so Leo could have a go. He stood by Leo's shoulder, with his arms crossed, watching.

Vidya looked away. Cataloguing information about Caleb had become automatic. Why was she bothering? It wasn't as though Udeni was going to be grateful. Her resistance to finding the father was just a passing fixation, like so many things were with her. Except the baby wasn't a passing thing, was it? The baby, when it came, was a permanent addition to the family. It would be reassuring to know Udeni understood that. It was ridiculous that Vidya was even having to worry about this.

Vidya sighed; her earlier elation had faded. This whole situation was bananas. It *would* be Udeni who got pregnant from a one-night stand with someone she didn't even remember properly. It would be with one of Vidya's work colleagues, rather than a random stranger, because heaven forbid that Udeni's recklessness should only affect her and leave Vidya out of it.

Udeni insisting that she was going to raise the baby by herself was all very grand, but she wasn't really going to, was she? Vidya was going to help. It was inevitable. And Amma and Thatha would rant and shout and probably chew Vidya's ear off for not 'looking after her sister', but once the baby arrived, they'd probably have to fight off babysitting offers from Amma. Udeni would be forgiven in an instant, but Vidya wouldn't be. It was all so damn unfair.

Udeni always got away with everything. There was something about her that made people think she was some sort of sweet angel, when really, she was an impulse-driven hot mess. Vidya was the sensible one who sorted out the messes. If Udeni had been less pretty or Vidya less plain, things would have been so different.

Vidya turned her gaze back to the two men. Leo was frowning with concentration and leaning towards the screen. Caleb was mirroring Leo's movements and muttering things like 'get him' and 'there' and 'yes!' She watched the way Leo's eyes darted around as he played. The firm set of his mouth. The sharpness of his jawline. She really liked this man. He was gentle and had a lovely voice and smelled of aftershave and clean laundry. She liked his fastidious work ethic, his very toned legs and his big, warm hands. But he was her work colleague – and she wasn't her sister – so she couldn't jump on him simply because she wanted to. He might not be interested in her, of course, but she couldn't take a chance to find out. It was so frustrating. She wished that just for once, the real world would just bog off and let her have what she wanted.

Leo's game ended. 'Drat,' he said. 'So close.'

Caleb sagged with exaggerated relief. 'Ha.'

'I'm only ten points behind you. That's what – two hits?'

'Still counts.'

Watching them bicker good-naturedly made Vidya miss Angie, the only person in the world who knew what Udeni was really like. Vidya glanced at her phone; there was no reception. Oh well. It was probably for the best. She may as well enjoy this little respite. Leaving the guys behind, she made her way to a driving game. She was usually pretty good at those.

Chapter 16

Two rounds of driving through twisty virtual terrain and trying not to fly off the track made Vidya feel much better. There was something about concentrating so hard that the real world disappeared. She should do this more often. Maybe not in a slightly fuggy seaside arcade, but just in general.

She found the guys strolling around looking for what to play next.

Caleb said, 'Oh look! Dance Dance Revolution 2!' He rushed forward, hand already in his pocket to get coins out.

'Really?' said Vidya.

'Oh, yeah,' Leo said. 'He loves that one.'

Just as Caleb reached to put his money in, a group of young men arrived at the machine and one of them pushed him out of the way.

'Hey,' said Caleb. 'That's my machine. I was about to put money in.'

'Ah, well.' One of the men, who was wearing, somewhat incongruously, a *Game of Thrones* jumper with 'Team Lannister' on it, squared up to him. 'Shame you didn't actually put your money in and bagsie it then, isn't it?' His friends stood behind him, trying half-heartedly to look threatening.

Leo quietly stepped in front of Vidya. She peered round him.

Caleb's eyes moved quickly, from one man to the other. 'Tell you what,' he smiled, 'since we both want it so badly, how about we have a dance off? Loser pays for the round and gets the machine for the next round.'

Leo sighed. 'I think it'll be okay,' he said to Vidya, quietly. 'I'd better—' He stepped up next to Caleb.

Lannister T-shirt guy sized up Leo, who seemed so stiff, he looked like he might creak if he moved. 'Okay, but not you and me, him …' He gestured to one of his friends. 'And him.' He pointed to Leo.

'Oh. I—' Leo began.

'Deal,' said Caleb. He patted Leo on the shoulder. 'Go on. It'll be fun.'

Vidya heard the edge to his voice. Caleb was amused? Leo would probably lose this horrifically. Why would Caleb do that to his friend? She ran through what she knew about him. Had there been any indication of this kind of malice before? Was there a sadistic streak she needed to make note of for the baby's sake?

Leo removed his jacket and handed it to Caleb. He pulled his keys and phone out of his pockets and gave them to Vidya. They were still warm from being in his pockets. He pulled his jumper over his head and handed that to Caleb too. Now, Leo stood, looking awkward in his chinos and collared T-shirt.

'Okay. Let's go!'

Leo got onto the machine, faced the screen and put his hands on the support bar behind him. Beside him, his opponent did the same. Both the screens in front of them lit up. Follow the instructions on the screen and put your feet on the relevant flashing red and blue squares on the floor in front of you.

A countdown appeared. Vidya watched Leo blow out his cheeks. The now familiar mask of concentration descended.

It turned out that Leo was incredible at it. He made a few false moves at the start, not hitting the flashing tile fast enough, then he seemed to find his rhythm. Vidya watched, entranced, as he danced, feet moving faster and faster as the game progressed. His eyes were targeted on the screen, his hands gripping the support bar. If she hadn't fancied him before, she would have definitely fallen for him now.

His opponent was good, but he wasn't keeping up in the way Leo was.

Vidya glanced at Caleb, who was watching with a hawk-like grin on his face. He had known, she realised. He had known that Leo was good at this and that the other guy was likely to choose Leo assuming he would be easier to beat than in-your-face Caleb. She had heard of darts hustles and pool hustles, but this was the first time she'd ever heard of a Dance Dance Revolution hustle. A giggle rose from her chest.

Leo let go of the bar and jumped round in a circle, turning his head to keep his eyes on the screen. Now he was dancing without holding on to anything. The tune reached a crescendo and blared out a final chord.

Leo leaned forward, his hands braced on his knees, and looked up at the scoreboard. Ninety-one per cent. The word 'winner' flashed above it.

His opponent scored eighty-four per cent. The two men shook hands and Leo stayed in place while his opponent stepped off. His hair was damp with sweat and his eyes were gleaming. He caught Vidya's eye and gave her a proper grin, like the one on the roller coaster. She felt butterflies flutter in her stomach.

'How …?' she said. 'How are you so good at that?'

'Lots of practice,' he said, loudly, so that she could hear above the holding track of the machine.

Caleb finished talking to the other men, took off his jacket and jumper, stashed them in the corner by Vidya, and stepped up onto the empty platform. 'Ready to go again?' he asked Leo.

Leo pushed his hair back, rolled his shoulders and said, 'Sure.'

She watched them. Caleb was a much more fluid dancer than

Leo and looked like he was having more fun. She thought about what Udeni had said, tall, funny, sexy and a good dancer. Apart from the tattoo placement, that was all she'd remembered about him. Even the photos of the guys on the website hadn't helped. Perhaps if Udeni saw a photo of them now, in the dim lighting with flashing lights, while they danced, it might jog her memory. Quietly, Vidya filmed a five-second clip. She would ask them for permission later.

When she lowered her phone, it occurred to her that tall, funny, sexy and a good dancer could apply to either of the two guys equally, albeit in very different ways. Caleb was exactly the type of guy that Udeni would find funny and sexy. Turned out Leo was more her own type. Funny and sexy were all a matter of taste.

There was still a chance that Caleb wasn't Udeni's guy. Until Vidya or Angie found out about the tattoo or got some other confirmation, it was still a fifty–fifty split between him and Piotr. Vidya rather hoped it was Caleb. Despite what her sister said about not needing to know anything about the father, Vidya was glad that she'd got to know him, at least a little bit. She liked him. He would make a good dad.

Maybe she should try and persuade Udeni to meet him. For a moment, Vidya allowed herself a little daydream, where she and her sister had boyfriends who got on well. Caleb could see his child, Udeni could have another person to help her, Vidya could hang out with Leo whenever the guys came round.

Then, like the inverse of a bubble rising, her feelings sank. Vidya remembered that she wasn't talking to her sister right now. And she wasn't going out with Leo. All she knew was that she liked him. She had no idea if he had any feelings either way about her. She turned her attention back to the dance machine.

The guys had reached the place in the sequence where they had to turn in a circle. They were perfectly in sync. She applauded.

The sound of more applause told her that the group of guys from before were still hanging around watching. When the round came to an end, everyone leaned in to look at the scores. Leo was at ninety-two per cent and Caleb had a respectable eighty-eight per cent. The guys fist-bumped each other.

'We've one more round to go,' said Caleb.

Leo held up his hands, panting. 'I'm out.' He looked across at her.

'Vidya, you should have a go.'

'I'm not very good at dancing.'

Leo jumped down lightly and came to stand next to her. He was still breathing heavily and glistened with sweat. She had a sudden mental image of running her hands through his shirt and feeling the muscles underneath. It brought with it a wave of heat. No. No. She had to surreptitiously pinch herself to shake herself out of the reverie.

'It's not dancing exactly,' Leo said, as he took his things off her hands. 'It's just a game. Try and keep up with the lights on the screen, or on the floor; it's easier to watch your feet. Have a go.' He touched her back, lightly. A featherlight touch that she felt all the way into her chest. 'You might enjoy it.'

'Come on,' said Caleb. 'It'll be fun.'

The crowd of onlookers dispersed. Vidya nodded. 'Okay, fine. But I'm warning you, I'm terrible.'

She tried. She really did. But she was, indeed, terrible. She looked at her final score of thirty-one per cent, next to Caleb's eighty-nine per cent and it was so out of kilter that she started to laugh.

Leo gave her an amused smile, one that lasted more than half a second. He seemed so much more relaxed now. Also, a bit rough and rumpled, which was so very attractive.

He handed Vidya her coat.

'I knew I was bad, but I can't believe I was that bad,' she said, in between giggles.

'You were pretty bad,' said Leo, as they reunited phones and coats with the right owners.

It seemed a strangely cosy thing to do, as though they were really comfortable with each other now – which they were, she realised. She had spent a lot of concentrated time with these guys. Even if she never got any closer to Leo, she felt like they both had become her friends. She'd never expected that to happen. You didn't get to make new friends very often once you started work and settled into a rut. It was nice to know that she still could.

'The important thing,' Leo continued, 'is that you had fun.'

Caleb joined them. They walked towards the exit. After that performance, any of the other games would be an anticlimax. The sun was low in the sky and the wind had picked up, making it much chillier. Vidya tucked her scarf firmly into the collar of her coat.

'How did you get so good at Dance Dance Revolution?' she asked. 'You're both really good.'

'There was this bar we used to go to when we worked together before. Years ago. They had a machine and we used it often.' Caleb grinned. 'Besides …' He jerked a thumb towards Leo. 'This guy had tap-dancing lessons forever.'

'You did?' She looked up at Leo.

He shrugged. 'My parents were theatre people, remember. We were taught to dance pretty much as soon as we could walk. I am, by my family's standards, a terrible dancer.'

'But you're great at it.'

'Only when I know the choreography. I can do footwork. But I can't emote and I'm not graceful. Apparently, I just look like I'm being tortured, but in a very musical way.' Leo's features softened. 'My little sister, Cordelia, is the one who got all the singing and dancing genes. She's a West End actress.'

'What about Rosie?' Caleb asked. 'She must have inherited some of the skills too.'

'She can sing. Wonderfully. She sings in a choir on Sundays, for … you know, stress relief.' Leo leaned towards Vidya and said, 'That's my older sister. She's an accountant.'

'You and Rosie,' said Caleb, shaking his head. 'The kids who ran away from the circus to become suits.'

'Watching bailiffs empty your house will do that to you,' Leo said, ruefully.

'Oh my God, that sounds horrible,' Vidya said. 'How old were you?'

'Quite young.' He gave it some thought. 'Cordy was a toddler, so I must have been about six.'

'You poor thing. How scary.' The urge to put her arms around him was incredibly strong.

His face remained neutral. 'Like I said, I was young. I remember Rosie being really angry with my parents for years, though. So was Grandma.'

Vidya dug her hands deeper into the pockets of her coat. Leo had turned away from her to look at the sea. She turned around too and watched the setting sun. There was something magnetic about the water. The dying rays of the sun tinted Leo's features gold. She tried to imagine him as a frightened little boy, watching his home being emptied.

'Is that why you grew up with your grandma? Because your parents lost your home?'

He nodded. 'Something like that. They took us to Grandma's and then went touring for a while, to make some money. Also, I guess it meant they didn't need a place to stay because they were moving as part of the tour.'

'That sounds harsh.'

He shook his head. 'Not for me. Living with my parents was difficult. They were always obsessed with their work. They would be in character at random times. I had trouble working out when they were in character and when they were real. And they used to make us do acting exercises all the time and ...' He shook his head. 'Anyway. Grandma did normal parenting stuff, like making us follow a routine and shouting at us to do our homework. She taught us all about budgeting, because she said that two people who were idiots with money was enough for one family.'

'She sounds amazing.'

'She was.'

'Did your parents just leave you there with her?' She tried to picture her own parents giving her and Udeni up to be raised by someone else. She couldn't even begin to imagine it. She was so lucky and she'd never even known.

'When I was about twelve, Mum and Dad were settled again and sent for us. Cordy was delighted, but Rosie refused to go and I didn't want to leave her. So … I stayed with her and Grandma. Eventually, Cordy came back to us too.'

'Your parents ran out of money again?'

He nodded. 'No sense of responsibility at all. They're still acting, and are also tour guides in Cornwall now.'

Vidya thought about her own parents, who took family responsibility very seriously. She'd had it pressed upon her throughout her childhood. 'I can't imagine parents who aren't serious about things,' she said.

'Oh, they were serious all right,' said Leo. 'Just not about looking after us or keeping an eye on money. They were serious about their acting careers. Everything and everyone else came second.'

Caleb nudged Leo. 'Tell her about your name.'

'Your name?' She glanced up at Leo in the failing light. 'Is your name not Leo?'

'It is. But it's short for Leontes,' said Caleb. 'But that's his middle name. You'll never guess what his first name is.'

Leo gave a long-suffering sigh. 'Caleb, really?'

'I want to know now,' said Vidya. 'I'm guessing Leontes is … something from Shakespeare?'

'The first Shakespeare character my dad played.'

'His first name begins with O,' said Caleb, grinning wildly. 'You'll never guess what it is.'

Her knowledge of Shakespeare was pretty rudimentary. 'O?'

136

Only one name came to mind. 'Othello?'

'No,' said Leo. 'Thankfully, not that. No. It's Oberon. After my mum's favourite character. I choose to use Leo instead. For obvious reasons.'

'Oberon? As in, the king of the fairies from *A Midsummer Night's Dream*?' Because she remembered that much.

'Imagine,' said Caleb. 'Might as well wear a sign saying, "Kick me".'

Vidya was looking straight at Leo, which was why she saw the quick tug of his smile.

'Right?' Leo said. His voice was so deadpan that it struck her as funny.

She couldn't help the giggle that escaped her. 'Wow. Your parents really hated you.'

'I'm glad my childhood misery amuses you.' There was a trace of laughter in his voice.

She laughed. God, she loved a man with a sense of humour about himself. It didn't hurt that he was handsome either. She looked up at him and wished …

They walked along, with the shops on one side and the sea on the other. The sun was lowering even further now and the beach was emptying. The stalls on the pavement turned on their lights, making everything a little more magical.

'Oh, look. Candy floss,' said Caleb. 'I haven't had that in years.' He dug out his wallet. 'Do you guys want some?'

'Ugh, no,' said Leo. 'Too sweet for me.'

'I'll pass too,' said Vidya. She was all for sweet things, but something that was pure spun sugar was too much, even for her.

'Suit yourselves.' Caleb practically ran to join the queue. 'I'll be right back.'

'Sometimes,' said Leo. 'It's like spending time with a ten-year-old.'

While they were waiting for him, Vidya and Leo leaned against the railings and looked out to sea. Caleb did remind her of her

137

sister. Udeni could be childlike … and childish, at times. The thought reminded Vidya of the argument that they were still having. All the fun had meant that she'd forgotten about it for a few hours. It came crowding back now.

Leo took a deep breath and let it out. 'So, do you want to talk about it?'

Huh? 'About what?'

Leo tilted his head to the side. 'Your argument with your sister. You're thinking about it again right now, aren't you?' He paused for a moment and added, 'You don't have to tell me, obviously. It's none of my business. But sometimes, it helps to talk to someone who won't judge.'

Vidya blinked. He might not judge her, but he might judge Udeni. No matter what Vidya's own opinions were on the matter, she wasn't going to let someone else be mean about her sister. When she narrowed her eyes, he seemed puzzled.

'I'm told I'm a good listener,' he said.

What the hell. Not talking about it was making her head hurt. 'I had an argument with her.'

'Oh, ouch,' said Leo. 'Did she do something to you or your stuff?'

'No. Nothing like that.' It was, on the face of it, a fairly trivial argument, but Udeni seemed to be taking it more seriously than expected. Did she really feel that Vidya was judgemental and superior? Was she? Udeni did do some thoughtless things without any care towards the consequences. But still … right now Udeni was fragile and not fully herself. 'I suppose I should be the bigger person and apologise.'

'Let me guess,' Leo said. 'You're often the one who apologises?'

'How did you know?'

'Something about the way you talk about her,' he said. 'You're very protective of her.'

Vidya thought about how protective she felt towards her sister, despite everything. She sighed. 'I guess I have to be.'

Leo said nothing, but he raised an eyebrow. He really was listening.

The wind picked up. She caught the edges of her wildly flapping coat and tamed them by zipping it up.

'When I was about eight and my sister was about five, she had an accident,' she said. 'We were in the playground and I was supposed to be looking after her. It was a pretty safe place, to be fair. But she fell off the top of the climbing frame and hit her head, hard enough to be knocked out. It was one of those frames like a pyramid and there was a space in the middle, you know, underneath. That's where she fell. It took the grown-ups ages to get her out and she was unconscious for a couple of days. They thought she might have brain damage or something.' Vidya remembered the weight of her guilt. Her parents hadn't said it was her fault, nor had they said it wasn't. She was supposed to be the one looking after little Udeni. Vidya should have been watching.

'That's hardly your fault,' said Leo, his voice tight.

'I felt like it was. I've been looking after her ever since.'

Leo nodded. He was quiet for a moment, then said, 'You're not still blaming yourself, are you?'

Was she? She wasn't sure. 'No …' she said, carefully. 'But I think the instinct to step in and stop her from doing anything too stupid is still strong.' A sudden sigh. 'And honestly, she does do a lot of things that are stupid.'

Leo made a thoughtful humming noise. 'Are you sure they're stupid? Or just things that *you* think are stupid?'

'What?' Vidya snapped. 'I don't judge her.' Well, okay maybe she judged her a little bit. But not so that it showed. She thought about her argument with Udeni earlier. What if it did show? What if she wasn't as good at hiding it as she thought she was.

'I'm just speaking from my own experience,' said Leo. 'Cordelia takes after my parents a lot. She tends to do impulsive things and often will run out of money, despite Gran and Rosie's best efforts. Sometimes, when Cordy explains why she did things, I

139

can understand her reasons.'

'Let me guess,' said Vidya. 'She always comes to you, rather than your big sister, because you're the sympathetic one?' Just like Udeni always came to Vidya first. If, or when, they told their parents, Vidya would be there in her corner.

'I suppose she does, yes,' said Leo. He frowned intently for a moment. 'I don't think I mind, to be honest. I'd rather she come to me than get help from a stranger. There are a lot of nasty people out there. Lots of nice ones too, don't get me wrong, but Cordy … she has no radar for that sort of thing.'

Oh, Vidya recognised that too. 'They just do things without thinking about the consequences. Then when the consequences come back and bite them … because they always do …'

'They come to you to sort it out.' He looked at her and she felt understanding move between them.

'Exactly,' she said, softly. Something loosened inside her chest. Somebody else felt the way she did. She wasn't being unreasonable or selfish.

He held her gaze. 'But we still do it,' he said. 'Every time, we step up. Why is that, do you think?'

Vidya looked away, because tears were gathering. 'Programming?'

Leo gave a little huff of laughter. 'Or love. I mean, I love my sisters. Both of them. And if they need me … I'm always going to be there. I'd like to think that if I needed them, they would be there for me too.' He glanced in the direction of the stall where Caleb was watching candy floss being wound around a stick. 'Same with Caleb.'

Vidya watched the shifting sea and thought about Udeni – about the evenings watching *Cobra Kai* together on Netflix, of the times Udeni had run out to buy painkillers when Vidya was doubled over with period pain, of Udeni covering for Vidya to their parents when she was late coming home. Udeni needed Vidya's help with big screw-ups, but Udeni did help in small ways. They loved each other. The argument was just an argument. It would pass.

'I should call her,' she said, quietly.

'Probably,' Leo said, kindly.

Vidya turned, so that she was facing him. He hesitantly moved so that he was half facing her.

'You're a good man,' she said.

'Thank you,' he said. 'I would say the same back, but "a good woman" just sounds weird and patronising.'

She laughed. 'Does a bit.'

'But you're very organised and professional. I like that.' His eyes met hers. 'I like—'

A movement made her flinch. Bloody seagulls. 'Dammit, Charlie.'

'I really do *not* like that bird,' said Leo.

She laughed. The moment was broken. She leaned her elbows on the railing again.

Caleb returned carrying a cloud of pink on a stick. Just looking at it made Vidya's teeth hurt. They resumed walking.

'Try some.' Caleb held the candy floss out to her.

'No, thanks. That's too sweet, even for me.'

'I'll pass too,' said Leo.

'You don't know what you're missing.' Caleb tilted his head to the side, trying to take a bite.

Vidya shook her head. This was exactly the sort of thing Udeni would do.

'Are you seriously going to eat all that? You'll feel sick,' said Leo.

'I'll be fine,' said Caleb.

'Hmm. Just don't make a mess in the car.'

Caleb made a humph noise. Both the others turned to look at him. 'Sorry,' he said. 'I got candy floss in my nose. Yuck. My face is all sticky now.'

Vidya stared at him, not sure whether to be amused or exasperated.

'Seriously,' said Leo. 'You really are a child.'

'You need to embrace your inner child more,' said Caleb. 'Here. Hold this.' He thrust the candy floss towards Leo and dug around in his pockets. He produced a tissue and started to rub his nose.

'You're lucky Charlie the seagull isn't here,' said Vidya.

'Even seagulls know not to eat candy floss,' Leo said.

For some reason, this struck Vidya as very funny. She laughed out loud. Both men looked at her and grinned, almost indulgently, like her happiness made them happy too. She saw that expression on Angie and Udeni sometimes. It made her feel loved.

Chapter 17

When Leo pulled into the hotel car park later that evening, Caleb leapt out of the car almost before it had stopped. He leaned back and took in huge, dramatic gulps of air.

'Is he going to be okay?' Vidya said, from the back.

'He'll be fine,' said Leo. 'After all that candy floss, no wonder he feels a bit queasy. Just watch though. He'll be back to beer and burgers in an hour.'

'Good.' She let herself out of the car. Leo followed suit and locked up.

'Um … listen,' Vidya said. 'Thanks for this afternoon. I was feeling a bit down and it's really helped.'

Leo moved out of the way to let her pass. 'It was my pleasure,' he said. 'Genuinely. I haven't been on a Dance Dance Revolution machine for ages. It's nice to know I've still got the skills.'

Her eyes sparkled. 'I'm so impressed.'

He gave, what he hoped, was a modest shrug that didn't give away the way his heart soared.

Caleb was walking around the car park swinging his arms.

'I'll stay with him,' said Leo. 'You can go and call your sister, if you want.'

Vidya's gaze followed Caleb as he paced. 'I guess I should.' She nodded, as though she'd just persuaded herself. 'Yes. I'll do that.'

Leo watched her leave, her head bowed as she looked at her phone. She seemed happier now. Hopefully, her chat with her sister would cheer her up even more. At least, arguing with sisters was something he could help with.

He thought about her laughter when the roller coaster ride ended. It was a thing of such beauty. If only he could make her laugh like that again. It had made him feel ... different. A fizz of something he hadn't felt in a long, long time. Not since Jessica. Everything about Vidya drew him to her. Her laugh, her competence, the way her hips swayed when she walked ...

Caleb came up to him and nudged him on the shoulder. 'Man, you have it bad,' he said.

Leo snapped his attention away from Vidya. 'What?'

'You. You're so into Vidya. Just look at you, watching her arse like a love-lorn puppy.'

'I was not watching her arse.' Embarrassment flared up to his face because, of course, he had been, hadn't he?

'Yeah, you were,' said Caleb, cheerily.

'She's a *work colleague*.' Leo turned away from his friend and watched the seagulls swooping around, probably looking for opportunities to steal food and ruin meaningful conversations.

'You know, that's not the barrier you think it is. Just because Jessica made your working life miserable, doesn't mean it'll always be like that.' Caleb nodded towards Vidya. 'You should ask her out. I reckon you're in with a chance.'

Leo opened his mouth to give his usual rebuttals, but something made him pause. Her hand clamped on top of his. The way she'd looked at him when he came off the dance machine. That unguarded laugh. Maybe ... 'You think?' he said.

'I reckon,' said Caleb. 'I have good instincts about this sort of thing, remember?'

He did. But ... 'She's always asking questions about you, though,' Leo said. 'Are you sure it's not you she's interested in?'

Caleb frowned. 'I don't get that vibe from her. But you're right, she does ask lots of questions. Have you considered that maybe she's asking both of us questions, not just me? Maybe … it's just me that actually answers while you get your moody man thing on and don't say anything.'

Leo's first instinct was to deny that, but he thought about it. Cordy was always telling him that he was too quiet, too 'moody' as Caleb so elegantly put it, that he should open up and show people how he felt. Every time someone said that to him, it fired off the part of his mind that stored memories of his parents, who played emotion so liberally that he'd stopped knowing what was real and what was not. *No, darling, don't look down, that makes you look insincere. You need to project your feelings. Show that you're happy. Really show it. Emote. No, not like that. Like this, see.*

He had never managed to produce the level of expression his parents wanted. Now he couldn't bring himself to put his emotions on display for people to see because he was no longer sure he wasn't lying about them.

'If you don't show people how you feel, how will they know?' Caleb said.

Leo sighed. 'But how do I know for sure? I'm attracted to her, but how do I know that's real? Not just a flash in the pan? Attraction changes, remember.' His feelings for Jessica had certainly gone from one extreme to another within minutes.

Caleb stood in front of him and put his hands on Leo's shoulders. 'Mate,' he said. 'You're my best friend. I'd like to think I know you, at least a little bit.'

Leo inclined his head. Caleb probably knew him better than anyone else.

'You're a great guy. You need to stop second guessing yourself and playing it safe.' Caleb glanced over his shoulder to where Vidya was standing, her back very straight, speaking into her phone. 'Vidya seems nice. She's serious, like you. Okay, a bit nosy, but generally sensible. She's good at her job, which I know you like. And, probably most importantly, she doesn't treat you like you make her want to run away and cry.'

'I don't make people cry.'

Caleb rolled his eyes. 'Okay. Maybe not cry, but you definitely upset people.'

'I don't mean to upset them. I just expect them to do their job properly. There's a difference.'

'Don't change the subject.'

'I—' Okay. He *was* changing the subject. He glanced at Vidya too. 'I'm still not convinced you're right. And if you're wrong, I'll have made things awkward with a work colleague, whom I respect. It's not worth the risk.'

'You are so stubborn,' said Caleb. 'Sometimes, I could just punch you.'

Leo looked into his friend's eyes. 'And I'd run away,' he said. 'Because I am much faster than you.'

Caleb laughed. 'One of these days …' He removed his hands from Leo's shoulders. 'But think about it. If you don't at least try, you'll really regret it later. It's not often you meet someone you genuinely like.'

All the way over at the spot where the driveway met the hotel entrance, Vidya was talking earnestly. Her hair flew around her face and she tried to tether it with her free hand. His attraction to her was hugely inconvenient. It messed with his concentration when he was supposed to be working and messed with his sleep at night. Caleb was right. It wasn't often this happened.

'But what if she likes *you*, really?' Leo said. All the times when she had just been friendly to him and then switched focus to Caleb; there had to be reason for that.

'Then I promise you, I am not attracted to her.'

Leo raised his eyebrows at his friend.

'No, seriously. I'm … really not interested.' Caleb frowned. 'I've been a bit less interested in general lately,' he said. He looked uncomfortable.

'Oh?' said Leo, glad to have the attention removed from him.

'Hmm,' said Caleb. 'I met someone who had a real impact on me. There was …' He wiggled his fingers. 'Something. A connection.'

'Who is this woman? Are you going to see her again? Why have I not heard about this before?'

Caleb shook his head. 'It's nothing. I don't think I'll see her again. It's complicated.'

'You haven't fallen for a married woman?' Leo narrowly avoided adding 'again'. Caleb had been quite upset by the whole thing last time. He was all for having fun, but he drew the line at married women.

'I don't think she's married—' Caleb shook his head. 'Never mind. Forget it. I think I'm just a bit obsessed because I know I won't see her again and it wasn't really my call, that's all.' Caleb's smile was back. 'Well … how about we focus on you this evening? We're not going to go back to work, are we? So why don't we go to the pub when Vidya finishes her phone call. It'll do us all some good to loosen up a bit.'

Leo drew a deep breath. 'Let's do that.'

'Who knows, maybe we could find a karaoke ba—'

'No.'

They ended up going to the same pub as before. Leo didn't want the day to end. His mission to cheer Vidya up had succeeded. She was currently sitting opposite him, slowly drinking a glass of wine, laughing at some story that Caleb was telling them. She was lovely. Leo took a sip of his pint and watched the way her cheeks rose when she smiled. Her face looked so full and soft. He wondered how it would feel to cup her face in his hands. To kiss her. To feel all that warmth and softness up close.

Work colleague though. He sighed. Next to him, Caleb nudged him. 'What's the matter with you?'

'Oh. Just the Sunday blues,' Leo said. 'There's a lot of work to cover. I was thinking about that.'

'Oh, man. Did you have to remind us? Now I'm depressed too,' said Caleb.

'Sorry,' Leo said, without any remorse.

'I guess we should go back to the hotel after this one drink,' said Vidya.

'That was the plan,' said Leo.

'You are both so boring sometimes,' Caleb said. He finished his pint. 'I am going to get another one.'

Leo watched Vidya shake her head, her expression more amused than worried. He knew Caleb well enough not to be concerned. He also knew that this relaxed time would end tomorrow. Tomorrow, they would be back to reading contracts and compiling lists of red flags. Tonight, they were still off. If he was going to talk to Vidya, he should do it now.

How did one go about flirting with a work colleague anyway? It had been so long since he'd wanted to flirt with anyone. How did you make conversation? He wasn't usually this bad at it. It was like his brain had deliberately deleted all the small-talk options. Hobbies. He could ask her about her hobbies. Wait, what were his hobbies? He must have some. Did running and keeping up the tap dance lessons as a form of exercise count as hobbies?

Vidya finished checking her phone and looked up at him with a smile. Now or never.

'So … uh. What do you do in your spare time? Do you have any hob—'

Vidya's attention was on something behind his shoulder. Her smile faded and was replaced by a frown. Leo twisted in his seat to see what was going on.

She was looking at the bar, where Caleb was talking to a pretty woman who was clearly interested in him. Caleb said something and the woman laughed and rested her hand on his arm.

'Oh.' Leo turned back to see Vidya was still frowning disap-provingly. While Caleb might not have any feelings for Vidya, she seemed to have feelings for him. Leo took a gulp of his drink and swallowed down the throat punch of disappointment. Ah well. At least he'd found out before he made a fool of himself. He took another sip of his drink. Thank heaven for small mercies.

Vidya looked at him. 'Are you wanting to get another drink?' she said.

'Hmm?' He looked at his pint. It was nearly empty. 'I … er, no. I was suddenly thirsty, that's all. I still don't intend to stay out much longer.'

She swirled her glass of wine. 'Me neither.' She took a large sip. There wasn't much left in her glass either.

Caleb came back, the woman he'd just met following behind.

'Guys,' he said. 'These ladies …' He gestured to his new friend and a group of laughing women sitting not far away. 'These ladies know of a karaoke bar.'

'No. No karaoke for me,' Leo said, holding up his hands.

Vidya shook her head too.

'Well, in that case …' said Caleb. 'Leo, would you mind walking Vidya back to the hotel? I might see how my karaoke skills are.'

'We start at nine tomorrow,' Leo warned. Not that Caleb needed reminding.

'I'll be there for breakfast as usual,' said Caleb. He clamped a hand on Leo's shoulder, turned so that Vidya couldn't see his face and gestured with his eyes towards her. He mouthed, *Go on.*

Leo tried to protest, but Caleb patted him on the shoulder and left, apparently more drunk than he possibly could be on one pint. Caleb was still under the delusion that Vidya wasn't interested in him. She clearly was. But Caleb was trying to push her and Leo together, and now he had left Leo to spend time with Vidya. What a mess.

Leo wondered about texting Caleb, but he knew that it wouldn't make a difference. Caleb would just accuse him of still being hung up on Jessica and too chicken to follow his heart. When Leo looked at Vidya, she was typing on her phone again.

She had sucked in her bottom lip as she concentrated. It was the most adorable thing he'd ever seen.

Still, there really was no use in pursuing someone whose eyes were set on someone else.

She raised those eyes while he was still looking at her.

'Er … did you want to head back now?' he said.

She nodded. 'Let's.' She drained her wine with a gulp.

He did the same with the remainder of his pint.

Chapter 18

It was fully dark now and there was a chill in the air. Vidya removed her handbag from around her neck, stuck it between her knees and zipped up her jacket.

'Would you like me to hold that for you?' Leo asked. He had done up his long coat too, but the ends of it flapped like an angry gull.

How inelegant she must look, with her bag clamped between her knees, in a half crouch. Ah, well, if she'd wanted to appear elegant in front of Leo, that ship had well and truly sailed. She pulled the zip up to her chin, retrieved her bag and slung it across her body again. 'All done,' she said, with a cheer she didn't feel.

'Shall we walk the back way? Or go down to the promenade and walk by the sea.'

'Oh, sea,' she said. Why would she want to walk through damp dark streets, when the promenade was available? She couldn't see the sea at home. Besides, it was a longer walk and she got to spend more time with him.

They set off. Both with their hands deep in their pockets. The thought that Caleb had gone off for another one-night encounter bothered Vidya. It's not like he was connected to Udeni in any way, but … it felt wrong. Udeni might be an annoying and ungrateful little minx, but she was at home, with her digestion and emotions thrown into chaos, because of his baby, and he was off having fun with some random woman he'd met in a bar. This gave Vidya a problem. Should she tell Udeni? What good would that do? Seeing as Udeni had been a random woman he'd met at a party when they slept together, Udeni knew what he was like.

Getting to know Caleb in the past week, Vidya realised that she'd started thinking of him as Udeni's potential partner. If he knew about the baby, he would care. She was sure of it.

'Does he do that often?' she said. Leo turned his head. It was too dark to see his expression clearly. 'Caleb. Does he regularly go off with random strangers?'

Leo was quiet for a few minutes. They reached the seafront and crossed the road so that they were walking parallel to the sea. 'Not … often,' he said, finally. 'When he's had too much to drink or … if he's upset about something, then yes.' In the yellow light of the streetlamps, she could see his eyes glitter.

Leo looked sad. 'Why do you ask?'

'I dunno.' She couldn't exactly blurt out everything. 'I guess I didn't realise he was the sort to … shag around like that.' Then, realising how it sounded, she added, 'Not that there's anything wrong with that.'

'No. He's single. If the lady is a consenting adult and also single, then no, there's nothing wrong.' He shook his head firmly.

'Yes. Exactly.' Vidya was pretty sure that was the view Udeni would take too. At least, it was what she would have said before. Did she feel the same way? Now that there had been consequences to her one-night stand. Really, did Udeni even fully appreciate that there was going to be a baby at the end of all this? It wasn't a fun game. It was a life. Two – because Udeni's life would never be the same either.

Her phone call to her sister hadn't gone well. Udeni had simply refused to answer. Vidya had ended up talking to Angie instead. Thank goodness for Angie, who was keeping an eye on Udeni and making sure she ate. Angie was doing her best to stay out of the argument between the two sisters, but it couldn't be easy for her. Vidya sighed. So many things to worry about.

'Are you upset about Caleb running off like that?' Leo asked. His eyes were on the path ahead.

What? Oh, right. That's what they'd been talking about. 'No,' she said. 'Just surprised, that's all.'

Another few minutes of silence. The easy atmosphere between them had gone. Leo seemed distant and tense again. Perhaps he didn't approve of Caleb gallivanting about when they had work the next day. Or perhaps she had somehow upset him.

'Thanks for walking me back,' she said. 'I appreciate it.'

A brief smile. That was a good sign. She couldn't believe she'd once thought he was cold and robotic. Once you knew how to read him, he was really quite expressive.

'I'm heading back to the same place,' he said. 'It's hardly an imposition.'

'All the same.' The wind blew Vidya's hair in her face and she pulled her hand out of her pocket to push it back. 'And thanks for letting us have half the day off.'

'Ugh,' he said. 'You make me sound like a tyrant.'

'You did make us work on Saturday.'

'I said you didn't have to.'

She scoffed. 'Right. Like I could have swanned off while you sat in that room, poring over documents.'

'Some might have done,' he said. 'But you're conscientious. I appreciate that.'

Talking about work was a safer topic. 'Do you think we'll get everything done in time?'

'Potentially,' he said. 'If not, we'll have to get Stella to scan everything we haven't read. It'll take her quite some time to do that.'

'Did you find anything in the land stuff?'

'A few things will need negotiating, but nothing that's a deal breaker. You?'

'A few penalties if they change suppliers, which I think they intend to do because they've got brand deals in place already. I'm manually listing those.'

'Your whizzy AI didn't catch them all?'

'It caught most of them, actually,' she said. 'But not all of them and it's too important not to check.'

His nod suggested that he approved of this assessment.

'Two more days to get it all read,' she said. 'It's a shame we can't extend it a couple more days.'

'Caleb and I fly out to Europe on Wednesday night, so there's not much choice,' Leo said. 'We have to leave here on Wednesday morning at the latest.'

They approached the hotel and started up the steep slope. A car drove up, which meant they had to step off the road into the rock-lined border. When the car had gone, they resumed their trek uphill. Vidya, who was less fit than Leo, was soon out of breath. He slowed down to keep pace with her, but the difference in the levels of effort was so embarrassing that she pushed herself. By the time she got to the top, her thighs were burning and she was so hot that she'd unzipped her coat. It flapped around her in the most irritating way.

Leo had stopped a short distance ahead and was waiting. She resumed walking, without paying attention to her feet. Something underfoot turned over and pitched her into the rocky border by the road. She went over with a shriek and landed with her hands in the middle of the plants and gravel. Her knee hit one of the rocks and sent a stab of pain through her.

'Shit. Are you okay?' Leo was by her side.

Oh, God, how embarrassing! She couldn't even walk up a road competently. 'I'm fine,' she said. 'I'm fine.' There was no graceful way to get up apart from pushing her backside first out of the shrubbery and slowly getting back to her feet. Her knee stung, so did her hands. She tried to brush herself down.

As if all this wasn't mortifying enough, the car returned, illuminating her in her soil-stained, scuffed-up glory.

'You're bleeding,' Leo said.

She looked down at her knees. A small bloom of red had appeared on the denim over one of them.

'I'll be fine,' she said. 'It's just a scratch.'

Leo offered her his arm. 'Let's get you inside and see if we can find a first-aid kit.'

'No. Really, I'll be fine.' She took a step and sucked in her breath at the pain.

'Can you put weight on it?'

She tried again. She could. 'I don't think I've broken anything.'

Reluctantly, she took the arm he offered. They walked up the hill slowly. Her knee hurt, but more insistent was the closeness of Leo. She was holding on to his arm, which meant that her own arm was tucked close to his body. Her fingers dug into his bicep every time she took a step on her injured leg. If it weren't for the pain, she would have easily melted into the warmth of him. So, yay, pain.

Once they entered the hotel lobby, Leo made her sit down on one of the plush chairs and disappeared to locate a first-aid kit. Vidya rolled up her trouser leg to look at her knee. It was oozing blood, but at least the jeans had kept the wound clear of soil and other debris. Her hands, however, were streaked with mud and dotted with tiny cuts.

Leo reappeared with a green box and knelt at her feet.

'It's not that bad,' she said.

He gave her a stern look that did really odd things to her stomach and inspected her knee. 'May I?'

He waited until she nodded before he touched her. He was only touching the back of her calf in a very practical way, but she still felt the contact through her whole body. Leo opened a pack of Steriwipes and cleaned the wound efficiently. 'It's nothing terrible,' he said, while covering it with a non-adhesive bandage.

'Now, let's look at your hands.' He held them, palms up, in his big hands. 'You've got some small stones in this cut.' He fished out a pair of tweezers and started to remove them.

'You're very good at this,' Vidya said to the top of his head.

Leo didn't look up. 'I used to be a first aider,' he said.

'Used to be? You mean you're not anymore?'

'I didn't renew my training. There. I think that's got everything.'

'I used to do a lot of cleaning wounds and scratches,' she said.

'Because you were looking after your sister?' He wiped her hands with an alcohol wipe.

'Ow. Yes.'

'Uh-huh.' Leo finished wiping and held her palm up to look at it closely. He ran his fingertips down the side of her palm and she forgot how to breathe. His eyes flicked up to meet hers. 'And who looks after you?'

In that moment, looking into his eyes, it felt like he was offering. The pain in her knee and her hands faded away and all she could feel was the thunder of her heartbeat and the roar of her blood. No one looked after her. Except that wasn't true. Right now, *he* was.

Vidya wanted to say something pithy or meaningful, but all she could do was look into his face and wonder what it would be like to be held by him. To kiss him. As if he had read her mind, his hand tightened gently around hers and she felt the smallest of tugs towards him.

'Oh, my!' said a voice. 'I think he's proposing.'

They both looked round. Leo dropped her hand.

The two older ladies, Jill and Linda, were standing a few metres away.

'Oh, no,' said Jill. 'She's hurt herself.'

'That's disappointing,' said Linda.

'I … I fell, just outside,' Vidya said. 'Leo was taking a look at my injuries.'

'Is that what we call it these days?' said Jill, beaming.

Leo started packing things away.

'Where have you ladies been?' Leo asked.

'We've been to York for the day.'

'Oh, lovely,' Vidya said.

'I'll just return this,' said Leo. He stood up and glanced at Vidya. 'Are going to be—'

'I'm fine.' She made a shooing motion with her hands.

Once he had set off, she carefully stood up and tested her knee. 'I genuinely am fine,' Vidya said to the ladies, who were watching her with concern.

The three of them started towards the stairs.

'He seems like a good one,' said Linda.

'Practical as well as handsome.'

'Oh, there's definitely nothing like that going on,' Vidya said, laughing.

'No?' Linda glanced back to where Leo was talking to the concierge. 'Are you sure he knows that?'

What was that supposed to mean? 'I'm pretty sure, yes.'

'Pity,' said Linda. 'Because I think he would like there to be more than just a working relationship.'

Vidya felt the heat rush to her face. 'Well, I'm sorry to disappoint you.' When they had reached the bottom of the stairs, Vidya said, 'I think I'll take the lift. So … good night.'

'I hope your knee doesn't bother you too much,' said Jill.

'Thank you.'

Vidya hobbled over to the lift and hit the button to summon it. She turned to look for Leo and saw that he was walking towards her. She felt an irrational surge of hope.

'I'm … heading up,' she said. Oh, nice, Vidya. State the bleeding obvious. In the back of her mind, a tiny voice said, *Come with me, come with me,* but she didn't say that out loud. 'Thank you for patching me up.'

'I'm glad you're okay,' Leo said. He didn't meet her eye. 'I guess I'll see you tomorrow.'

'Um. Yes.'

The lift arrived and the doors opened. She put her hand out to stop them closing. She didn't want the evening to end just yet. 'Good night, Leo.'

He was moving his weight from one foot to another. He clearly had more he wanted to say. Vidya's heart picked up. Maybe …

He raised his head. 'Vidya—'

A movement behind Leo distracted her. It was Caleb, coming back in. She noticed but returned her focus to Leo. He turned to see what she was looking at.

'Oh,' he said, and took a tiny step back, away from her.

Wait, no! Why was he stepping back? Damn. Caleb had terrible timing. What was he even doing here? He was supposed to be off hooking up with the woman from the bar.

Leo took another step away from her and said, 'Good night, Vidya. I'll see you tomorrow.'

Vidya stepped into the lift. 'Tell Caleb I said good night too.'

As the door closed, she watched him turn around and greet his friend. Alone in the privacy of the lift, she leaned against the wall and willed her heart to calm down. She wasn't sure which would kill her first – embarrassment or frustration.

Chapter 19

Two days later and it was the last day. Vidya wasn't even sure if she was going to get through all the documents she needed to read and log. Leo and Caleb were conferring about the more complicated agreements, which was distracting. Well, if she was being honest, Leo was distracting her simply by existing. So, she had asked Stella if there was somewhere else she could work, which was how she'd ended up in the tiniest office imaginable – it was little more than a cupboard with a desk in it. But it didn't have men loudly discussing whether clause 22 of one contract caused a conflict with clause 89 of another, so she could get on with her work. The pile of files on the to-do side of the desk was diminishing slowly and the 'to return to the file room' pile on the floor was growing.

She glanced at the clock on the computer monitor. 12 p.m. Time for a break. She stretched her arms above her head.

She took her phone off 'do not disturb'. Udeni was still leaving her messages unread. It was near enough lunchtime, so she called Angie.

'Oh my God, you're alive!'

Vidya heard doors opening and closing and the sounds from the office receding. 'Why weren't you answering your messages?'

Angie's voice took on an echoey quality, suggesting that she'd ducked into the stairwell to take the call.

'I was working. It's the last day. I have a lot of stuff to get through. I put my phone on do not disturb.'

'You could have told me.'

'Is Udeni okay? If there was a problem, I told you, call me. Your calls will always come through.'

'Oh, she's fine. Still sulking, but basically healthy. I'm just concerned about you. How are you doing?'

Vidya took a deep breath and rubbed her eyes. 'I'm okay,' she said. 'Tired and worried, but fine.'

'I am keeping an eye on her,' Angie said. 'She's in a bit of a strange mood, but I don't think there's anything to worry about.'

'Good.' When Vidya got home, she would talk to Udeni, face to face, and iron all this out. It wasn't something you could do over the phone.

In the pause that followed, Angie said, 'Are you sleeping okay?'

'Not bad. I'll be glad to be back home, in my own bed.'

'Speaking of other people's beds,' said Angie. 'What's happening with Leo? Any advance on him administering first aid to your knee a couple of nights ago?'

She knew she shouldn't have mentioned that in the chat. 'No. I told you. There's nothing going on. There can't be now. It's our last day and we have a ton of work to do.' Vidya thought of his fingers stroking her palm and sighed. Leo had been awkward around her ever since Sunday. Even though the three of them ate together each night, it felt like Leo barely said anything to her. She had no idea what had caused the change in him. 'It's probably for the best. Workplace things can get awkward. I'm getting weird mixed signals from him now anyway.'

'It's not like you to be shy.'

'It's not that I'm shy,' Vidya said. 'It's more … oh, I don't know. I can't read him properly. Plus, it feels complicated – he's best mates with the man most likely to be Udeni's guy. How would

160

that work? He would find out and then he'd tell Caleb. So, she wouldn't be able to keep it a secret, like she wants to.'

'Oh. I see what you mean. That would be awkward,' Angie said.

'Uh-huh.' Vidya leaned her head back against the chair and tried not to think about how she was turning away from something she wanted, just to protect the interests of her sister. Again. 'How are you getting on with Piotr?'

'I met him. He seems very nice and friendly. I didn't get anything conclusive, but we know he was at the party and he was drinking.'

'We knew most of that already.'

'I know. I'll have another go this evening. I'll try and bring the conversation round to tattoos somehow.'

Vidya groaned. 'I wish she could remember who it was. And then just tell them. It would make things so much easier for everyone.'

'That's kind of up to her, really,' said Angie. 'But getting back to you and Leo. He's not Udeni's guy. You can't use that as an excuse—'

'I'm not. It genuinely would be so difficult if Caleb turns out to be the one. And, to be honest, I'm almost convinced he is.'

'And? Just because things *might* get weird for Udeni, you're not going to take a chance on something that would make you happy? You have such a martyr complex.'

'I do not.' Vidya was being practical.

'Don't you? You complain about Udeni leaning on you all the time, but don't you think at some level, you like that she does?'

'That's the stupidest thing I've ever heard.'

'Is it though?' said Angie. 'I love you, but think about it. Every time something goes wrong for Udeni, you step in to fix it. And you offer yourself as a buffer between her and your parents. Don't you think … Maybe that's the reason your parents still act like you're in charge of her screw-ups? How is she supposed to take accountability for her actions, if you always do it for her?'

'I …' Vidya's mind flew back to something Leo had said outside the arcade two days ago about her still blaming herself for her sister's accident. Was that what she was doing? Had she really carved herself a role that inserted her between her sister and her parents?

'I'm sorry,' Angie said. 'Have I upset you?'

'It's okay,' said Vidya. 'You just want the best for me, right?'

'Too right. And I want you to get laid – with this man you have the hots for.'

Vidya laughed. 'Not much chance of that today. We have so much work to do.'

'Don't work too hard,' said Angie. 'And when you finish up and go for drinks, you totally should jump on Leo and see what happens. You can always claim that you were drunk.'

Vidya chuckled. 'We'll see.'

There was a knock. The door opened and she turned to find Leo peering in. *Lunch?* he mouthed.

She nodded. Thank God, she hadn't had Angie on speakerphone! 'I've got to go. Bye.'

'Oooh. Has he just arrived? Is he looking sexy?'

'Bye.' Vidya hung up. Leo opened the door fully. He was wearing his immaculately pressed suit, as usual, and he did indeed look sexy. She bit back a smile as she rose and collected her coat.

'How's your leg?' Leo asked.

'Okay, actually. A bit sore, but otherwise, fine.' She pulled her coat on and followed him out. The door locked itself behind her.

'I'm making progress,' she said. 'I think, with concerted effort, I'll have all the details from the files by the end of the day. I'll probably have to wait until I get back to the office to do the analysis of it and work out the full costs of changing things, but that's okay, right?'

Leo nodded. 'Yes. Caleb and I are still working through the property leases and local covenants. Like you, we should have all the information gathered by this evening.'

'Where is Caleb?'

'Phone.' Leo rolled his eyes.

'Is his mother okay? She calls him a lot.'

'Oh, I don't think it's his mum this time. He's looking for a new flat – the landlord is selling the one he's in at the moment. So, he's lining up some viewings for when we get back from Brussels.'

They walked across the foyer, Leo slightly in front.

A voice called out, 'Excuse me, young man.'

Leo didn't bother looking round, but Vidya did. A middle-aged man in Bermuda shorts was waving towards Leo trying to catch his attention. Someone had mistaken him for a member of staff again.

'Hey. You there!'

Leo's pace increased. Vidya grinned and ran to catch up.

'If you wear a dark suit …' she said.

'It's what I wear for work,' he retorted.

'Well, the service is shocking,' the man bellowed.

'He's going to complain, isn't he?'

'And he'd be right,' said Leo. 'There should be a member of staff at reception.'

They got to the front door and Leo slowed down a bit.

'Would you have stopped if it was an old lady?'

Leo glanced at her, eyes crinkling with amusement. 'Depends on the old lady, but yes. Probably.'

Caleb, who had been sitting on the half wall, looking out at the sea, came and joined them. 'Your mate Charlie the seagull's been around,' he said to Vidya. 'Stole a kid's bread roll right out of his hand. Brazen robbery in broad daylight.'

'Dammit, Charlie,' Vidya and Leo said in unison.

Vidya laughed.

'So, boss. Where to for lunch?' Caleb fell into step with them.

'Since it's our last day, let's grab lunch and eat it by the sea, shall we?'

It was cold again, but the sun in a cloudless sky made

everything feel brighter and more colourful. The air was filled with the sounds of shop awnings flapping, the steady wash-hush of the sea and, of course, the gulls. They bought Cornish pasties from a stall manned by a woman in a pirate costume and wandered down the steps at the end of the promenade to the beach. The tide was out, leaving a rock-studded stretch of sand. They picked their way through it until they had passed the worst of the seaweed smell.

Vidya sat on a rock and hunched up to protect her lunch. The guys did the same. Sensing food, a gull landed near them and wandered around, with mad red eyes alert for crumbs. When Vidya was full, she threw the last bit of remaining crust out as far from them as she could, resulting in a pile of noisy gulls.

'Thanks,' said Caleb. 'You drew them away from us.' He quickly finished his own lunch and sat back, chest out, head tilted to catch the sun. On the rock next to him, Leo brushed crumbs off his jacket.

'So, Vidya,' said Caleb. 'How have you found this week and a bit?'

'It's been busy,' she said. 'And a bit dusty, but not too bad, all considered.'

'I heard you volunteered to come with us. No one ever does that, apart from Sarah,' said Caleb. 'What made you?'

You, she thought. *I had to find out about you. I still don't know if you're the man with the chest tattoo, but I'm glad I met you. I just wish Udeni could have got to know you, instead of me.* Out loud, she said, 'I'd been stuck in a bit of a rut at work. Some time away from the office, near the sea, sounded nice.'

'Hah,' Leo said. 'And you ended up stuck in a meeting room, not actually seeing much of the sea.'

'We went to the funfair,' Caleb protested. 'And had fish and chips. And I'm guessing Vidya has had more than enough of the seagull experience.'

'That's true,' said Leo. 'We did do that.'

'And then there's this,' said Vidya. 'I know it's only a lunch break, but it's different to sitting in a London park. Or worse, eating lunch at your desk.'

'Leo always goes for a walk after lunch,' said Caleb, snarkily. 'He can avoid talking to people that way.'

'Rude,' said Leo. 'What about all the times I meet you for lunch?'

'That was before I came to work at Askew, Else and Thomas. We rarely do lunch together now.'

'I see you all blooming day. Lunch is a good chance to get away from you.'

Vidya listened to them bicker like an old couple and smiled. Sarah was right. They were lovely when you got used to them. Vidya sneaked a glance at Leo, looking incongruous in his buttoned-up suit and long coat, and sitting ramrod straight on a rock. His mouth was set in a thin line, but his eyes were laughing. Maybe Angie had a point? Maybe she should forget all the reasons she shouldn't try with Leo and just see what happened.

Leo looked at his phone. 'We should get back.'

Everyone sighed, but they stood up and dusted the sand off their bums anyway.

Back on the promenade, as Vidya reached the top of the steps, the two men parted in front of her and a little boy ran in between them. Vidya moved out of the way too. The boy reached the top of the stairs. He was dressed in what looked like swimming shorts, a jumper and sandals. In his hand was a tiny bucket.

Someone shouted, 'Archie! Wait!' And the little boy stopped at the top of the steps and turned around. Vidya turned too. A young woman was hurriedly pushing a pushchair with bags on it where the child should be. A baby was strapped to her chest. 'Sorry,' she said, as she passed Leo and Caleb. 'Archie, you're supposed to wait for me and not run off.' She took the boy's hand.

'Do you need some help?' Leo said. 'I could carry the pushchair down for you. Might be safer.'

165

The woman looked at him, her expression one of profound gratitude. 'Could you? That would be so kind.'

'Of course. No problem.' He stepped closer to her and picked up the pushchair, bags and all.

'Thank you so much.' The woman started descending the steps, the toddler taking them slowly.

Vidya watched. Would Udeni be like this soon? The woman was young and pretty, but her hair was escaping her ponytail and fluttering around. There were bags under her eyes and a stain on her shoulder. Anxiety radiated off her, even as she helped her son jump down the last step.

How would Udeni deal with being a mother? Her life was about to change dramatically and she didn't even know it. Drinks and dancing would be replaced by sleepless nights and a baby who depended on her for their every need. How on earth would Udeni cope?

Then, in a flash of realisation, Vidya understood that she would never be the same again either. It wasn't her baby, but she was going to be involved. She had been so focused on Udeni and the practical aspects of it all that she hadn't really absorbed her own feelings about the baby. She was going to be an aunty. There was going to be a child and she would love him or her with everything she had. The enormity of it hurt her throat. The beach blurred behind tears.

A baby was coming into their lives. Not one of them was ready for it.

'Aw,' Caleb said. 'That's a cute kid.'

Vidya glanced sideways at him. If only he knew. She looked back at the little boy, now hopping around on the sand. How could anyone prepare for that?

Leo walked across the sand behind the boy and his mother and deposited the pushchair. Vidya blinked away tears. She saw him hunker down and say something to the boy, then give him a high five, before he walked back, his coat flapping in the breeze.

He would make a good dad.

She glanced at Caleb, who was looking at his phone. What kind of dad would Caleb be if Udeni gave him the chance?

When Leo reached the top of the steps, he stopped. 'Vidya? Is everything okay?'

To her horror, she realised that there were tears on her face. 'What? Oh. Yes. Just sand. In my eyes.' She quickly brushed her knuckles across her face and made a show of blinking rapidly. 'I think I've got it now.'

Leo nodded.

'So, good Samaritan thing done for the day?' Caleb teased him. 'And it wasn't a little old lady this time.'

'It would have been dangerous for her to try and drag the pushchair down and keep an eye on the kid and hold the baby,' Leo said.

They started walking back. He kept looking at Vidya. She turned her face towards the sea until she had her emotions under control.

'What did you say to the little kid?' Caleb asked. 'He looked very serious about it.'

'Oh, nothing much. I just told him to be good,' said Leo.

'Why would he listen to you?'

'Because I'm a stranger in a big coat,' said Leo. 'You always listen when a stranger in a big coat tells you to listen to your mum. You never know who they report to.'

Caleb laughed. 'Really?'

'That's what my nephew tells me. I think he's afraid they might work for Santa.'

They walked back along the seafront, past various stalls selling food and postcards and random things.

'You should see him with his nephews,' Caleb said to Vidya. 'They've got him wrapped around their little fingers.'

She grabbed the opportunity to find out more. 'How about you? Do you like kids?'

Caleb shrugged.

'Do you want to have kids of your own some day?'

This garnered a surprised glance from Leo. It must have sounded like a weird question to ask a work colleague. Oh, well, she had already established her nosy-cow credentials. May as well lean into it.

Caleb took it in his stride. 'Not really thought about it,' he said. 'When the time comes … with the right woman, I guess.' She noticed his glance at Leo, who merely looked down and carried on walking.

Oh, yeah. It would be weird if she didn't ask him too. 'How about you, Leo?'

'Never thought about it,' he said, gruffly. 'You?'

Her? Had she ever wanted to be a mum? She wasn't sure she had. 'A bit like Caleb said. It's not something I've desperately wanted, but … when the time comes.' The time was coming in about seven and a half months. Vidya would be the co-parent to this baby, no matter how much Udeni insisted she would do things on her own. She always needed help. Vidya always helped. Because she loved her sister and she would love the baby too.

The smell of doughnuts wafted past. Vidya turned her head to follow it. She was feeling raw and fragile. Hot sugary carbs might be just the thing.

'Oh, look, doughnuts.' She changed direction and headed towards the red-and-white-striped cart.

The guys followed her. They had the choice between large doughnuts or a bag of mini ones. They all chose the mini ones. The walk back to the hotel was conducted in happy sugary silence. Having the mini doughnuts in the bag meant that they were easier to keep safe from marauding seagulls too. When they reached the hotel, Caleb went on ahead, while Leo and Vidya paused to dispose of their empty doughnut bags.

'I guess it's back to the grindstone,' said Vidya. She crumpled the bag up and dropped it in the bin. She still had sugar on her fingers. Without thinking, she licked it off. Hearing a small sound from Leo, she looked up and her eyes met his. She slowly moved her hand down.

He cleared his throat. 'You … er …' He indicated his cheek. 'There's some sugar.'

'Oh. Right.' *That's* what he'd been looking at. She rubbed her cheek with the side of her hand and looked back at him. 'Did I get it?'

He shook his head. 'May I?'

'Please.'

Leo stepped closer. His hair was tousled from the wind. This close, she could smell a faint trace of his aftershave. Suddenly, the air felt thicker and heavier. He had the most beautiful eyes. Today was the last day that she would get to see them. Angie's words about jumping on him and seeing his reaction echoed in Vidya's mind.

Leo raised his hand and brushed her cheek, the touch of his warm fingertips sent tingles down her spine. She raised her eyes to look into his. He was so close now that it would take almost no effort to close the space between them and kiss him. Or for him to kiss her. She really, really wanted him to kiss her. His lips were slightly parted and so tempting. For a second his fingertips hovered just above the skin on her cheek.

Vidya's heart pounded. The world narrowed until there were only the two of them, the teasing warmth of his fingertips millimetres away from her skin. Then, he tilted his head and gently rested the tips of his fingers against her face. Her heartbeat was almost deafening now. His gaze moved from her eyes to her lips and, very gently, he stroked his thumb across her lower lip.

The sensation that flashed from her lips to her belly was so strong that Vidya gasped.

The sound seemed to startle Leo. With a sharp breath, he jumped back. 'I … I'm so sorry,' he said. 'That was—' His eyes were wide and panicky. He shook his head. 'That was so inappropriate of me. I'm sorry.'

'Leo.' She shook her head. 'Leo, it's fine.'

'No. It's not.' He seemed to have recovered himself now, his usual guarded expression back in place. 'If you want to make a report to HR, please do. I shouldn't have touched you like that. I'm so sorry.'

'Le—'

'I'll leave you in peace to get back to work.' He turned away.

No. This won't do. 'Leo.' She grabbed his arm. He turned back and looked down at her hand in surprise. She let go.

'Leo,' she said, firmly. 'You asked. I gave you permission.'

How was it best to play this? What she wanted to tell him was that she was fine with him touching her face. That if he wanted to kiss her, she really wouldn't object. But his reaction to his own actions had been so extreme that she didn't think that would help right now. 'So. Don't worry about it. It's fine. Shall we go back to work?'

Leo gave a look that she couldn't read. 'Yes,' he said. 'Let's do that. And … thanks for understanding.'

She followed him back inside and peeled off to go wash the last of the sugar off her hands … and her cheek if there was any still there. In the bathroom, it took a few minutes for her heart to stop hammering. Putting her hands on the sink, she looked at her flushed face in the mirror and swore. Disappointment plumbed through her. She had come this close to kissing him. So close. So. Damn. Close. How could she keep resisting him?

Chapter 20

Four hours later, Leo closed the file with a snap. 'I think that'll have to do.'

Caleb finished typing the note he was making and said, 'I concur.' He scrolled up in his document. 'We haven't covered everything, but we've made notes on all the things that are held here.'

It had taken all Leo's will power to concentrate this afternoon. Vidya wasn't even in the room and she was taking up space in his thoughts. He checked the time. Nearly five. This would be the earliest they'd finished on a weekday in the time they'd been here.

'Great. Let's go see how Vidya is getting along.' Caleb bounced to his feet.

Oh, God. Leo still wasn't over the embarrassment of what had happened. At least he had come to his senses before he'd kissed her! He knew she must be interested in Caleb and not him. All that talk about kids should have confirmed that, if nothing else. She hadn't cared about Leo's views, she'd only asked him to be polite, as an afterthought.

What had he been thinking?!

Caleb was heading for the door and expecting Leo to follow. 'We should get all this onto the filing trolley first,' Leo said. He could ask Stella to do that, but it was a nice, relatively mindless activity that he could pretend was still work. It meant that Stella could file them quicker the next day. 'Maybe we could save Stella a job and file them too.'

He set about putting the files in the right order. He couldn't face Vidya now. He really couldn't.

Leo shoved a file with unnecessary force. He knew exactly what he had been thinking. He had been thinking about how lovely she was. How plump her lips looked. How soft and warm her cheek felt under his fingertips. How she would taste of sugar and doughnuts. How he only needed to move a fraction to kiss her.

'Earth to Leo,' Caleb said.

Oh. Right. Filing. He was supposed to be putting them away. 'Sorry. Tired. Yes, let's carry on.' Leo trailed behind Caleb, pushing the trolley and watching as his friend used his key fob to access the file room. Even this room reminded him of Vidya.

Caleb started talking about what he was planning to do at the weekend. Leo made the right noises without actually listening. Between them, they got all the files back into the right places fairly quickly.

'I haven't done filing in ages,' said Caleb. 'It's like being a trainee all over again.'

'I guess it does us good to do these things from time to time,' said Leo. 'Although, economically, not really.'

'Fee earners should do fee-earning work,' said Caleb. 'I know. I know.' He put his hands on his waist. He looked around. 'Well, we're done here. We should go find Vidya now.'

'She's probably busy.'

'We can help.'

'I think we'd probably just get in the way if we try.'

'What is wrong with you? Anyone would think you're trying to avoid her. What's going on?'

'Nothing. There's nothing going on. It's just been a long day, all right?'

They left the file room, carefully pulling the door shut behind them.

'You know what we should do,' said Caleb.

What now? 'Not karaoke.'

'No. I was thinking we should go out for a nice meal. We've all worked very hard. The company could stand us a decent meal as a reward.'

Leo would have to sit with Vidya, watching her watching Caleb. It would be a hellish way to spend an evening. But he couldn't say no without it looking mean. He would go with it for now and find a reason to leave early. 'Sure.'

Vidya was still in her tiny cupboard office. As Caleb knocked and entered, she closed a file and added it to a stack on the floor. She gave them a vague smile, but didn't make eye contact. Leo really had messed everything up with his lack of self-control.

'We're calling it a day,' Caleb said.

'I still have some more work to do.' She indicated a much smaller stack of files on the desk.

Leo stayed outside in the corridor, holding the door open. There wasn't room in that tiny office for him *and* Caleb.

'Can we help?' Caleb said. 'We could take a couple of files each and—'

'No.' She looked affronted. 'It'll take me longer to explain my system than it would to do it myself.'

Leo almost laughed. That was exactly how he felt when people tried to help at the last minute. Finally, a woman who could understand him! He caught Caleb's eye and raised his eyebrows.

'That's fair.' Leo nudged Caleb with his foot. 'Come on. I'll buy you a drink while we wait for Vidya to finish up.'

Caleb made a face at him. 'How long will you be, do you think?' he asked Vidya.

She gave the remaining files an assessing glance. 'Another half hour, maybe forty minutes?'

'Okay, great. We'll meet you in the lobby at seven. Since we've all been working so hard, we get to go and have a fancy meal on the company card.' Caleb shuffled backwards out of the office; there really wasn't any other way to leave the tiny space.

As they walked down to the bar, Caleb said, 'Tonight's your last chance to talk to her properly, before we're all back in London and our busy work schedules get in the way. You should ask her out.'

'Will you stop that.' It came out snappier than Leo intended. 'She's clearly more into you.'

'I told you; I'm not getting that vibe. She keeps eyeing you up when she thinks you're not looking. And that day at the arcade, I honestly thought you were in there.'

Leo had thought so too, briefly. But that was just wishful thinking on his part. He could have styled it out and hidden behind the professional veneer, but he had blown that too this afternoon. Stupid. Stupid. Stupid.

'Can you leave it? Please,' Leo said, tiredly. Tonight was going to be a nightmare of awkwardness.

Vidya finally got to the end of the files on her desk, updated her spreadsheet and made sure she'd saved it. She looked at the stack of files on the floor and groaned. These were going to need refiling. Ugh. She stood up and stretched. There was plenty of time before she had to meet the guys.

When Vidya got to the file room, she video-called Angie and put her on speakerphone so that she could chat while she filed. She recounted the face touching, lip-stroking incident and smiled indulgently at the squeals from the other end of the line.

'So, what happens next?' said Angie.

'Apparently, we're all going out for dinner. Like that won't be weird at all.'

'Are you going to make a move on him?'

'I don't know. Like I said, it would be weird, wouldn't it – if I start seeing Leo and if Udeni's baby is secretly his best mate's kid. He'll figure it out. He's clever.'

'Wow,' said Angie. 'Start seeing Leo? An office romance? That's serious talk. I thought you just wanted to jump his bones.'

'No. I mean, yes, I do. But I also like him. He's nice.'

Angie made a hmm noise. 'Tell me what you like about him.'

Vidya pushed the last two files in her load into their hangers and came to stand by the desk where she'd propped her phone. 'Obviously, I think he's good looking. And he's clever. And really good at what he does.'

'Which we know you have the hots for, because you're a weirdo,' Angie agreed.

Vidya ignored that last bit. 'He's a little bit quiet, which comes across as grumpy, but he's actually just a bit awkward and shy. His sense of humour is quite dry, which, if you're not used to it, might be taken as humourless. I mean, I thought he was snarky and grumpy until I got to know him.' How had she been so wrong? 'He's kind and likes to help people,' she continued. 'He has lovely eyes and this smile ... you don't see it often, but when you do, it's amazing.' She stopped talking and looked at the screen to see her friend had her hands clasped under her chin. 'What?'

'Your face! You had this lovely dreamy little smile,' Angie said. 'You really do like him a lot, don't you?'

'I do. We get on really well and there's something about him that makes me want to hug him. I'd do it just to wind him up and he'd probably pretend to be mortified but secretly like it anyway.'

'You absolutely have to tell him how you feel. If your little encounter today is anything to go by, he must feel the same way.'

'I don't get it, though. He goes hot and cold. Some days he's really warm and approachable, flirty even. Other times he's just stiff and awkward. I don't know what to make of it.'

'But from what you said about today ... I'd say he does like you. There's something bothering him, maybe. You should find out what that is.'

Vidya leaned her arms on the table and hung her head for a moment. 'That's not the main thing I was supposed to find out on this trip,' she said. 'I still don't know for sure if Caleb is the guy.' She'd had over a week. She knew a lot about him now, but she still didn't have anything useful.

'Actually, I have some news on that,' said Angie.

'You found out something about Piotr?'

'No. Udeni remembered what that tattoo was of. It's a dragon.'

'A dragon?' Okay. That made sense. It was a magical creature.

'She said it was a dragon taking flight. About three inches long. A solid black tattoo, no colour.'

'That's useful. But I'm still not going to be able to see Caleb's chest …' Ideas whirred in Vidya's mind. 'But now that I know some details, I could straight up ask him.'

'Indelicate, but … you could,' Angie agreed. 'If you do it subtly.'

'I did try before, but the conversation sort of got away from me and I didn't want to make it weird.' Vidya thought about that. 'Or weirder, I guess.'

'Sometimes the direct approach is best.'

'I can't tell him why I need to know, can I? It's not my secret to tell.'

'Unfortunately, no.'

'Not unfortunately,' Vidya pointed out. 'If it were my secret to tell, then it would be me that was pregnant and that would be a completely different conversation. I would remember who I slept with, for a start.'

Angie gave a small laugh. 'Fair point.'

'Don't tell Udeni I said that.' Vidya closed her eyes and grimaced. 'And yes, I know I am judging her. It's just … such an enormous thing and she's acting like it's a trivial little mistake. It's a whole life. Several lives. The baby's, hers, mine. Nothing is going to be the same again.'

There was a silence at the end of the line that went on for so long that Vidya came to check the screen to see if Angie had disappeared.

'Ange?'

'Are you going to ask me to move out? You'll need the space when the baby arrives …'

Oh, crap. She hadn't even thought about that. 'Do you think you'll want to move out?' she said, cautiously. 'Babies are noisy and messy.'

'I love living with you guys, but it's going to change things, isn't it?'

Vidya sighed. 'Probably. Yes.'

'And you guys are family and I'm not, so …'

'Family is what you make of it,' Vidya said, firmly. She thought suddenly of Leo, being brought up by his grandmother because his parents weren't able to. 'You would be an awesome aunty. Found family counts.'

'Aargh. I'm only twenty-eight. I'm too young to be an aunty.'

Me too, Vidya thought. But when was anyone ready to be an aunt, really? Or a mum? 'Yeah. Sorry about that.'

Angie huffed out a laugh. 'You should probably talk to Udeni before you commit though.'

Vidya was about to reply that Udeni would feel exactly the same. The three of them had shared that flat for a few years now. Angie was practically another sister. But Vidya couldn't predict Udeni's feelings anymore. 'Yes, you're probably right. We should have a meeting, all three of us, when I get back.' It would force Udeni to talk to her properly too. That could only be a good thing.

Vidya checked the time. 'I should go. I need to have a quick shower and get changed before I meet the guys.'

'Vid. If you have to choose between making sure about Udeni's guy and getting your guy. Go for your guy, okay?'

'Normally, I would, but … a baby is kind of a big deal, so …'

'Vidya. So is you falling for someone.'

'I'm not falling for him.'

'Every phone call, you've talked about him.'

'I've talked about Caleb too.'

'That's because you have to talk about Caleb. It's part of your

177

mission and we keep asking. But you didn't have to talk about the other guy. At the start of all this, Leo was just some cranky dude, heading up the project, who you found aloof and annoying. Things are a little different now, right?'

How had she ever found him aloof and annoying? She thought of all the emotions that she'd seen in his eyes. The quiet humour, the kindness. People only thought he was aloof because they saw his guarded expression and didn't notice his eyes. She noticed them though. She could look into them forever. Angie was right. She was falling for him. Shit.

'Vidya, you okay?'

She pulled herself together. 'Yes. I'm fine. I'd better go.'

'Think about what I said, okay? I know you love Udeni, but you can't let your worries about her get in the way of your happiness.'

'Yes. I'll think about it. Love you, bye.'

After Vidya had hung up, she put her phone away and spent a few minutes staring at the wall. She was falling for Leo, wasn't she? She'd told him about her and Udeni and how she felt responsible. She rarely talked about that with anyone, apart from Angie. Yet she'd felt comfortable telling Leo. Was Angie right? Should she just go for it and damn the consequences for Udeni's secret?

Why was she even thinking about this? Her sister came first. No man was going to get in between them. She'd made a promise to help her sister and right now that meant finding out as much as she could about the baby's father. Tonight was her last chance to do this. She needed to get it done, her attraction to Leo would have to wait.

Chapter 21

The restaurant they ended up going to for their final dinner in Waterloo Bay was a lively little Italian place that Stella had recommended. There was bright lighting and cheerful music and, thank goodness, wine. Now that they'd come to the end of their stay, Vidya realised that she was very tired.

The conversation that evening had been stilted. Leo was still being awkward. It didn't escape her notice that he'd made sure that he had kept a healthy distance from her when they'd walked to the restaurant that evening. He'd barely made eye contact with her. She had told him she didn't mind what had happened, so why was he being so weird about it? Had he taken all the stern warnings from HR about appropriate behaviour in the office to heart?

Speaking of which, she needed to carefully broach the subject of tattoos to see if she could find out for sure whether Caleb had a dragon on his left pectoral.

'I'm thinking of getting a tattoo,' she said.

Both men looked at her wide eyed.

Leo, predictably, recovered first. He picked up his wine glass. 'Well, that seems very unlike you, but … that's nice.'

She kept her eyes on Caleb. 'Do you have any tattoos?' she asked him.

'Me?' Caleb shrugged. 'Sure. I have a few.'

'Where?' Okay that was too direct. 'I mean, they're not visible.'

'Um … various places. My back, calf, chest. Most of them are small, even the ones I had done when I was drunk.' He glanced at Leo, who raised his eyebrows and nodded.

She was committed to this line of questioning now. No backing out. 'Chest? That's an unusual place. What did you have done on your chest?'

'I don't think that's an unusual place for a tattoo.' Caleb looked at Leo. 'Is it?'

Leo took another sip of his drink. 'I don't think so, no.'

Dammit. She'd made the classic mistake of giving him something to get distracted by. Again. She leaned forward and smiled, hoping that would make this less weird. 'So, what did you have done on your chest?'

Caleb and Leo exchanged another glance. Something seemed to pass between them. Caleb looked sad. Leo's face was completely blank. He drank more wine.

'I'm a little uncomfortable with this line of questioning,' Caleb said, without his usual bonhomie.

Shit. Okay. Her mind wheeled. This was still a work setting. 'I … I'm sorry,' she said. She looked down at her wine. 'I guess I'm more of a lightweight than I thought. I'm so sorry.'

'It's fine.' Caleb's smile crept back. 'Why are you so invested? If you don't mind me asking.'

The politeness felt like a punch in the guts. She had come to think of these guys as her friends and Caleb was the friendliest and most laid-back person she'd ever met. His retreat to formality hurt. Leo still wasn't looking directly at her, but there was a small crease between his brows. This evening had suddenly gone wrong.

She needed an answer to his question. One that didn't involve Caleb's one-night stand with her sister and an unexpected pregnancy. 'I was thinking of getting something tattooed on my shoulder,' she said. This was her one chance to be direct, so she

180

added, 'Mythical creature, maybe. Like a dragon.'

There was a weird silence. Vidya held her breath.

Then Leo said, 'Good luck with that. Word of advice, don't get it done when you're drunk.'

Caleb shook his head. 'I still can't believe that guy did it. He should have taken one look at us and sent us away. We were clearly too drunk. The risk.' He shuddered.

Vidya turned to Leo. 'You were with him and you let him get a tattoo while drunk?' she said. 'I find that hard to believe.'

Leo shrugged. 'Alcohol has a lot to answer for,' he said, darkly.

The rest of the meal passed relatively quietly. She had single-handedly ruined the atmosphere and she *still* didn't know if Caleb had a dragon tattoo on his chest. But now she knew that he had *something* tattooed on his chest. The chances of him being the father rather than Piotr had just gone up.

Caleb tried to keep the conversation going, wittering gently about work. Leo had withdrawn completely and was only giving the blandest comments. Vidya just wanted to cry.

When the meal was finally over, they unanimously agreed that they would go back to the hotel.

While she waited for Leo to pay the bill, Vidya checked her phone. A message had arrived from Angie: *Finally spoke to Piotr. It isn't him. He doesn't have any tattoos and he only stayed for an hour at the anniversary party. Looks like Caleb's our guy!*

Vidya looked up at Caleb and felt a mixture of warmth and sadness. On the one hand, she liked Caleb. She couldn't think of a nicer person to be the father of Udeni's child. On the other hand, it made life so awkward.

After tomorrow, everything would change. Once they went back to work, she wouldn't be able to hang out with them again. If Udeni decided to tell Caleb about the baby, then everything would change again. Leo was already being awkward around her. How much worse would it be once he knew about Udeni and the baby?

They were walking along in moody silence when a gull swooped down and pooped. Vidya gave a shriek and leapt backwards. Her knee twinged.

'Goddammit, Charlie!' Caleb shouted.

'Did it get you?' Leo asked.

She checked herself. 'No,' she said. 'Just missed. Thank goodness. I don't want more clothes ruined.'

Caleb grinned. 'The first time we met you, Charlie had just pooed on you.'

'Right. I suppose he thinks that he should try and get me on my last day too.' She glared at the birds in the sky. 'I am definitely not going to miss those damn birds.'

Caleb laughed. 'No. I can't say I blame you.'

'I will miss you guys though,' she said.

They both nodded but neither replied.

'I'm sorry I made things weird,' she said. 'I didn't know you guys at all, and it's been really great getting to know you.'

'Yeah, we get that a lot,' said Caleb. 'Actually, I don't. Leo does.'

'Thanks,' Leo said, dryly. 'And the feeling is mutual, Vidya. It has been good to work with you.'

'You should have seen how pissed off he was when he heard Sarah wasn't coming and they were sending us someone else,' Caleb said.

'I rate Sarah's competence highly,' said Leo. 'I'm glad that you were just as competent.'

'Coming from you, that's quite a compliment,' Vidya said, hoping for a smile. He didn't smile, but somehow the atmosphere between them felt a little lighter.

They went up the hill to the hotel entrance and crossed the foyer without anyone mistaking Leo for a member of staff. At the lifts, Leo pressed the call button.

'Actually,' Caleb said. 'You guys go ahead. I think I'm going to get a bit more sea air while I still have the chance and check in on Mum.'

She couldn't see Leo's face but saw Caleb grin and clap him on the shoulder before he left.

Well, at least she had a chance to talk to him now. She opened her mouth to apologise again for ruining the evening.

'I'll take the stairs,' Leo said. 'It's only a couple of flights for me, so it's just as quick. I'll see you tomorrow, Vidya.' He made for the entrance to the stairs, which was next to the lifts.

Wait. No. If he was avoiding her now, he would avoid her tomorrow morning and then she'd have to find him at work if she wanted to talk to him and that would be difficult. 'Leo.' She ran after him. 'Leo, wait.'

He stopped with one foot on the stairs and turned around. 'Yes.' Everything about him screamed wariness and it hurt to see that directed at her.

'Why are you avoiding me?'

'I'm clearly not avoiding you,' he said. 'We've just been out to a restaurant together and now we're standing in the same stairwell.'

'You know what I mean. You're taking the stairs so that you don't have to be alone with me.' She took a step forward and saw him flinch and lean slightly towards the stairs. When it was clear she wasn't coming any closer, he seemed to relax.

'I thought,' he said, carefully. 'That, given what happened earlier … it would be best if you and I weren't alone together.'

Vidya put her hands on her hips. 'Why? Are you worried that I might have thought you were inappropriate?'

He pinched the bridge of his nose and murmured something that sounded like, 'It's not you I'm worried about.'

'That's not it.' He sighed. 'I'm not given to losing control, okay? And for me to touch you like that was … unforgivable.'

'I gave you permission.'

'To wipe sugar off your face. Not fondle you.' He sounded disgusted with himself.

'I said it was fine.'

He took his foot off the stair and turned to face her. 'But it's not fine, is it, Vidya? Yes. I like you. That's my problem, not yours. That's no excuse for me to take advantage of your trusting nature like that. Especially when I know you're interested in Caleb!'

There was so much clamouring for attention there that Vidya only stared. 'Wait,' she said, latching on to the last thing he said. 'I'm not interested in Caleb.'

'Aren't you?' Leo drew his eyebrows up. His body language said angry, but his eyes were full of pain. 'You can't stop staring at him.' He counted off his fingers. 'You're always asking him questions or asking me questions about him. You use any excuse you can to find out more about him.'

Leo had noticed. Of course he had. He was clever. She obviously wasn't. 'No. No.'

'What other explanation is there?' he said.

She couldn't answer that. What could she say without letting on about her sister?

Leo took her silence to be an admission. 'See.' He lowered his hands. 'It's okay. Caleb is … handsome and friendly and … socially functional. It's only natural that you should want—'

Vidya shook her head. Frustration pressed against her eyes. She didn't want to cry now. 'You're wrong.' She was almost shouting. 'I don't want Caleb.'

Leo looked exasperated. 'Then what do you want?'

'I want you!' It came out before she could censor it.

It was out now. She waited for his reaction, her heart in her throat.

He seemed frozen to the spot, eyes wide and dark, lips parted. She noticed that his chest was moving like he was breathing hard too. When she looked into his eyes, she could see his pupils dilate.

'Say something …' she said.

Muscles in his forehead twitched. He stepped closer to her. Slowly raising his hand, he placed it on her cheek. Not just his fingertips like before, but his whole palm.

Vidya felt tension drain away from her shoulders. She leaned her face against his hand.

'Yeah?' His voice was lighter now, his eyes alive with need.

She smiled. 'Yeah.'

Slowly, almost unbearably slowly, he stroked his thumb across her lip. Sensation zipped through her, earthing itself in her belly. She reached forward and grabbed the lapels of his coat.

He kissed her, one hand still caressing her face. His kiss was gentle and restrained, just like he was. She thought of the ferocious concentration of him on the dance machine. There had to be more than that. She let go of his lapels and slid her arms inside his coat, so that she could feel the warmth of his body. He wrapped his free arm around her and pulled her closer. The kiss intensified until all she could think about was the feel of his mouth against hers, the movement of the muscles in his back against her hands, his fingers in her hair. She lost all sense of time or rational thought. All she could think was more. More. More!

She dug her fingertips into his back and he made an extremely un-Leo-like sound deep in his throat.

He moved his mouth away from hers and kissed the side of her neck. She closed her eyes and groaned, tipping her head to the side.

The door to the stairwell opened and through her lust-filled haze, she heard a woman exclaim, 'Oh! Oh my!'

'See,' said another voice. 'I told you. You owe me a cake.'

The voices disappeared as the door shut behind them with a soft thump.

'I think we should go to my room,' Vidya whispered.

'Mine's closer.' His lips were just by her ear.

'Okay.'

He moved back and she shivered with the loss of contact. He kissed her and gave her a brilliant smile. 'Come on.' He tugged her hand.

They ran up the stairs and down the short stretch of corridor to his room. He unlocked it and ushered her in. She shrugged off her coat as she waited for him to lock the door. She barely registered anything about her surroundings apart from him.

'Are you sure?' He was shrugging off his big coat too.

'Yes,' she practically yelled.

Because he was still Leo, he hung his coat up. Because she knew him, Vidya handed hers to be hung up as well. He said, 'It's a terrible idea.'

'That too.' She reached up and pulled his mouth to hers.

They kissed, with her back pressed against the wall until the need for more was overwhelming. She fumbled at his jumper and he tried to remove hers. It was clumsy work.

She pushed him back a bit. 'I'll do mine. You do yours.'

She saw the flash of approval in his eyes and felt a wave of affection. Giving him another kiss, she sat on the bed and pulled her jumper off over her head. Leo did the same with his, but instead of dropping it on the ground like she did, he flung it onto the chair. Watching this man, who was normally so fastidious, slowly lose his control made her feel amazing. Powerful. She bent her head to undo the buttons on her blouse.

When she looked up, he was peeling off his shirt. He had turned aside to throw it onto the chair, so she admired his lean body. He turned back to her with a smile.

The sight hit her like a bucket of ice.

There, on his chest, just under the collarbone, was the tattoo of a dragon taking flight.

Chapter 22

'What's wrong?'

Leo had no idea what was happening. Vidya was staring at him, with both her hands clamped over her mouth, her eyes huge.

'Vidya?'

She shook her head, hands still over her face. 'I have to go.' She scrambled to her feet. Her blouse was open, she gathered it up in one hand, pulling it over her lacy bra. With her free hand, she grabbed her jumper off the floor.

He could see she was leaving, but he had no idea why. 'Vidya, what's wrong?' he asked again. 'What happened?'

He stepped back so that she could go past him and unhook her coat and handbag.

'Did I hurt you?' Had he? He couldn't think how. Maybe he'd trodden on her foot in his haste? Was that possible?

When she looked at him, her eyes were full of tears, which frightened him more than anything. Something was clearly very wrong. He took a small step towards her. 'Vidya. Talk to me.'

But she was already opening the door, with her things clutched to her. Just before she left, she turned. 'It's not you,' she said. 'Not your fault.'

Then she was gone.

He stood, frozen in the middle of the room, not sure what to do. Should he go after her? Should he just leave her be and see if he could talk to her in the morning? He looked around the room. What on earth had she seen to make her react like that?

It dawned on him that he was standing there with no shirt on. He looked down at his own chest, in case he had a weird rash or something that he didn't know about. No. He wasn't exactly ripped, but he didn't look that bad, surely.

He was still standing in the same place, twitching indecisively from one direction to another, when someone knocked on the door. Oh, thank God.

He pulled the door open. 'Vid—'

It was Caleb, who looked him up and down, then looked down the corridor and said, 'What the hell is going on?'

The sight of Caleb kicked Leo's brain back into operation. He stepped back and let Caleb in. Remembering that he was bare chested, Leo went over to the chair and picked up his jumper. Was it because he was careful where he put his stuff? No. It couldn't be that. Could it?

Caleb said, 'I just saw Vidya running down the corridor in a state of …' He looked around the room. 'Well. Anyway. She looked upset.'

'Did you talk to her? What did she say?' Leo pulled his jumper on. It felt strange and prickly, as though his skin was highly sensitised.

Caleb shook his head. 'I was coming out of the lift and she was running into the stairs. She saw me and I saw her, but I didn't think I should follow her. I thought I'd come and ask you.'

'Ah.' Leo picked up his coat from where it had fallen off the hook when Vidya had grabbed her own coat. Her scarf lay on the floor. He picked it up and stood there with it, not sure what to do. Hanging it up on top of his coat seemed like a transgression.

'So, what happened?' Caleb moved the shirt onto the desk and sat down in the chair.

Leo gave up and put the scarf on the desk, on top of his shirt. He sank onto the edge of the bed, exactly where Vidya had been sitting only moments ago. 'I don't know.'

Caleb made a winding gesture with his hands, as though telling him to go on.

'We … er … after you left, she confronted me about being a bit distant this evening.'

'A bit,' said Caleb.

'And I told her I liked her. She said she liked me. We kissed and … things progressed.' He could still feel her, taste her skin against his lips. He couldn't think about that now. He shook his head and carried on. 'We came here. We agreed it was a terrible idea, but we were going ahead anyway. I took my shirt off and then she suddenly … looked sick and ran away.'

He braced himself in case Caleb brought out his sense of humour. He didn't. He simply listened before weighing in. 'Nothing else happened? You didn't say anything weird that might have triggered a reaction?'

'No.' There hadn't been much talking. They'd been busy. He thought it through. There had to be a trigger. 'I was standing there.' He pointed. 'I took off my shirt. Turned around to put it on the chair. When I turned back to face her. That's when she freaked out.'

He looked at what he could see from his position. There was nothing that might cause alarm. Was there something he simply wasn't seeing? His brain wasn't exactly working at full capacity right now. Leo shook his head. 'I don't understand.'

'Didn't she say anything else?'

'Oh. Yes. She said it wasn't me; it was her. And then she ran away.'

'Well, that's something at least,' Caleb said. He sounded genuinely relieved.

Leo looked up, offended that Caleb might have suspected him of doing something bad to a woman. Then he remembered that he'd suspected himself of mistakenly hurting her. She had said it wasn't him. So … if he took her words at face value. Perhaps it wasn't anything he'd said or done. It was something to do with her.

'So, what now?' Leo said. Letting his guard down enough to kiss Vidya was not something he'd done lightly. The last time he'd done that, he'd been with Jessica, only for her to very publicly cheat on him and then dump him. The public nature of their breakup meant that everyone in the office had been whispering about it for weeks. The humiliation had taken away two things he'd loved – Jessica and his work – at the same time. He'd had to move jobs to get away from it all.

He groaned and fell backwards onto the bed with his hands over his eyes. He should have known better than to get involved.

'Hey, hey,' said Caleb, gently. 'Don't beat yourself up about it.'

'I should have just held it together for one more day,' Leo said from behind his hands. 'Just one more damn day and I'd have gone back to London. I wouldn't have had to see her, apart from random glimpses. I would have got over it. What on earth possessed me?'

'You fancy her. She fancied you. You've been working together under pretty intense conditions, for over a week. It's only natural. It happens all the time.'

'To you, maybe. Not to me. I can't mix my work life and love life. It was always going to end in disaster. It always does.'

'If our roles were reversed,' said Caleb, 'you'd tell me that there isn't evidence of a connection. What is it? Correlation is not connection?'

Leo parted his fingers to glare at his friend through the gap. 'Causation,' he said. 'Correlation is not causation. And you're not helping.'

He closed the gap again and stared at the darkness under his hands. 'Just one. More. Day. And I would have been okay.'

They stayed like that, silent, for a minute, then Caleb stood up in a determined sort of way.

Leo sat up, alarmed. 'Where are you going?'

'I'm going to take Vidya's scarf back to her.'

'No. Don't. You'll make things worse.' Leo stood.

'How could I possibly make things worse?'

'I don't know, but I wouldn't want you to. I seem to have upset her by mistake. It's entirely possible that you'll do the same.'

'But don't you want to know *why*?'

'Of course I do. But she has the right to change her mind. She doesn't owe me an explanation.'

Caleb stared at him. 'I'm worried about her, though,' he said, finally. 'And she's a friend too.'

That was a good point. Maybe she needed a friend right now. 'Okay,' said Leo. 'But don't make her feel bad. I'll be fine.'

Caleb's expression was full of pity. 'Okay, mate. If you say so.' He picked up the scarf. 'I'll just go see if she's okay.'

'If there's anything she needs help with …' Leo said. 'Obviously, I'll help.' He sighed heavily. 'I'd come with you, but it's all too awkward right now.'

When Caleb had left, Leo changed into his pyjamas and carefully packed the rest of his clothes, ready for tomorrow. He didn't know what he'd done to precipitate her reaction, but he hoped that Vidya was okay.

He sank down on the bed. Suddenly, all he wanted was to talk to his grandmother. Except, she wasn't around anymore. He took out his phone and stared at it. He could call his sisters, but … how on earth would he explain what had happened when he didn't understand it himself?

Vidya sat scrunched up on her bed, knees drawn up, arms clasped around them. How had this happened? How?

The moment that Leo had turned towards her, so that she saw his pale chest with the dragon tattooed on it, kept replaying in her mind. She felt nauseous. She had almost slept with someone who had slept with her sister! The father of her sister's baby.

How could she have been so wrong?

Her heart picked up speed and her breath came short. This was terrible. Pain writhed inside her. She had really liked Leo, she realised – more than she'd admitted to herself. She had really, really liked him. She was suddenly boiling hot. She couldn't breathe. Oh. Shit.

Panic attack. This was just a panic attack.

'No one ever died of a panic attack. No one ever died of a panic attack.'

She'd been here before. She knew what to do. Blowing out exaggerated breaths, she forced herself to breathe slowly. Inflate the lungs until they were really big. Exhale everything. Let them fill up again. See. She could breathe. She was okay.

Eventually, her body came back under her control. She unclasped her arms from around her knees. Everything felt cold and clammy as she cooled down. Slowly, she tucked her legs under the duvet and hugged a pillow, so that she could rest her chin on it.

How had this happened? They had discounted Leo from the running early on.

The clues Udeni had given them were so few – one of the white male lawyers in Team B, who had been at the party. That narrowed it to three. The only real defining feature had been the tattoo. Angie had said it couldn't possibly be Leo because … well, Leo was so unlikely to have a one-night stand. Vidya would have agreed with that assessment until a few minutes ago. They'd been too quick to dismiss him.

She had assumed that he'd left the party early because she'd seen him walk towards the exit, but she hadn't actually seen him leave.

The rest of the clues – tall, funny, sexy, can dance – fit Caleb and Piotr, who were charismatic and outgoing. People you easily associated with being funny and sexy and good at dancing. But

Leo was all of these things too. You just didn't see them at first glance.

Had Udeni somehow seen straight past the facade and immediately seen Leo for who he was? Had Leo been drunk enough to show her?

Vidya groaned. It didn't matter, did it? What mattered was that she had made a snap judgement and let everything else be guided by it. All the research she'd done on Caleb. What a waste of time! What did she know about Leo? He was shy and thoughtful and kind and … kissed like a dream. No. She couldn't think that. Tears pushed against her eyes. She closed them and rested her face on the pillow. But could she forget?

She had wanted him so much. All the times she'd watched the way he moved, the way his forehead creased when he was worried, the way he twiddled his pen in his fingers when he was thinking, the way he let her share his chips because a seagull had nicked hers. She had tried to keep her distance, tried to give up what she wanted and focus on her sister, because Udeni always came first. In this case, quite literally, apparently.

She had finally found a guy she liked, who liked her back, but she couldn't have him because of her sister. It was so unfair. Tears seeping out from under her lashes, Vidya allowed herself a moment of angry resentment. She didn't ask for much. She was willing to do anything, give up her evenings to babysit, take on more of the financial burden with the flat – anything – for her sister. But again everything revolved around Udeni. Vidya couldn't even have just this one thing?

Vidya gasped out a loud sob. Why had they discounted Leo so early? Why hadn't she made sure? If she'd worked it out about the tattoo earlier, she wouldn't be in this position now. She gave up and let the tears fall.

When, a few minutes later, someone knocked on the door, she nearly jumped out of her skin. She dragged a palm over her face. Who was that? What if it was Leo? She couldn't see him. Not like this. Not like anything. She just couldn't bear it.

What must he have thought? She had been completely in the moment with him and then she'd run away without any explanation.

Whoever it was knocked again. Oh no no no no. Go away.

Another knock. 'Vidya, it's Caleb.'

Caleb. Okay. She could probably handle seeing Caleb.

'Just a minute.'

She went to the bathroom and looked in the mirror. Her crying hadn't been pretty. It had been dreadful, eye-reddening, face-inflating, snotty, ugly crying. She splashed some water on her face and dried it. It made no difference. She still looked red eyed and puffy. Couldn't be helped.

As she made her way to the door, she tried to think of an explanation, which Caleb could convey to Leo. She couldn't tell him the truth, but there really wasn't anything else that was acceptable.

She hauled the door open. All the crying and the aftermath of the panic attack had left her feeling hollow. She leaned against the door.

Caleb stood outside, looking worried.

'Hi,' he said. 'I just … came to see if you were okay.'

'I'm fine,' she said. Her voice was croaky and sad.

He didn't look convinced, but he nodded. 'That's good.' He held something out. Her scarf. She must have left it in Leo's room.

Embarrassment and remorse rose. 'I'm so sorry,' she said. 'I … I wish I could explain, but …' She took the scarf. 'How is he?'

If she knew Leo half as well as she thought she did … he would be angry and sad and probably worried.

Caleb made a face. 'Well, not exactly happy. And he is concerned about you.'

'Did he send you to check on me?' she asked.

Caleb didn't reply. He didn't have to. His expressive face said it all. Leo might be worried about her, but Caleb was worried

194

about Leo.

'Please can you tell him that I'm sorry. It's not him. It's me. I have … baggage that I have to deal with.'

Caleb studied her, solemnly. She wasn't used to seeing this side of Caleb. He was the happy-go-lucky one. Seriousness, on him, seemed wrong. 'Vidya,' he said. 'I love Leo like a brother, and I hate to see him hurt.'

'I didn't mean to.' It was such a weak thing to say. 'I feel awful. I honestly …' Her throat closed up and tears rose. She swallowed hard so that she could speak. 'I wish I could explain, but I can't. Just tell him I'm sorry.'

Caleb nodded. 'I will.' His eyes searched her face. 'And you're okay, right? Not … hurt.'

'I'm fine.' Vidya tried to smile and failed. 'Just a bit emotional. Like I said … baggage. It's not Leo. I'm sorry he got caught up in it.'

Caleb nodded. 'If you need anything, just ask, okay. I mean, Leo's my best friend. But you're my friend too. And … uh … if you need help with anything, we're both here for you.'

'I know.' She did. Which made everything so much worse.

'Okay. Well, good night.'

'Good night.'

She watched him walk away. 'Caleb,' she said.

He half turned.

'Look after him.'

This time, he did smile. 'Always do,' he said.

When Vidya got up the next morning, she felt like she had the worst hangover. Her head hurt, her eyes stung and her skin felt too tight for her face. She'd just got dressed and was standing in front of the mirror wondering how on earth she was going to face Leo that morning when a text arrived from Caleb.

Going back early. Won't see you at breakfast. Have a safe train journey home. C

195

Well, that solved that problem. She need not worry about running into Leo for another forty-eight hours.

Instead of going straight into the office, like she'd intended, Vidya had called in claiming sickness. She had done it over Zoom, so that her line manager could see her tear-ruined face. She really did look like she had come down with a terrible cold. 'I know we're on a tight deadline,' she said, before he could say anything. 'I'll work from home.'

She forced down some breakfast and waited to see Stella to say goodbye before checking out. Her bill was already covered by the company, and Leo had pre-booked and paid for a taxi from the hotel to the station for her. Her heart twisted at the sight of his name at the bottom of the payment voucher.

The train journey home was … useful. Being in public meant she was less likely to cry and feel sorry for herself, so it forced her to think and plan.

Her mistake was obviously terrible, but what could she do about it now? One option was that she distance herself from Leo as much as possible and make sure that he never saw Udeni. Ever. Given that Vidya and Leo worked in the same company, and were currently on the same project, avoiding him completely would be difficult.

She stared out of the window and tried to imagine never seeing Leo again and, by extension, Caleb too. There was a hollow in her chest. She liked them. They had been her friends. If she hadn't given in to her feelings and kissed Leo, he would still be her friend. By wanting more, she'd ruined everything.

But there was no going back now.

Could she work with him, dispassionately, as a professional? She wasn't sure. Leo, she was sure, would be able to put on his mask and carry on working as normal, but she couldn't do that.

Besides, she had hurt him. The confusion on his face when she had run out! Caleb had been clear that she'd hurt Leo. She knew she had. For all his sang-froid, he was sensitive. She owed him an explanation, ideally one that would let him down gently and not involve her sister in any way. But whatever she said, it would be a lie. She didn't lie much, because her guilty conscience nearly always gave her away. She didn't have Udeni's ability to rewrite the world to fit whatever story was her truth on the day. Vidya would always know that she'd lied to Leo. He would probably find out and he would be hurt all over again.

She sighed. Then there was the matter of the baby. She thought of Leo helping a stranger with her pushchair and children, simply because she needed help. Of him hunkering down so that he was on the same level as the small boy when he talked to him. Of him carrying bags upstairs for two old ladies, even though he didn't have to. He was a good man, and he would be an excellent father. If Leo ever discovered he had a child and hadn't been involved in raising it, he would be devastated. He, of all people, knew about neglectful parents.

That wasn't fair on anyone. Least of all the baby.

It seemed to her that the best thing for everyone concerned was that Udeni should tell Leo. Or better still, Vidya could tell him herself and combine it with an apology. This was, objectively, the best outcome, but ...

Vidya blinked back sudden tears. She was amazed that she still had any left after last night's crying.

But ...

But she wanted Leo. She cared for him, and the idea of Leo and Udeni being parents together ... being a family ... it made her want to howl. She didn't ask for much. Seriously. Couldn't she have this one thing? Just once.

Her eyes continued to fill with tears, so she pinched herself to distract herself. Maybe taking the day away from the office wasn't such a good idea. She needed something to take her mind off this.

Chapter 23

Vidya took her laptop into the living room of her empty flat. Once she got home, she'd had another good cry, then taken a hot shower and got into her comfiest tracksuit. She was starting to feel better. She decided to try and finish her work, so that she hadn't wasted the entire day moping over a guy she couldn't have.

Vidya sat down at the dining table, with a nice, strong coffee next to her. She had her back to the front door, so that she could see the sky through the glass doors that led out to the balcony. After the vast sky and the twinkling sea, the view looked very dull indeed.

She wondered what Leo was doing now. Was he frowning at his work, in that intense way of his? Was he twiddling his pen in his long fingers? Was he thinking of her?

No. She had to stop thinking of him like this. It couldn't happen. She had to move on. She forced herself to concentrate. Eventually, she got into the right headspace and was typing up observations when her phone pinged.

It was her parents. *Are you free now?*

Oh, she may as well be. Using her laptop as a support, she propped her phone up and called her parents.

'Hello, darling, how are you?' Her mother peered at her from behind sunglasses. 'Are you and Udeni okay?'

'We're fine,' Vidya lied.

Her mother's demeanour changed and she leaned closer to the phone and removed her sunglasses. 'Are you sure?'

Too late, she realised that she must look dreadful. Plus, she was a terrible liar. 'Ah. I'm coming down with a cold, I think,' she sniffed. It wasn't hard, because her voice was still a little heavy from all the crying.

'Have you taken a Samahan sachet?'

Vidya sighed. 'Not yet. But I will. As soon as I've finished talking to you. I promise.' She meant it as well. The little sachets of traditional medicine were pretty good for making you feel better in general. The combination of those and painkillers had seen her through many an illness.

'How is Udeni? Is she okay?'

The question made Vidya's chest squeeze. Udeni was fine, in some aspects, because pregnancy wasn't an illness. But at the same time, Udeni would never be the same again. It wasn't Vidya's secret to tell, so she said, 'Yes. She's fine.'

Amma probably noticed the little pause before Vidya answered. That woman had almost supernatural instincts when it came to seeing through her. So, Vidya carried on quickly.

'How's the holiday going? Where are you now on your travels?'

'We are in Mexico, near … where is it?' Amma raised her head to ask Thatha.

'Tulum.' Thatha came on the screen. He looked well, his grey hair a little too long and tousled. 'We went to see the ruins by the sea. It's very interesting. Not very big.'

'That sounds lovely.'

Thatha sat down next to Amma. 'Did you know, there's a lot of Asian imagery in the Mayan temples? There's one of a Mayan sitting on a lotus flower.'

This made Vidya smile. Her father was always finding ways to link everything to South Asia. 'That is interesting, yes.'

'And there are people here in the Yucatán who look a lot like us.'

'Wow.'

Amma leaned in again. 'I got some lovely silver jewellery,' she said. 'I've always had gold, but I think I should try wearing silver more often.'

'This experiment is costing me a bloody fortune,' Thatha said, without any rancour in his voice.

Amma scoffed at him.

'Well, I'm glad you're having a nice time,' said Vidya. 'You deserve it.'

Amma nodded, serious again. 'How is work? You said you were going away for a few days. Did that go well? Were the new team nice?'

How did she answer that? She stared at a spot above the screen. Could she even talk about Leo without crying again?

'Vidya?' There was concern in her mother's voice.

She looked back at the screen. Amma had leaned close to the camera now, all Vidya could see was a close-up view of Amma's eye and cheek. This made her smile.

'Sorry. Got distracted,' she said. 'Work is fine. I got back from Waterloo Bay a few hours ago and I am working from home this afternoon.'

'Still?' said Amma. 'What time is it there?'

She glanced at the clock. 'Er … six. Well, nearly.'

'Why is your sister not home? Shouldn't you be cooking your dinner?'

Yes. She probably should. She could barely remember having eaten anything all day. 'I should.'

'I hope you girls are eating well.'

A key rattled in the lock. Vidya turned in time to see Udeni hurtle through the door, hand clamped over her mouth, and dash to the bathroom. A second later there was the sound of someone throwing up.

Oh no. Vidya turned slowly back to the screen. Amma had

seen that.

'Is your sister ill? What is wrong with her?'

Shit. Shit. Shit.

'Um … probably something she ate. Let me go and check that she's all right. I'll text you back in a bit.'

'No. Call me. Tell Udeni to call me. I hate to think that you're ill and I'm not there to—'

'Bye, Amma. Bye, Thatha.' Vidya terminated the call.

Oh dear. Now they'd have to explain why Udeni was throwing up. Vidya rose from her seat and closed the front door, which Udeni had left wide open. She picked up the handbag her sister had dropped in her dash to the loo and hung it on a coat peg.

Then she got a glass of water and went to see her sister.

Udeni was sitting on the floor next to the toilet, looking pale and miserable, still wearing her coat.

'Hey,' said Vidya. 'Is it morning sickness?'

Udeni didn't respond.

Vidya put the glass of water down on the floor next to her and stepped back again. 'I got you some water …'

Udeni reached out an arm and pushed the door closed.

Vidya stared at the door as it clicked shut. Oh. Like that, was it?

Suddenly, the anger was back, roaring through her. She had just ruined her own life for this brat and this was how Udeni treated her?

'Fine,' Vidya shouted at the door. 'Be like that!' She turned to leave, then turned back. 'For your information, I know who the father of your child is.' Then she stormed off to her room and shut the door.

Sitting on the bed, Vidya hit a moment of paralysis. She didn't want to see Udeni, but her laptop was out there. She didn't want to do any work. She didn't want to think about Leo. What did she do now?

She dug the heels of her palms over her eyes. 'Aarrgh.' If only everything would just go away.

Her phone rang. Reluctantly, she eased it out of her pocket and glanced at the screen. Amma. She declined the call. Seconds later, Vidya could hear Udeni's phone ringing. It stopped.

A beep told Vidya that she'd got a message.

Why are you both not answering your phones? Is Udeni sick? What is wrong?

Vidya stared at it for a minute. She was tired of being the responsible one. Tired of covering for her sister. Tired of it all.

She replied: *Why don't you ask her?*

Then she put her phone on silent and burst into tears again.

This was all such a mess. Her sister was being a cow. Her parents were on her case and Leo was … She didn't know what Leo was right now. Angry with her? Confused? Sad? All of those things all at once? Her options were to never see him again and hope he never found out about the baby or … tell him and watch him become a family with her sister. She couldn't bear either of those scenarios.

Her life had been fine before all this. Boring, yes, but fine. She hadn't asked for any of this. It was all so unfair.

Someone hammered on the door, making her jump. The door opened, and Udeni barged in, waving her phone. 'What did you tell Amma?'

Vidya looked up, but she couldn't formulate a reply. A huge sob escaped her and she buried her head in her hands.

There was a moment of silence. Then, 'Shit.' The bed dipped as Udeni sat beside her. 'What's wrong? Akka?'

Vidya shook her head, her face still in her hands. Udeni put an arm around her, the argument seemingly forgotten. 'Seriously. You're scaring me.'

Vidya took a deep breath and tried to speak, but another sob came out instead. She never cried like this. Drama was Udeni's thing, not hers.

As she tried again, there were footsteps and Angie appeared in the doorway. 'What's going on?' She sat on the other side of Vidya.

She had to pull herself together. Angie thrust a wad of tissues into her hand. It reminded Vidya of Leo helping her on the first day, which prompted a fresh bout of tears to erupt out of her.

Udeni's arm tightened around Vidya. 'I don't know what's upset you, but whatever it is, we'll fix it, okay?' she said. 'I'm here for you.'

If only that were true.

Angie rubbed her back. Udeni was still hugging her with one arm. She could sense the worried glances being exchanged over her head.

After a few more attempts, Vidya gained control of herself. She raised her face and wiped the tears off it. She looked at Udeni. 'We need to talk.'

Angie looked from Vidya to Udeni and back again. 'I'm going to make us all a nice cup of tea,' she said, firmly. 'And then we're going to talk. Come on.'

Vidya trailed obediently after her friend; Udeni followed, looking subdued.

Several minutes later, Vidya squeezed the peppermint teabag against the side of her sister's mug. Udeni had disappeared into the bathroom again, clearly to be sick again. Vidya was making her peppermint tea, which handily gave her some extra thinking time.

The baby had to come first. Her own feelings were irrelevant here. Udeni's too, maybe. Vidya thought about Caleb, the guy who had never known his father and carried around that lack of acknowledgement buried deep beneath his happy-go-lucky facade. She thought of Leo, who was essentially abandoned by his parents and would be devastated, and furious, if he found out he had a child that he knew nothing about. She thought of Udeni herself, who would valiantly raise a child the best way she could but would be shattered if the child resented her decision. All this pointed to one thing. They had to tell Leo. When they'd thought Caleb was the father, it had been almost excusable not to tell him. Caleb was laid back and spontaneous. If he'd found out later, he would cope. But Leo. No. This sort of secret would hurt Leo deeply. Especially as other people knew and he didn't.

And yes, it affected Vidya too. She would be one of the people who had deceived him. She cared for him too much to do that. Okay, he might be confused and upset about what happened the other night, but that would be nothing compared to the hurt of finding out he hadn't been told he was a father.

'I think that teabag's been bashed enough.' Angie smiled at her. She was holding two mugs of caffeinated tea for herself and Vidya. Angie's expression was cautious, as though she expected Vidya to dissolve into tears at any moment.

In all honesty, Vidya wasn't sure she wouldn't. She extracted the teabag and threw it in the food waste bin.

In the bathroom, the toilet flushed again. Angie pulled a face. 'Has she been throwing up again?'

When Vidya nodded, Angie said, 'She's been all over the place these past few days. Throwing up, not sleeping, crying. She was really upset when you two argued.'

Vidya pressed her lips together. They might be arguing again soon. Angie gave Vidya a long look, then put the mugs down and hugged her. 'Whatever it is that's going on, we will sort it out. Now we're in the same place and talking to each other again.'

Udeni returned, looking a bit pale. 'Thanks.' She took a tentative sip of her peppermint tea. 'So, what did you want to talk about?'

There was no point stretching this out, so Vidya took a deep breath, then said, 'We were wrong. It isn't Caleb.'

Both the other women said, 'What?'

'It's Leo.'

They stared at her for a moment, then Angie said, 'Oh, honey.'

Udeni was still staring at Vidya.

Vidya said, slowly, 'The father of your baby … it's Leo.'

'You said it couldn't be him. Because of my description. And you thought he left the party early.'

'Well, you said he was tall, funny, sexy and a good dancer and he had a tattoo on his chest of a dragon taking flight. That was your description. The first four things obviously described Caleb.'

'Or Piotr,' said Angie.

'But they describe Leo too, when you get to know him.'

'That can't be right,' said Udeni. 'You like Leo. Angie told me.'

'Well, he has the tattoo on his shoulder.' She held a forefinger and thumb above her own left breast. 'About here.'

'And you found this out … how?' said Angie, quietly.

Vidya had a sudden memory of looking up at Leo's toned body, reaching out to touch him, and then, the tattoo coming into view. Her chin wobbled. She cleared her throat to try and pull herself together. 'He took his shirt off and … there it was.' Her voice cracked and tears came. She dabbed her eyes.

'Oh, Vid. That must have been such a shock.' Angie rushed over to hug her.

Vidya tried to say that she was fine, but the words just wouldn't come out.

'Oh, no.' Udeni shook her head, her eyes huge. 'That's awful. I'm so sorry, Akka.'

Vidya sniffed. 'Not your fault.'

'If I'd remembered more about him …' said Udeni.

There was no arguing with that. Vidya sniffed again. So did Udeni. So did Angie.

'Why are you crying?' Vidya asked Angie.

'You're both hurting and I love you guys. This is awful.' Angie let go of Vidya and fetched the kitchen roll, which she put in the middle of the table. She tore off a sheet and dabbed her eyes. 'What a mess.'

It took a few moments for them all to get their composure back.

'So, what do we do?' said Angie. 'You,' she said, pointing at Vidya, 'are in love with the guy that you,' she pointed at Udeni, 'can't remember sleeping with but got pregnant by. This is so messed up.'

'Well,' said Vidya. 'I think that we have to tell him.'

'What? No,' said Udeni. 'I told you. I can do this alone. I don't need—'

Vidya raised a hand. 'I know what you said, but it's not just about you. You have to think about this baby. You're going to need financial help to start with. The baby … at some point, is also going to become a child who will want to know who their father is.'

'But—'

'And Leo would be devastated if he found out that he had a child and hadn't been involved.' Vidya leaned forward and took Udeni's hand. 'He's a good man, Nangi. Kind and gentle and caring. He will be a great dad. He would want to be involved. I know he didn't intend for this to happen. Neither of you did, but I think you owe it to him to tell him.'

Udeni narrowed her eyes. 'But if he knows, he'll be around all the time. You'll have to see him and it'll upset you. Do you want to keep seeing him?'

Vidya closed her eyes, counted to five, then opened them again. 'I don't want to keep seeing him. It hurts me to see him. I want to put all this behind me and never think about it again, but I can't. Because actions, your actions, have consequences. There will be a baby and that baby deserves to have a father. Especially when that father will love them.'

Udeni blinked at Vidya with her big doe eyes.

Vidya lowered her voice. 'I hurt him and humiliated him. I owe him an explanation. It won't make things okay and I know that he and I can't ever be anything now, but … I owe him an explanation as to why I ran away when I saw his tattoo. He has … some past trauma and I think this has dug it up.' Her voice wobbled and another tear ran down her face. 'I can't do that to him.'

Her sister looked down at her mug for a long time. When

Udeni finally looked up, she said, 'You really like him, huh?'

'That's not relevant anymore, is it?' As much as it hurt to admit it, the needs of Udeni and the baby were bigger than her own. She would get over Leo. She had to. 'You have to tell him.'

'Why do you feel so strongly about this now? You were happy to go along with it before.'

'Because I met them. Both Leo and Caleb. I've seen what can happen when a child grows up abandoned by one or both parents. I would hate for my niece or nephew to have to deal with that.'

The other two looked puzzled, so Vidya explained about Caleb's absent dad and Leo's irresponsible parents. 'So, if Leo ever works out that he was a father and didn't get to be a part of raising that child all along, he's going to be devastated,' she said.

Angie said quietly, 'She has a point, Udeni.'

Udeni rested her forehead on the table. 'Let me think about this,' she said. 'It's all so hard.'

That was probably the best outcome Vidya could hope for. Udeni was impetuous and stubborn, but she wasn't so headstrong that she couldn't be persuaded. She would come to the right conclusion eventually.

Vidya finished her tea. Angie gave a huge sigh. 'I'm so sorry, Vid,' she said. 'I wish there was something more we could do.'

Udeni looked up. 'We could tell him and then see what he wants to do. If he likes Vidya as much as she likes him, maybe he'd still want to be with her anyway.'

'But he's having a baby with my sister. Udeni, that's just weird.'

'Sure. But that doesn't mean it's impossible. If you want him and he wants you – you can make it work.' Udeni gestured between them. '*We* can make it work.'

Vidya didn't know how to respond to that. Could they make it work? 'It's just so … weird and embarrassing.'

Udeni shrugged. 'Like I said before. I don't need him to acknowledge that he's the baby's dad. No one needs to know.'

'The baby does.'

Her sister waved a hand. 'Not for years. They could just be a fatherless child who has a really lovely uncle as a father figure …'

'No.'

Udeni sighed. 'You are very stubborn.'

That was rich coming from her.

'I've never seen you upset like that,' Udeni carried on. 'If you're that sad – you must really care about him. That's important too.'

Did she care about him? More than just physical attraction? Vidya thought about how comfortable she was when she was with Leo. The warmth of him. The way he had asked 'who takes care of you', while he was taking care of her. Almost as though she deserved to be taken care of, and he was offended that no one was already doing it. Leo was a very private person, who didn't let many people near him. When she saw him smile, free and unguarded, she knew him well enough to recognise what a gift it was.

'I do care about him,' she said. 'But I still don't think it'll work.'

'But … how about you tell him and see what happens?' said Angie.

'Yes. I think that's a plan. Do you agree, Udeni?'

Udeni nodded.

For a moment, there was silence. Then Angie said, 'Now that we've got that sorted, I'm going to go have a shower. You two should probably talk about the other stuff that happened this week.'

Once she'd left, the two sisters didn't speak for a few minutes.

'I'm sorry,' Udeni said. 'I was … It was wrong of me to lash out like that. I was feeling rotten and I took it out on you. You were only trying to help.'

Vidya nodded. 'I'm sorry too. You're right. I do judge. And I tend to try and swoop in and help whether you want it or not. I'll try not to do that.'

'I love you, you know that, right?'

Vidya hadn't been expecting that. 'Oh.'

'I know I'm a bit rash sometimes and I say things without thinking them through. I don't do that with everyone, mostly just you. Because you've always understood and been there and … well, sisters argue, right? It's normal.'

'I guess so. You know I'm always here for you though. Whenever you need me.'

'I know.' Udeni frowned. 'So … is this us making up?'

Vidya smiled, weakly. 'Uhuh. If you'll have me.'

This was the problem with having a little sister you loved. You loved them even when they annoyed you. Or took you for granted. Or leaned on you too heavily. You still loved them. It was time to stand up for herself though. She opened her mouth to speak, but Udeni beat her to it.

'I did take you for granted. I'm sorry. I know you'll always help me. I know you don't have to, but you will. And I do appreciate it. I just … sometimes it's hard being the failure of the family, you know.'

'You're not a failure. Don't be ridiculous. You made a mistake. It's not the end of the world. We'll deal with it.'

Udeni looked down at her hands. 'I'm scared,' she said, suddenly. 'I don't know anything about raising a child and I'm scared I'll do it wrong.'

A hundred different answers swarmed around Vidya's head, but none of them were the right one. Finally, she said, 'I think all you can do is your best.'

Chapter 24

Leo sat in yet another hotel room. A well-appointed city hotel in Brussels this time. He and Caleb had only left Waterloo Bay that morning, but it felt like a hundred years ago. Back in the distant past, when he'd accidentally believed that he could have a normal relationship.

He changed, wearily, into his pyjamas and brushed his teeth. Everything felt like a huge effort. Had it only been last night that he'd kissed Vidya? Just before everything went wrong. Again.

It felt like he had a gaping wound in his chest and everything hurt. He crawled into bed and lay on his back, staring at the darkened ceiling. Try as he might, he couldn't think what had caused Vidya's sudden reaction. He wished he could work out what he'd done, so that he could stop doing it.

As they often did, his thoughts went back to Jessica. That had been his first real relationship. They hadn't moved in together, but they'd been a couple. It had been a fairly steep learning curve for him. Caleb, for all his teasing, had been a great help at the time. Jessica had seemed happy. With hindsight, he realised that she'd seen him as an oddity that she could fix. A challenge. Then, when she realised that he was always going to be reserved, that she couldn't suddenly unlock a dramatic, tap-dancing, sparkling persona in him, rather than talking to him maturely, like a sane person would do, she'd cheated on him.

Leo had thought that Vidya was different. She had seemed relaxed around him. She found his jokes funny – which was rare; most people didn't even notice when he made a joke! He had hoped that she saw him as he really was and liked him anyway. So, what on earth had happened to scare her off like that?

He sighed and checked his phone. It was late. He should get some sleep. He and Caleb had a client meeting first thing. After a full day, they would be heading home and on Friday, Leo would have to report to Charlie about the work they'd done in Waterloo Bay. Vidya would be at that meeting. He needed to pull himself together before then.

He closed his eyes and an image of Vidya's horrified face, her hand over her mouth, her eyes wide, formed behind his eyelids. Leo sighed again and punched his pillow into a different shape. He was never going to get to sleep tonight.

On Friday morning, Vidya dressed extra smart. She even put on heels that were slightly higher than her usual one-inch mules. Today, she needed all the extra confidence she could find. She had a meeting with both Leo and Caleb, as well as their line manager, Charlie, to update him on the progress of the project.

For the last two days, the guys had been in Brussels and the wait for them to come back had been agony. Today she was going to have to talk to Leo and tell him about Udeni. The idea of seeing him again was wreaking havoc with her mind, and she had been too anxious to sleep much last night. This was a terrible thing to have to do. How did you tell a guy you'd almost slept with – and who you thought you might love – that the woman he'd had a one-night stand with two months ago was your sister and … that she was expecting his child. Ugh. Vidya had to remind herself that she was doing the right thing.

This was for her sister and her unborn niece or nephew …

and for Leo himself. Vidya drew herself up to her full height. Embarrassment and self-pity had no place here. She was an impenetrable fortress. She could do this. She could. She checked herself in the mirror one last time and set off for work.

Vidya got to the meeting room ten minutes early. She had printed out hard copies of her report and the summary that Leo had put in the shared drive last night. For all the talk of going paperless, some people still preferred paper copies of things.

The idea of sitting in this meeting with Leo made her queasy. She took a deep breath. Right now, her issues weren't as important as this meeting was. This was the first time they'd used the AI assistant in an actual project. If Charlie disapproved, then some of that was on her. Looking around, she decided that the best place to sit was facing the door. This meeting room looked very different to the big room in the hotel in Waterloo Bay she'd spent the last week in, everything was more polished, including the dark wood table. The view was of other buildings, and the birds were pigeons, not gulls. She pulled out a chair and sat down.

The door opened and Caleb came in. He looked tired, but he gave her his usual cheerful smile. 'Hey, Vidya, how's it going?'

She felt an unexpected surge of relief that he was still talking to her. There was no reason to think he wouldn't … but it was still nice to know.

He took a seat next to her and poured himself some water. 'Looking forward to this?'

'No, are you?'

'Depends,' he said. 'I don't think Charlie is expecting us to have managed all the work we've done. So, I'm looking forward to seeing his face when he finds out. I fully expect him to kick up a fuss about using AI.'

She nodded. 'I think you're right.'

Caleb was quiet for a moment, then whispered, 'Have you spoken to him?'

She didn't need to ask to know he was talking about Leo. 'No.'

'Hmm. He's been so grouchy lately, he—'

The door opened again and Charlie, Mr Charles Bexworth Huxley, came in. Behind him came Diane Askew, a formidable lady, who was one of the founding partners of Askew, Else and Thomas. Caleb glanced at Vidya and widened his eyes. If the big boss was here, this upped the stakes for this meeting considerably. She plastered a smile onto her face.

Leo entered last and closed the door behind him. 'This is the rest of my team for this project,' he said. 'My colleagues Caleb Fotherill and Vidya Munasinghe from the paralegal admin team.'

Ms Askew nodded and sat down, so did Charlie. Leo didn't make eye contact with Vidya at all. He came round and sat next to Caleb. Her heart cracked a little more. Any chance of friendship they'd had was now clearly gone. He was freezing her out and only interacting with her in a professional capacity. It was understandable after what had happened.

All she could do now was show him that she could be a professional, even if they were no longer friends. Which meant she had to focus right now. This wasn't about her. This meeting was about the work, and, it seemed, about proving Legal Team B's competence.

While the others sat down and glanced through the paperwork, Vidya skimmed her notes. Her phone buzzed; she took it out to put it on silent. The message was from Leo. It said: *Remember, you know more about querying the AI than any of us. You are the expert in this room. But it was my call to use it. If needed I will take the flak.*

Vidya leaned forward to look at him. He gave her a subtle nod, unsmiling. She understood. Whatever they were outside this room, in here, they were a team. She gave him a small smile and returned her phone, now safely on silent mode, to her pocket. She sat a little straighter. Next to her, Caleb leaned forward.

'Let's get this started,' said Charlie. 'Vidya, please take notes.'

She nodded, but Leo interjected. 'Actually, there will be some sections where Vidya will be taking the lead with the explanations. So, Caleb, would you mind assisting and taking notes when Vidya's talking?'

'Happy to.' Caleb made a show of uncapping his pen.

Leo stood up and passed around the copies of his summary. He started by outlining the scope of the project. 'Obviously,' he said, 'this is a substantial amount of work. We estimated the work would take thirty-five to forty person days, we had only twenty-one.'

'Why was this the case?' said Ms Askew.

'There was a time barrier, in that the work needed to be done for today, before Charlie met with the company this afternoon,' said Leo. 'And Caleb and I had to fly out to Brussels on Wednesday. We got back last night.'

'Well, why not put more people on it, then? This is a big project. Important.'

'That, I can't answer,' said Leo. 'When the timescales changed, I requested a team of five.'

Ms Askew turned to Charlie and raised a quizzical eyebrow. He blustered a bit and said, 'That was all we had available. There are several other cases with imminent deadlines and I felt that Leo had overestimated the time needed.'

'But you got the work done?' Ms Askew asked Leo.

'Yes. But we needed to enlist the help of the AI assistant.'

'Why are we using a major client's work as a guinea pig for testing out AI capability?'

'I didn't authorise it,' said Charlie, smugly. 'This was Leo's call.'

'We had a task that was repetitive but needed to be done accurately. There weren't enough people to check everything manually. The hotel had scanned documents, but they weren't cross-referenced in any sensible way,' said Leo. 'The connections between agreements and suppliers were known to one manager, who has left the company, taking her knowledge with her. With

214

all due respect, if we were to do this on time, with the number of people we had, we didn't have a choice but to use the AI to filter out the boilerplate agreements from the ones that needed scrutiny. Luckily, we had someone who was trained in writing AI queries with us, which made it possible.'

'It's still a risk,' said Charlie. 'The machine is a blunt tool. What about hallucinations?'

'That's most common in generative AI,' Vidya said. 'This isn't generative AI.'

Ms Askew frowned and took a few seconds to look at the paperwork in front of her. 'And you trust a machine to do this work?'

'Within certain parameters, yes.' Leo looked at Vidya. She knew that he was passing the baton to her as the AI expert in the room to explain.

'Let me explain what we did.' Vidya quickly outlined her strategy for getting the AI to sort the standard agreements from the nonstandard ones and the checks she'd put in place.

Somewhat unexpectedly, Ms Askew listened. When she asked questions, it seemed that she knew a little bit about the AI assistant and its limitations. Finally, she said, 'Carry on.'

Leo went through their findings, including the conclusions that, while taking over the hotel would incur quite a lot of costs, their client would probably still make a profit, according to their own projections, within five years.

Leo stopped talking. He glanced first at Caleb and then at Vidya and gave them a solemn nod. Vidya knew that was him acknowledging a job well done. Even now, when he was barely speaking to her, Leo was treating her like a professional. She wouldn't have expected anything less, but she was pleased nonetheless.

Ms Askew closed the report and looked up. 'You take responsibility for this?' she said to Leo.

'I do.'

Across the table, Charlie looked smug.

'Good. This is excellent. You had a difficult problem and you solved it using the tools available. We'll take this to the client this afternoon. Good work.' Ms Askew stood up.

Charlie's face fell. He got to his feet.

Vidya and the guys stood too.

'Now, Charles,' Ms Askew said, as the two of them headed for the door. 'We need to discuss why there were only three people available for the project.'

The door clicked shut and the three of them let out a collective breath.

'That went well,' said Leo. 'Thank you, team.'

'Did you collar Askew beforehand and tell her that Charlie made you do something impossible?' Caleb said to Leo.

'I couldn't possibly say.' Leo collected his paperwork and folder. 'Right. I'll see you later.'

'Leo,' said Vidya.

But he had already walked out, his long legs making short work of crossing the room.

She turned to look at Caleb.

'I need to talk to him,' she said.

'I don't think he wants to talk to you though. Not about anything other than work anyway.'

'Can you—'

Caleb shook his head. 'No. I tried, but he's definitely not in the mood to listen to me. He has been cranky as hell the past few days. So, if you could hurry up and talk to him, that would be awesome. I'm not sure how much more of this I can take.'

Vidya sighed.

Caleb patted her on the shoulder. 'Good luck.'

Left alone in the meeting room, she gathered all the papers and notes and fought down the urge to cry. It was all so damned unfair. Now that the meeting was over, Leo's coldness towards her really hurt.

She left the meeting room and headed back to her cubicle. As she passed, Angie looked up with a quizzical expression on her face. Vidya shook her head. Once she'd dumped everything on her desk, she opened a document to write up her notes. She stared at it for a few minutes. No. This would not do. She finally had Udeni's permission to tell Leo and now he didn't want to talk to her. This was bigger than her feelings. She had to tell him. In fact, she would do it right now. She stood again. A few people looked up, but no one really paid any attention to her. She marched out.

The legal teams were two floors above, so she took the lift. Here, where it was much quieter and the offices were bigger, no one seemed to care that she was there. She had to stop and ask for directions to his office. When she got there, it was empty.

The momentum that had carried her up there drained away.

She walked on a few steps until she could see the secretary's desk. 'Hi. I'm looking for Leo.'

'He's gone out to grab a coffee,' said the woman who was sitting there. 'He'll be back in a few minutes.'

'Should I wait?'

The secretary glanced at the clock. 'Come back in fifteen minutes, maybe.'

Vidya nodded. 'Thanks.' She walked back out. Now what? How should she waste fifteen minutes? She didn't want to go back to her desk. No. She would go downstairs and catch him as he came back in.

Chapter 25

Leo strode into the office building with his coffee and knew from the expression on the security guard's face that he was scowling. He tried to rearrange his face so that he looked neutral. He knew that he'd been a pain to work with the past couple of days. Even Caleb's usual joie de vivre had faded in the face of Leo's intense focus and nitpicking. Oh, he could convince himself he was just being thorough, but he knew he'd been micromanaging. He couldn't help it. He'd needed to keep busy. How else would he stop thinking about Vidya?

The idea of coming into the office today had kept him up all night. Even though he logically knew that there was no reason anyone would have heard about what happened between him and Vidya, the memory of what had happened with Jessica was still too vivid. He imagined the pitying looks, the conversations that stopped when he walked in, the overheard snippets of speculation about how long she'd been cheating on him for, and how on earth he hadn't spotted it.

Leo liked this job. He would hate to have to leave and start again somewhere else because he had terrible luck with women.

As bad as all his worrying had been, actually seeing Vidya had been so much worse. For a split second, he hadn't cared about the meeting or getting one up on Charlie or even the project. All he'd wanted was to kneel at Vidya's feet and ask her what he'd done wrong. Thankfully, he'd pulled himself together in time. He'd had to pause to take a minute before he went in, but he'd done it.

The effort had left him feeling scattered and exhausted. His concentration was shot to bits. Hence the need for this very, very strong coffee.

He reached the lifts and hit the button. It would be okay. He just needed to soldier on. If he remained his usual, professional self, no one would know anything had gone awry. Vidya was completely different from Jessica. Their encounter had been private. She wouldn't tell anyone about it. Neither would Caleb. It should be fine.

'Leo.'

He startled so violently, he almost spilled his precious coffee. Vidya had appeared next to him. He'd been so engrossed in his thoughts that he hadn't noticed her approach. He couldn't bring himself to look at her. He stared at the light on the lift.

'Leo, can we talk?' She said it quietly.

'If it's about the project, I think we have everything we need. Once you and Caleb hand in your meeting notes, we should be done.'

'It's not about the project,' she said.

The lift doors opened. Vidya stepped in. Leo didn't. 'I'll take the next one.' He took out his phone and moved away.

Someone else arrived, the lift doors closed. He left it a minute before he turned around and pressed the button to summon the lift again. Heat flooded to his face. That was childish. Surely, he was better than this.

More people arrived and when the lift doors opened this time, he got in. Wait. Why was Vidya down here? Had she been waiting for him? She had been, hadn't she?

Oh. If she was that determined to see him … an uneasy feeling

219

crept up his spine. The lift arrived at his floor and he got out. She was waiting for him. Part of him was impressed.

When he beeped himself into the office floor, she followed him.

A few heads rose as they walked past, he walking quickly, she practically skipping to keep up.

'I don't want to talk about it,' he said, in an undertone.

'I think we have to,' she said, also speaking quietly.

No one was looking at them. Leo got to the small office he shared with Caleb and put his hand on the door handle. It was still dark in the office. 'Caleb's in a meeting.'

'I don't need to talk to him. I want to talk to you,' Vidya said, quietly but firmly. 'You can let me talk to you in your office, or I can shout through the door at you. I'm not going away.' She folded her arms. Her chin went up.

He finally looked at her. This streak of defiance was part of what had drawn him to her in the first place. He knew her well enough now to understand that she wouldn't be this adamant if she wasn't fairly sure she was right about whatever it was she wanted to tell him.

'Fine.' He went into his office.

Vidya followed and shut the door behind her. She hovered for a moment. There were two chairs in the office. His and Caleb's. When he'd hung up his coat, he said, 'Take Caleb's chair.'

Leo sat in his own.

'I … think I'll stand,' she said.

Now that he looked at her properly, he could see that she had bags under her eyes. She looked drawn and, perhaps, a little grey. Despite his better judgement, concern stirred. It would be a stupid question to ask if everything was okay, given their circumstances. So, he said, 'Are you ill?'

'What? Me? No. Just …' She pushed her hair behind her ear. 'Just a bit stressed.'

'About …?'

'Leo. I owe you an explanation.'

He clasped his hands in front of him. 'No, you don't. You can change your mind for whatever reason, whenever.'

'There was … there was a reason.' She was shifting her weight from foot to foot. Clearly nervous. He was curious now. This was not what he had been expecting. What exactly had he been expecting from her? He didn't know how to respond, so he said nothing.

Vidya closed her eyes and opened them again. 'Okay,' she said. 'There's no easy way to say this. You're going to be a father.'

O … kay. This was getting quite weird. 'I hate to tell you, but we didn't—'

'Not me,' she said. 'My sister.'

What? That made no sense at all. Was she having some sort of psychotic episode? 'I've never met your sister.'

'You have. You had a one-night stand with her a couple of months ago.'

He shook his head. 'No. I definitely didn't. I would have remembered.'

'Are you sure? She doesn't. Remember, I mean. Not well, anyway.'

He was definitely worried now. Looking carefully, he could see that she really didn't look healthy. Something was very wrong. He glanced at his phone. Should he call for a first aider? Who would he trust to handle this? He unclasped his hands. 'Vidya,' he said, gently. 'That doesn't make any sense.'

She gave him a hollow-eyed look of desperation.

'Maybe you should sit down,' he said. 'Try again.'

Her eyes looked to the ceiling. She took a couple of deep breaths, which made her chest heave in ways he really shouldn't notice right now.

'The company anniversary party,' she said, finally. 'You arrived late with Caleb and Piotr, and the rest of the team. You were all wearing rabbit masks.'

'Yes. The masks were Caleb's idea. I was just going to go as I was.'

'Right. Right.' She nodded. 'Then you met a girl dressed as a Disney princess. You guys drank a lot, danced a bit, then slept together.'

Leo slowly shook his head, drawn into this story despite himself. 'No ... I went home after a couple of drinks.' Then, just to be clear, he added, 'Alone.'

She shook her head too. 'My sister couldn't remember your name or much of what you looked like, but she said the guy was tall, funny, sexy and a good dancer – and he had a tattoo, beneath his left collarbone, of a dragon taking flight.' She tapped her own shoulder, at roughly the same place that his tattoo was. 'Just here.'

Realisation dawned. 'Caleb. That was Caleb. Not me.' He had no idea about the sleeping with a Disney princess part, but it was the sort of thing Caleb did when he was very drunk. And he had mentioned meeting someone at the work party.

'I thought that at first, but the description matches you. The tattoo.'

Things suddenly fell into place. Her reaction when he had turned around to face her. That must have been when she saw his tattoo. Oh. No wonder she had run away. To think that she was about to sleep with a guy who had already slept with her sister ... poor Vidya. 'It wasn't me. It was Caleb.'

'But the tattoo—'

'We both have the same tattoo.'

She opened her mouth. Then closed it again. Then shook her head rapidly for a few minutes. 'What? How? Why?'

'It's a long story. It was a few years ago. We were both going through some stuff. We got drunk. It was meant to be a phoenix, but we weren't clear and ... well, I quite like the dragon now.'

She looked even greyer than before. Was she going to faint?

'Seriously, Vidya. Sit down.' He hurried around her and dragged Caleb's chair so that it was behind her.

She sank slowly down into it. 'So ... you *and* Caleb have the tattoo?'

'Yes.'

'And the guy who slept with my sister after the party is ... Caleb. Not you.' Vidya's shoulders seemed to drop.

'Caleb did meet someone that night, but he said she was blonde.' He doubted her sister was blonde, but who knew. 'I think her name was Elsa.'

A fleeting smile. 'Yeah. That's Udeni. She was dressed as Queen Elsa. Blonde wig and all.' He must have looked blank because she added, 'Elsa is from *Frozen*. The Disney film?'

'Right.' His brain niggled at him. There was something it wanted him to pay attention to. But the more obvious thing came first. 'Your sister is pregnant?' That must have been what the argument a few days ago had been about.

'Yes.'

'And she's sure Caleb is the father?' He was speaking quietly because gossip got around this place like wildfire.

Vidya shrugged. 'She knew it was a guy from Legal Team B. Piotr doesn't have a tattoo. It's not you. So, it must be Caleb. The dates match up and she hasn't been with anyone else in a while, so yes.'

Leo's first instinct was to protect Caleb. 'Okay. I assume there is a baby coming at some point.'

Vidya nodded. 'She didn't want me to tell the father. She just wanted me to confirm that it was him and find out a bit about him. She wanted to know what kind of a kid she might have. I ... agreed, because ... well ...'

'Because you're her big sister and that's what you do,' Leo said. More things fell into place. The look on her face when she'd seen that child, for example. 'That's why you were asking Caleb questions all the time.'

She nodded again. 'Not because I fancied him. I was just gathering information.'

'And why are you telling me now?'

She twisted her fingers together. 'Partly because I owed you a proper explanation. But mainly because you had shitty, absent parents. If we didn't tell you, we'd have made you into a shitty, absent parent too, through no fault of your own. If you ever found out, which, let's face it, we work in the same building, you might have found out. You would have been furious and so upset. I … I couldn't do that to you.' Vidya looked up at him when she said it and he felt like she'd scooped something out of his chest.

'But it's not me, it's Caleb,' Leo said. 'Does that change things for you? Or for your sister?'

Vidya thought for a moment before she answered. 'I think Caleb would feel the same way as you would … if he was forced to be an absent dad.'

This was true. In fact, it would be worse for Caleb, who carried around a seething hatred of his absent father. Leo was annoyed by his parents, but he didn't hate them. He and his sisters kept them at a distance out of necessity, but they still cared.

'I'll have to talk to Udeni,' Vidya said. 'Tell her that things have changed. Or rather, my conclusion was wrong.' She gave him an apologetic look, her brows knitted, her expressive eyes sad. 'I'm so sorry. That must have been such a shock. I was so sure … It never occurred to me that two people could have the same tattoo in the same place. I'm so sorry.'

'Understandable.' He really did understand. He had a more immediate issue though. 'Caleb will be here soon. Do you want me to tell him?'

She stared at the floor and was quiet for a moment. The only sound in the little office was of them breathing.

'I think … I think I should tell him,' said Vidya. 'My sister is going to meet me in a coffee shop near here later this afternoon. Could he come and meet her then?'

Almost without thinking Leo reached for his computer.

'You have an hour between your lunch meeting and your

meeting with Somersby.' She sounded weary. 'I've sent you a meeting request already. It should say Waterloo on it. I thought that once you knew, you'd probably want to meet her to talk to her.'

He moved his hand slowly back. 'You've thought of everything,' he said. Despite the appearance of barely holding it together, Vidya was still organised. He admired that.

She raised her eyes to his and he felt a pang of longing. All this time he'd been hurt and angry at what he'd thought was her rejection of him. Now he understood why she had reacted the way she did, but he couldn't unsee the look of horror on her face. The awfulness of that moment was etched so clearly into his mind that he wasn't sure he could ever go back to the way things had been before. No matter how much he wanted to.

'I guess I should tell him today, then,' Vidya said. 'There's never going to be a good time to tell him, is there? It's pretty earth shattering.'

'I've always thought that becoming a parent was a binary thing. One minute you're not and then you are and you'll never be the same again.' Then Leo thought of his parents and added, bitterly, 'At least that's how it should be.'

'I think it's a lot of work.' She sighed.

'Yes.'

They sat together in silence for a moment, separated by a few feet of carpet and a whole gulf of misaligned emotions. The door opened and into this awkward silence came Caleb.

He stopped, door still open, when he saw Vidya.

'Oh,' he said. 'Should I leave?'

Leo shook his head. 'No. No. Come in. Close the door.'

Caleb did as Leo asked. As he approached Vidya, he said, 'What's going on? Has Charlie been shit-stirring again?'

She looked at Leo, the message in her eyes was clear, as if she'd spoken out loud, 'What do I do?'

She herself had said, there was no good time.

Leo stood up. 'Vidya has something to tell you, Caleb. I think you should sit down.'

Vidya quickly repeated what she'd told Leo about the events of the party. She was more coherent than she had been before. Probably because it was the second time she was saying it. Or maybe because telling Caleb wasn't nearly as stressful as when she'd thought Leo was the baby's father.

'Elsa!' Caleb looked delighted. 'I thought there was someone you reminded me of. I just thought you were familiar from seeing you around the office.' He clasped his hands together. 'So, her real name's Udeni?'

'You thought her name was really Elsa,' Leo said. It wasn't a question. It was too silly.

'That's what she said it was at the party,' Caleb said. 'When I tried to ask again, she sang "Let It Go" at me.'

Yes, well, that tracked. That was the sort of thing Udeni would do. Should she tell him about the pregnancy? She glanced at Leo, who was leaning against his desk, next to where Caleb was sitting with his arms crossed. He looked unfairly handsome. He gave her an encouraging nod.

'Um. Caleb,' she said. 'The thing is … Udeni is pregnant. We're pretty sure it's from that night.'

Caleb stopped. His mouth was frozen in a silent 'oh'. He looked back at Leo, who put a gentle hand on his shoulder.

'I'm sorry to spring this on you,' Vidya said. 'You're going to be a father.'

Caleb still wasn't saying anything.

'Uh. Udeni didn't want to tell you at first. She doesn't want you to think there's any pressure. She doesn't need you to be involved. It just seemed like the ri—'

'How can I not be involved?' Caleb said, loudly enough that Leo glanced outside the office. Responding to Leo's pressure on his shoulder, Caleb dropped his voice and said, 'If it's my baby,

I want to be involved. I'm not going to be some sort of arsehole dad who isn't there for his kid.'

Which was exactly what she'd thought he'd say. 'I know,' she said. 'I thought you'd see it that way. My sister … she can be very stubborn, but I think she understands what this would mean to you now.' She really hoped this was true. Udeni was probably going to be furious that she'd told two people instead of one. It didn't matter. Caleb was her friend and this meant a lot to him. So, she would deal with whatever Udeni threw at her. Besides, the baby would miss out on an adoring father, which seemed unfair.

She explained about the meeting. 'I'll change the meeting request to Caleb,' she said to Leo.

Caleb looked from one to the other. 'Wait a minute. What does Leo have to do with any of this?'

Vidya groaned and dropped her face into her hands. Ugh. As if she hadn't been embarrassed enough already.

Thankfully, Leo came to her rescue. 'It's a long story,' he said. 'I'll fill you in later. Can we focus on the important part – about you meeting with Udeni?'

Caleb nodded. 'Right. Right. Yes. Er … I'll be there.' He looked back at Vidya and suddenly seemed scared and young.

She patted his hand, which was gripping the arm rest. 'Thank you,' she said. 'It'll be fine. She's not expecting anything of you. So don't stress.'

'Easy for you to say,' said Caleb. 'A girl I met once, who didn't even get around to telling me her real name, is going to have my baby. That's the definition of stress, surely.'

She smiled. 'I suppose it is.' It was time to go. Her own feelings were in turmoil right now. She needed some time to sort those out. Besides, she had actual work to do. She stood up. 'I'll see you later.'

Vidya glanced at Leo, whose face was giving nothing away. He was clearly focusing on Caleb right now. That was probably a good thing. She said her goodbyes and left, trying not to cringe. How on earth was she going to get over the embarrassment of her actions? She had jumped to a conclusion, blown her chance with Leo, then told him he'd got someone pregnant, only to find out that she'd got the wrong guy. He must think she was a lunatic.

Chapter 26

Three hours later, Leo was still dealing with Caleb's random responses about Vidya and her sister. He flipped between 'How can this be happening?' and 'I can't believe Vidya thought it was you'. Right now, he was staring into space saying, 'I'm sure we used protection. I always use protection.'

Leo sighed and minimised the document he was working on – he was clearly not going to be able to get anything done. 'But you can't remember for sure. You said yourself, you'd had far too much to drink.'

'She'd already been drinking, so I had to catch up,' Caleb said.

This made no sense to Leo at all, but he let it slide. 'And condoms don't work a hundred per cent of the time.'

'I know, but … I didn't expect it to happen to me.'

'No one ever does.'

Caleb was quiet for a moment. Leo cautiously opened his work document again.

'Leo?'

'Yes.'

'Do you think she'll like me?'

Leo peered around the screen. 'What?'

Caleb leaned back in his chair. 'Well, she was drunk when we met. We had a great time, but she can't even remember what I looked like. And if we're going to co-parent this kid, we're going to have to see each other. Do you think she'll like me when she meets me … you know, sober?'

Leo had no idea how fragile Caleb was right now, so he said, 'You said there was a connection when you met. Something special. So, I'm sure she will like you.'

'That's a good point.' Caleb moved out of his line of sight again.

They worked in silence for a bit. Leo got to a point where he could save his work and call it done. He checked the clock. It was nearly time to go. A flare of something like panic shot through him.

Why was he getting worked up? This meeting was a big deal for *Caleb*. He himself had no reason to be stressed. He had a mental image of Vidya, looking out at the sea, her hair blowing back away from her face. Now he knew why she had run out on him, it was still upsetting, but not humiliating anymore, not really. In her place, he would have run away too.

As if reading his mind, Caleb pushed his chair around to the side of the desk, sat down and said, 'What are you going to do about Vidya?'

Leo blinked.

'I mean, you know why she reacted the way she did,' said Caleb. 'Are you going to forgive her?'

'There's nothing to forgive, really,' Leo said. 'I'm relieved that she didn't find me repulsive or something.'

Caleb made winding motions with his hands. 'And … are you going to talk to her about it?'

'Probably. Eventually. When it's the right time.' How did he bring it up without them both dying of embarrassment? Would she even be interested now that things had gone so drastically wrong? What if the sight of the dragon tattoo made her think of Caleb and her sister? That was just too awful. He rubbed his fingertips on his shirt, above the tattoo.

'Oh, come on,' said Caleb. 'There's never going to be a right time. You have to seize the day.' He leaned forward, his elbows on his knees. 'You like this woman, Leo. It's not often you fall for someone. Don't let her get away.'

'Like you're the expert on relationships right now,' he snapped. The minute he said it, he felt bad.

Caleb's face fell.

'I'm sorry. I didn't mean that,' Leo said. 'You had no way of predicting this would happen.'

'But it's true, isn't it?' said Caleb. 'How long have you been telling me that getting drunk and getting laid aren't going to solve my problems? I guess you were right. This is how it's come back to bite me.'

'I'm sorry,' Leo said, again.

'But … buuuuut,' said Caleb. 'Maybe this isn't a disaster. I guess we'll find out when I meet Elsa.'

'Udeni.'

'Sorry, yes, Udeni. I mean, Vidya's great, so her sister must also be okay, right?' He brightened. 'Hey, this means I get to have Vidya as my sister-in-law, of sorts. That's cool.'

Leo didn't know what to say to that.

Vidya arrived at the café ten minutes before the meeting time. Udeni, who was working 'from home', was sitting at a table, tapping away on her laptop. She was looking healthier today and was smart in her work clothes. It wasn't often Vidya saw her in work mode. Udeni looked professional.

Vidya had a moment of cognitive dissonance. She had always thought of Udeni as someone young and vulnerable. Someone she had to look after. Looking at Udeni now, it struck Vidya that Udeni was an adult. Choosing to keep this baby may have seemed like a whim, but she had really committed to it. She had bought books on baby care and was giving everything some serious thought. Perhaps she was ready. Or ready as anyone ever was for a baby.

Caleb was a nice man. With his support and, of course, her own, Udeni would be okay. Vidya felt the load on her shoulders lighten a little.

She had worked through lunch, so she ordered herself soup and a roll, and took it to the table where her sister was working.

Udeni noticed her. 'One second,' she said. 'Let me just send off this email.'

Vidya sat down next to her and made herself comfortable. From where they were sitting, they could see out of the window. The café wasn't too busy. There seemed to be quite a lot of people also working. Most of them had earbuds in. This was a good place for a meeting.

Her sister finished what she was doing and closed her laptop. Vidya had told her all about the mix-up, that Leo wasn't the father and it would be Caleb coming to see her.

'How are you feeling?' Vidya asked. 'Nervous?'

Udeni nodded. 'Yes, but also … not so bad, you know. You were right. Telling him is the right thing to do. And now you've found out it wasn't Leo, it's helped clear the misunderstanding between you, so that's an added bonus.'

Vidya groaned. 'I'm so embarrassed about that.'

'Why? It was an honest mistake.' Udeni nudged her. 'It means that you can date him now.'

Vidya cast about for something to say. Of course she'd like to try again with Leo, but … quite literally running away the minute she saw his bare chest wasn't something that was so easy to recover from. She looked out of the window and, to her relief, saw two familiar figures walking down the street. Leo must have come with Caleb for moral support.

'It's them,' she said. 'There they are.'

'The two suits?' Udeni said, craning her neck to see.

'Yes. Looks like Leo came too.'

Udeni stared for a moment. 'Caleb is the one on the right?'

'Yes. Why? Do you remember him now?'

'I recognise the way he moves.' A small smile touched Udeni's face.

Vidya didn't want to know what she was thinking about.

Udeni turned suddenly. 'What if he doesn't like me? He thinks I'm a blonde-haired Elsa. What if he sees the real me and doesn't want anything to do with me?'

He didn't have to like her. He just needed to want to be a part of the baby's life. Actually, he didn't even need to do that. 'He'll like you,' Vidya said. 'I can't imagine why he wouldn't.'

'What if I don't like him? I don't remember that much about him – I mean, I must have found him attractive but—'

'Tall, sexy, funny and a great dancer,' Vidya said.

'Yes, but I had vodka goggles on then. What if I don't like him now?' Udeni's eyes were wide and a little panic stricken. This was a genuine worry? At this point in time?

'Caleb is nice,' Vidya said, kindly. 'I like him. I'm pretty sure you'll like him too.' She rubbed her sister's forearm. 'Relax. Okay? It'll be fine. For what it's worth, I think you two would have made a really nice couple if you met under more normal circumstances.'

Udeni gave her a long look. 'You approve of him?' she said.

'We've become friends. So, yes.'

'That's good to know.'

The two guys entered, Caleb first, then Leo. Caleb scanned the café. When he turned their way, Vidya waved. Leo said something to Caleb and went to the counter.

Caleb came towards them. His eyes were on Udeni. 'Elsa,' he said.

'Rabbit head.' Udeni smiled.

'Caleb, actually.' He smiled back and extended a hand.

'Udeni.'

They shook hands and he sat down. His gaze slid towards Vidya for a second and they nodded to each other. Then his attention was straight back to Udeni. This, Vidya felt, was a good sign. She turned her attention to eating her soup quietly.

For a moment, there was awkward silence. Then Udeni said, 'I guess this is a bit of a surprise. I thought you should know about the baby, but you don't need to—'

'I want to know,' Caleb said, quickly. 'Obviously, it's unexpected, but I want to be a part of it.'

'We'll do a paternity test,' said Udeni, firmly. 'Once the baby is born. Because that's less risky.'

Caleb nodded. 'That makes sense.'

Vidya blinked. Udeni sounded very calm and in control. Vidya had seen Caleb switch from happy-go-lucky to serious and organised before, but this was the first time she'd seen Udeni do it. Perhaps she had underestimated her sister.

'So, how far along are you?' said Caleb. 'Because they count two weeks before too, don't they?'

'Eleven weeks,' said Udeni. 'More or less.'

'And everything is okay?'

'I think so. We'll know more when I have the twelve-week scan next Thursday.' Udeni glanced at Vidya, who smiled back.

Leo arrived with two coffees and slid one in front of Caleb. He introduced himself to Udeni, who shook his hand and looked him up and down.

'Nice to meet you, Leo,' she said.

'He's one of my best friends,' said Caleb. 'We both work with Vidya.'

Udeni smiled. 'I know.'

Leo made eye contact with Vidya briefly and looked away.

She assumed Leo was here because Caleb had asked him to come. Should she be talking to him to give the other two some space? Did he even want to talk to her after her ridiculous accusation? Heat rose up her cheeks. What must he think of her? She must have looked like such an idiot.

Caleb asked if he could go with Udeni to the twelve-week scan.

Udeni said, 'It's okay; Vidya's coming with me.'

A brief look of disappointment passed over Caleb's face, but he recovered well. 'Oh, that's okay then. You won't be alone.'

'I won't at all,' Udeni said. 'I have my sister.'

Vidya smiled her most 'supportive sister' smile. Caleb gave her a funny look.

'I know,' he said. He wrapped his fingers around the coffee mug and looked at Udeni over it. 'So, tell me about yourself. What do you do?'

'Er … I work in arts fundraising. I'm twenty-five. One sister, as you know.' She gestured towards Vidya, who resisted the sudden urge to make jazz hands.

'Well, I'm twenty-nine. Lawyer. Only child.'

They stared at each other for a moment, then Udeni giggled. Caleb laughed too. 'I guess most people already find out this stuff before they have a baby together.'

Vidya relaxed. Laughing was good. They were getting on. She turned her gaze back to Leo and saw that he was watching them too. His expression was thoughtful. As though sensing her eyes on him, he looked in her direction, then almost immediately tensed and turned away.

Great. He really did think she was unstable and strange. He looked down at his coffee and studied it with exaggerated interest. Vidya felt something shrivel up in her chest. Hope, she realised. She had hoped that if Udeni and Caleb got on okay, she could try again with Leo. But it seemed like she had blown her chances with him completely.

She hadn't realised quite how badly she wanted things to go back to the way they had been. Oh, they might make it to being friends again. That was quite likely, in fact, since they were connected now, through her sister and his best friend. But she wanted more. He made her feel like she was a delicate and beautiful creature. He had looked out for her the whole time they'd been in Waterloo Bay, and he'd cared for her when she needed help. She knew what it was like to kiss him, to feel his body against hers, and she wanted so much more of that.

She took a long look at him, trying to memorise the contours of his face. Then she too pretended to study her food, so that he wouldn't see how close to tears she was.

Leo checked his watch. It had been the most excruciating half hour. He was sitting across from Vidya, but he couldn't work out how to talk to her. They had sat there, quietly drinking coffee and eating soup respectively, contributing to the conversation if Caleb or Udeni needed them to, but otherwise, keeping to their own awkward bubble. Vidya was clearly tired and sad. He should say something. Maybe reassure her that things would be okay. But he just … couldn't.

More than anything, he wished they could just scrub out the last few days, and return to that moment in the stairwell when she'd said she wanted him and he'd let her know that he wanted her just as much. He wasn't good at grand declarations at the best of times, and this was a complicated situation. Vidya was a woman who knew what she wanted. Judging by how intently she was avoiding eye contact, the last thing she wanted right now was him.

He didn't blame her, not really. She'd left his hotel room, because she'd had a shock. But what had he done at the time? He had had a massive sulk, left her behind and driven back. He was her boss for that project, he was supposed to look after his junior colleagues. He was better than that, normally, but he had lost his cool.

Leo sighed but tried to do it quietly. Checking the time, he cleared his throat. 'I … er … I have a meeting in twenty minutes, so I really should be heading off.'

Caleb looked at the clock on the café wall. 'Oh. Right. I need to be there too. I'm so sorry to cut this short,' he said to Udeni.

They both stood up. Caleb said, 'Um … can I have your

number, Udeni? It … would be nice to get to know you properly.' Was he flirting with her?

Spots of colour appeared on Udeni's face. Oh. If Caleb was flirting, then it seemed to be working.

As Caleb and Udeni swapped phone numbers, Leo wondered if he could mend bridges with Vidya in the same way. Maybe. Except he wasn't sure he knew how to flirt. Besides, he already had her phone number, and before he could say anything, it was time to leave. He said polite goodbyes to the sisters and followed Caleb out.

As they were walking back to the office, Caleb said, 'That went well.'

Not for Leo it hadn't. But he was there for Caleb, so he said, 'It did seem to. I don't think you have to worry about the two of you getting along. I think if you'd met under different circumstances, you'd probably have asked her out anyway.'

Caleb nodded, enthusiastically. 'She's so pretty. And dainty. Exactly like I remember … apart from the blonde hair thing, obviously. I can't believe I didn't realise that was a wig.'

Leo tried not to roll his eyes. Alcohol. Low light. Lots of reasons for that. They kept up their brisk pace and turned the corner.

'I think,' Caleb said. 'This might work out.'

'Excellent. I'm happy for you.' He really was.

'We could have a relationship, we're just going about it back to front.'

'Most people meet, get to know each other, date a bit, then have a baby together. You'll start at the baby and move backwards.'

'Yes.' Caleb stopped so suddenly that Leo carried on past him for a few steps before he turned back. 'Leo,' Caleb said, 'when I saw her, I recognised her.'

Leo frowned. 'That's not that surprising …'

'No, I mean I really recognised her. That connection.' Caleb tapped his sternum. 'I felt it here. I think we're meant to be together. Even if we are doing this back to front.' He beamed.

Leo stared at Caleb for a moment, breathing through the feeling that washed over him, which felt an awful lot like envy. 'That's fantastic.'

Caleb punched him lightly on the shoulder and strode into the building.

Leo followed. He had meant it. Caleb being happy really was fantastic. His friend had always lived spontaneously, embracing things as they happened. It wasn't a lifestyle Leo could adhere to, but it seemed to have served Caleb well so far. Maybe this chaotic beginning was the best way for him to find a long-term relationship. If everything worked out, he could end up with a family that just sprang up from one night of fun.

Emotion wriggled inside him. Jealousy? Leo was surprised at himself. Surely, he wasn't jealous of Caleb's current predicament. He thought of Vidya and how inaccessible she'd seemed. Maybe he *was* jealous. He wanted love and stability and, who knew, maybe a family eventually. It had come so effortlessly to Caleb. But then, he jumped in, feet first, without overthinking it.

Leo walked into the building deep in thought. Perhaps it was time for him to take a leaf out of Caleb's book. It was a risk to talk to Vidya about his feelings. But if he didn't, he would hate himself for letting her go. He had to at least try.

He scanned his pass. He would ask her out. It seemed a little old fashioned, considering everything that had happened, but it was as good a way as any.

Things had gone wrong the first time because of an unfortunate mix-up. But what if … Suddenly the thing that had been nagging at the back of his mind all day fell into place. Vidya's description that she had been given of Udeni's one-night stand: *Tall, funny, sexy and a good dancer. All those things apply to you too.*

She had thought he was sexy. Leo looked down at his feet. Huh. A smile rose from somewhere in his chest and made it to his eyes. Maybe it wasn't such a risk after all.

When the men left, Udeni let out a long breath and slumped in her seat. Her earlier brightness dimmed.

'You okay?' Vidya was worried again. Had all that relaxed happiness been an act?

Udeni nodded. 'Let me just go to the loo.'

When she came back Vidya said, 'So. That went well, I thought.'

'It did,' said Udeni. 'I can't believe I forgot him. I mean, how could I forget a guy who looks like that?' She touched her tummy. 'At least the baby will be beautiful.'

'I'm glad it all worked out.' The moment Vidya said it, she felt a rush of relief. It felt like a knot had been untied. 'I'm really not built for keeping secrets,' she said.

Udeni laughed. 'I know. You were right though, and I'm glad I let you persuade me to meet him. He seems really excited at the idea of being a dad.'

'I told you, he has … some hangups to do with fathers,' said Vidya. 'But I think they'll result in him trying really hard, not anything bad.'

'And what about you?' Udeni tipped her head to the side and gave her a concerned look. 'I noticed you and Leo didn't talk to each other.'

'Ah. Well, yes. That's awkward.'

'You should at least try to talk to him. Go for a drink or something? Clear the air.'

'Maybe.' Vidya gathered her stuff. 'I'd better get back to work. I've been away too long. I'll have to stay late to catch up.'

'Okay. We won't expect you home until late then. Text me when you leave.'

'Will do.' She gave her sister a little hug and practically ran back to the office.

Back at her desk, Vidya tried to focus, but in her mind's eye she kept seeing Leo sitting stiff and uncomfortable across from her. What could she do about him?

When she had spoken to him earlier and cleared up the

misunderstanding, she had got the impression that he was very relieved her reaction had been to his tattoo, and it wasn't anything to do with him. But it seemed that this wasn't enough. Leo was still clearly uncomfortable around her. She understood. He had opened up to her and she'd hurt him. He was reluctant to do it again.

She could ask Leo out, but she would have to persuade him to take another risk. What on earth could she do to show him that he could trust her?

Chapter 27

It was nearing time to go home and Vidya was nowhere near finished. All the work she had been doing on the Waterloo Bay case meant that all her other projects had backed up. She stifled a yawn and took another sip of coffee.

On her phone, she opened her messaging app and wrote to Angie: *Definitely going to have to work late tonight. Udeni knows. You'll be home as normal, right? She's had a big day.*

Angie replied: *Yes. Don't worry about Udeni, she'll be fine. She's more with it than you give her credit for.*

Vidya craned her neck to see Angie's desk, which was at the other side of the open-plan office. She gave her friend a thumbs-up, which was rewarded with a grin.

Vidya put her phone facedown and looked at her work again, but she still couldn't concentrate. Angie was right about Udeni. She had been so well composed today, not at all like the devil-may-care girl she normally was. If she carried on in this vein, this whole thing wouldn't be a disaster. Her parents would still try and blame her for Udeni's 'trouble' though. That was just something she'd have to deal with when the time came.

With a sigh, she scrolled to the bottom of the spreadsheet that she was pulling data from.

Her phone buzzed. She turned it over to see a message from Angie. The preview said, *Heads up! Incoming!*

Vidya's head shot up to look at the door, half expecting to see her parents. It was Leo, striding towards her with his expression set. Uh-oh. She glanced at the document open on her screen. As he neared, she said, 'I'm working on it. I'll get it to you tonight, I promise.'

A frown flickered across his brow, then cleared. 'That's good,' he said. He placed a hand on her desk and leaned down. 'Can I talk to you for a moment?'

She looked up at him, surprised. He was very close. Nothing inappropriate for an office discussion, but for Leo … close. She could smell his aftershave and a lingering hint of coffee. What was this about? Work? Or Udeni and Caleb? 'Er … sure,' she said.

He glanced about the office. A few people were watching them. Past his shoulder, she could see Angie craning her neck from her seat, trying to get a better look.

Vidya pushed her chair back. 'We can use the meeting room.'

The meeting room had a small table and four chairs. It was really just a partitioned-off area with glass walls. If you spoke in a normal tone of voice, anyone sitting outside could hear everything, but it gave the illusion of privacy.

She led the way. Tension radiated from Leo. She could feel her own nerves prickling between her shoulder blades. Once inside the little room, she said, 'Is this about work?'

He shut the door and shook his head.

So, Udeni and Caleb then. She put her hands on the back of one of the chairs and braced herself for whatever surprise was to come.

Leo straightened his suit jacket. 'It's … er … I think we should talk. About … about us.'

'Here?' she said. 'Now?' Because that was the stupidest idea she had ever heard.

'No. Obviously not now.' He glanced at the activity outside the

242

glass partition. 'I was thinking after work. Maybe over dinner.'

Oh. She relaxed a little. Oh. *Oh.* She searched his face. His eyes were worried and pleading. She understood what he was trying to say. He was asking her out, in a very Leo sort of way. 'That would be nice,' she said. 'I think that's a good idea.'

Some of the tension left his shoulders and face. 'Great. Is … tonight too soon?'

'I have to work late tonight,' she said.

She saw the disappointment before his neutral expression set in. 'I'll be done by about seven though, I think.' Maybe they could meet for a drink.

Leo brightened. 'How about I cook dinner? That way, you can turn up when you've finished.' He pulled out his phone. 'Here. Let me send you my address.' His thumbs tapped furiously and then her phone buzzed in her hand.

'That's great.' She had intended to play it cool but she couldn't stop the grin that spread on her face. Leo's eyes lit up.

'I'll see you later then.' He turned and put his hand on the door handle. She made to follow him.

He turned around, hand still on the door handle. 'Vidya, just to be clear. This is a date.'

'I know,' she said. 'And I'm pleased to accept.'

He gave her a proper smile. For a moment, nothing else existed, just this handsome man and his rare, bright smile. Then his face resumed its normal guarded expression and he said, 'I'll see you later then.'

Her brain scrambled to adjust to the haze of happiness. She followed him out, not entirely sure how to act now. Leo merely gave her a polite nod and left the office. He seemed entirely nonchalant, as though he hadn't just reopened a door that she'd thought was closed forever.

As Vidya reached her desk and sat back down, her phone buzzed in her hand. It was Angie: *What did he want? What's going on??*

Vidya bit her lip to stop grinning and typed back: *Don't wait up for me tonight. I have a date.*

She heard the squeal from across the office. She didn't look up. Her phone buzzed again. Angie had sent her a string of emojis that were entirely inappropriate for work. She wrote back: *Got to get my head down and get this done. I can't leave until I've finished it.*

Angie: *Won't Leo cut you some slack if you're late with reports? After all, he knows what you're going to do instead.*

It only took a moment's consideration to know that he wouldn't be impressed at all.

Vidya: *No. He won't. I wouldn't be either. I've spent enough time out of the office today. Now shut up so I can focus.*

Angie sent her more suggestive emojis.

It was past seven when Vidya finished her work. She emailed off the documents, then messaged Leo to say she was leaving the office. She also sent a message to Udeni, out of habit.

Udeni's response was predictable. *Don't do anything I wouldn't do. And remember that condoms aren't always 100%!*

Which was a little optimistic, Vidya thought.

Leo's reply was more understated: *I will have dinner ready for you. See you in about 30 minutes.*

It took slightly longer than thirty minutes because she wasn't exactly sure where she was going, and she had to stop on the way to buy a bottle of wine. Leo lived in a block of flats. She buzzed up and Leo's voice said, 'Hi. Come up. I'm on floor six.'

Soon, Vidya was standing outside a nondescript door. She knocked and he let her in. He had changed out of his suit into jeans and a Henley shirt with the sleeves pushed up to his elbows. It hugged his shoulders in interesting ways. She tried not to stare at his forearms.

Leo took her coat and hung it up on the rack. The apartment was small and tidy. They were in a hallway that had coat hooks, a bicycle leaning against a wall and a small table with keys on it.

Three doors led off the hallway. Two were open, and she could see they led to a bedroom and a living room. The other must be the bathroom, and she asked if she could use it.

Once she'd washed her hands, Vidya patted her face with her damp hands and wondered if there was anything at all she could do to look less tired. Short of getting some sleep, she had no other answers. She gave herself a reassuring smile and went out.

In the living room, Leo was setting two places at a table with two chairs on either side. There was barely enough space for the table, chairs and a sofa. One side of the room was taken up by a kitchen. The opposite wall was a huge glass window through which she could see the lights of the city. There was something missing, but she couldn't put her finger on what.

Leo straightened up and looked tense. He had a tea towel slung over his shoulder. She breathed in and something smelled delicious. Her stomach growled.

Mortified, she said, 'I'm sorry.' She suddenly realised that she was starving.

This seemed to spur Leo into action. 'Sit down,' he said. 'Let's eat.'

While Vidya sat, he dished up two plates and brought them over. 'It's tuna pasta bake.'

'That sounds lovely,' she said. 'I'm so hungry.'

'Tuck in.' He picked up an open wine bottle and poured her a glass, which she gladly accepted.

The pasta bake was delicious. 'Mmm,' she said after a few minutes. 'This is good. You can cook.'

A brief smile. 'My grandmother didn't raise slackers,' he said. 'We all had to take turns cooking.'

'I am very grateful,' she said. 'I was too tense to eat much of my soup at the café, and this tastes like the best meal I've ever had.'

'Well, it has been a busy and, frankly, a roller coaster of a day,' he said.

'Worked out okay in the end though. Thankfully.'

Leo swirled the wine in his glass. 'Yes. Caleb seems very happy. Which I wasn't expecting, if I'm honest.'

'No, me neither. Udeni has gone from being completely against his involvement to okay with it. I was expecting things to be more tense than they were.' Vidya paused, fork suspended over her meal. 'I think … I think they might actually like each other. For real. Not just in a drunken fumble kind of way.'

'I agree,' Leo said, quietly.

Vidya resumed eating. As she finished her meal, she noticed that Leo was mostly pushing his food around the plate.

When she was done, he took the plates away and tidied up.

'Can I help?' she asked.

It didn't take them long to load the dishwasher and wipe down the surfaces. They chatted while they did it, discussing work and the meeting at the coffee shop earlier. Vidya was amazed at the gentle domesticity of it. She knew him well enough already to feel comfortable around him. The only thing that made things awkward was her overthinking things. And his overthinking things. They both worried too much. She had a sudden vision of how their future together would be. They were careful, methodical people. He would never push her to do anything she didn't want to do, and she had no doubt that he would support her in whatever she did. Clearly, she would never have to tidy up after him or rescue him from his own bad decisions. It would be a partnership. Wasn't that what she'd always wanted?

Vidya watched him fold the leaves on the table and put it away. Then there was the added bonus that he looked so buttoned up all the time and she got to see him like this. Dressed in jeans and a Henley that suited him so much better. Relaxed enough to smile unguardedly. Her own private Leo. She could get used to this.

Taking a gulp of wine, she said, 'So …'

'So.' He took her hand. 'I guess we should talk about us.'

'Yes. We should.'

'Well … I like you. A lot. You know that already. I … want this to go well.'

Vidya smiled. 'I want this to go well too.'

'That's good to know.' Leo looked up, meeting her eyes for the first time and her heart went wild. He ran his thumb over her knuckles and a dart of heat ran right through her. She put down her glass.

Leo stepped closer. A quick tug on her hand brought her close so that she had to put her free hand on his chest to steady herself. She looked up at him. He smiled his lovely, precious smile, and kissed her.

It was a gentle kiss that slowly unwound her. She slipped her arms around his neck. He wrapped an arm around her waist and pulled her snug against him. His other hand cradled the back of her neck. The kiss deepened gradually. When they finally moved apart, she felt light, like she'd been spun around in a warm cocoon.

'See,' she said. 'No reason for nerves at all.'

A smile touched the corners of his mouth. 'I dunno. The last time I took my shirt off, you looked like you were going to throw up.'

She laughed and laid her head against his chest. 'I'm really sorry.'

'It's okay. Now I know why, it's fine.'

She looked up at him again. 'So, are you going to take your shirt off?'

Leo walked her backwards out of the room and into the bedroom. 'And hopefully, you will do the same.'

'We'll see,' she said, still smiling.

He let her go and, in one swift movement, pulled his Henley off. Vidya's mouth went dry. He quickly folded the top and put it on a clothes rack. She reached up and touched the tattoo that had caused so much trouble. Her touch sent a tremor through him.

'Well,' he said, 'you're still here. We're doing better already this time.'

247

She laughed and took off her jumper. She was about to throw it into a corner when she remembered that Leo didn't really like mess, so she folded it and put it on the clothes rack too, next to his top.

'Oh my God, I think I love you.'

Vidya turned to look at him. He looked a little surprised too, as though he hadn't intended to say that out loud.

'Why?' she said. 'Because I folded my jumper?'

He gave a small nod.

'But you don't like it when things are all over the place. Has no one else done that for you?'

Leo sighed. 'I know I'm weird, Vidya. I'm uptight and awkward and strange. There aren't many people who look past that.'

He said it lightly, but she could see the weight in his eyes. He had been told this by someone he cared about. The idea that anyone could do that to him made her angry.

'Did your parents tell you that?' How could someone who was supposed to love him damage him so much? She put her hands on his shoulders. 'Leo, you *are* uptight and awkward and strange. But I'm not looking past that. I'm looking at it. It's part of who you are and I like you. All of you. Including your quirks.'

His eyes studied her face. She gave him what she hoped was a reassuring smile. He grabbed her waist and pulled her to him to kiss her. This kiss was nothing like before. It was all ferocity and need. Vidya threw her arms around his neck and kissed him back.

This time she was definitely not running away.

When Vidya woke up, it took a moment to remember where she was. Leo was asleep next to her, his breathing deep and even. His hand rested on her hip. She cautiously sat up. What time was it?

A small digital alarm clock glowed on the bedside cabinet on Leo's side. She leaned across to see. It was nearly seven a.m.

'Shit.'

Leo made a quizzical 'mmmpf' sound.

'I should go home,' she said. 'I promised Udeni I'd go to the community centre with her to look at mum-to-be classes.' Vidya slipped out of bed and started looking for her clothes.

Leo turned the bedside light on. She froze, realising that now he could see her. He pulled a T-shirt from under his pillow and passed it to her.

'Thanks.' She pulled it on. It was better than scrabbling around naked. The good thing about putting things neatly on the clothes rack was they were much easier to find in the morning.

'I'll order you a cab.' Leo got out of bed and put on a pair of pyjama bottoms.

'Thank you.'

She finished getting dressed, while he sat on the bed and typed on his phone. He looked up. 'It'll be about fifteen minutes.'

His hair was messed up, from where she'd run her hands through it. He was shirtless and barefoot, his pyjamas sitting low on his hips. He looked absolutely delectable. Vidya smiled.

'What?' he said.

'Nothing. It's just that you look … messy.'

Leo put his glasses on and looked down at himself. 'Oh.'

She went to him and put her hand on his bare chest. 'I like it. I feel like there aren't many people who get to see you like this.'

He picked her hand off his chest, brought it to his mouth and kissed the backs of her fingers. 'Hardly anyone, in fact,' he said, pulling her closer.

'Well, I'm honoured.'

He kissed the tip of her nose. 'We should do this again sometime.'

Vidya giggled and nuzzled into him. 'We should.'

'How about tomorrow?'

'You mean, today?'

He looked at the clock. 'Oh, yes. This afternoon maybe?'

She chewed her lower lip. She wanted to, really she did. But she couldn't just disappear like that. 'I want to …' she said. 'But …'

'You need to spend some time with your sister,' he said. 'I understand. It was a pretty big day for her yesterday.'

She looked up and rested her chin on his chest. 'I'm sorry, Leo.'

'It's okay.' He moved a strand of her hair away from her face and tucked it behind her ear. 'I should probably see how Caleb is coping too.'

She hugged him tight, and he hugged her back and held her for a long moment. Then he said, 'I'd better put more clothes on so that I can walk you down to the taxi.'

She nodded and let him go. It was cold now that his warmth had gone. So, she went and found her coat and put that on too.

A sudden thought occurred. 'About work,' she said.

Leo was putting on his shoes. His head shot up. 'Can we keep this a secret? At least for a bit. I don't think anyone needs to know.' The habitual frown, which had disappeared for a few hours, returned and Vidya felt sad for being the one to put it there.

'It's not that I'm ashamed of us or anything. But I dated someone at work before,' he said. 'It all went badly wrong and I don't want—'

'Us,' said Vidya, smiling. 'So, there's definitely an us then?'

'Of course.' Leo looked surprised. 'Did you think there possibly wouldn't be? What do you take me for?'

Vidya laughed. 'I'll take you as often as I can have you.'

She was rewarded with one of his smiles. Whatever he was going to say next was forestalled by the phone buzzing. 'That'll be the taxi,' he said.

He opened the door and they walked hand in hand out of the flat.

Chapter 28

Vidya put her elbows on the dining table and tried to zone out. Her mother was still talking at top speed. To be fair, most of it was aimed at Udeni now, who was arguing back. Vidya sighed. This was meant to have been a nice evening. Leo was going to take her out to dinner to celebrate being together for a month. Her parents had turned up before she'd even had a chance to get ready. So here she was, wearing a nice dress, but with hair that she hadn't even had a chance to brush properly. Thankfully, she had managed to text him that her parents had arrived. Hopefully, he wasn't too disappointed their date was cancelled.

Her mother turned back to her. 'I can't believe that you—'

'I told you,' said Udeni. 'It had nothing to do with her. It was my mistake. She's already told me off for it, and we've moved past it.'

'But how can you ruin your life like this!'

'My life isn't ruined. Please. It's not the 1950s anymore. Or the 1990s. Women can have children and still have careers. I work from home half the time anyway, and I'll fit it around childcare.'

'You'll spend your entire salary on childcare and then what will you live on?'

'Hang on,' said Vidya, wearily. 'She has a place to live already.

251

And I'm here to babysit sometimes. Anyway, there's no point crying over something we can't change, is there?' She put an arm around her sister's shoulders. 'How about we show her some support instead?'

'But to raise a child. Without a father—'

'I didn't say that,' said Udeni. 'I said I wanted to raise the baby myself. The father … he'll be around.'

'Are you going to get married?' This was from their father, who had been frowning the whole time.

'God, no. We're not together. But he wants to be there for the baby.'

'He's a good guy,' said Vidya.

'Can't be that good.' Her father glowered.

'Oh, come on,' said Vidya. 'He doesn't have to marry her. They aren't even together … anymore. But he'll be there for them. People do that, you know.'

'The embarrassment!' said Amma.

Udeni stood up suddenly and walked off.

Everyone looked at each other.

'Where is she going?' said Amma.

Vidya had no idea. So far, today, she had tried very hard to resist the urge to jump in and protect her sister, but now might be the time to help. 'Look,' she said. 'I know it's not what you wanted for her. You always say that life is what happens while you're making other plans. So … this has happened. Maybe we should make the best of it. You've always wanted grandchildren. Haven't you?'

'Yes, but …' Her mother sighed. 'It's hard, bringing up a baby. It was hard enough for us and there were two of us. How is she going to manage?'

'I'm here for her. Caleb – that's the baby's father – will be too. So will Angie. And Udeni has you. She's not alone. There's never a good time to have a baby, is there? Maybe this is as bad a time as any.'

Both parents stared at Vidya. They weren't arguing with her … so … that was a good thing.

'You've met him? This Caleb?' her father asked, cautiously.

'Yes. I like him. He's a good guy.'

'Then why doesn't Udeni want to marry him?' Her mother shook her head.

'Because she doesn't love him and he doesn't love her. They're more like … friends.'

Before her parents could say anything more, Udeni came back and slapped something on the table. It was the ultrasound photo. She slid it across to Amma, who picked it up.

For a moment, no one spoke. Both parents stared at the grainy black-and-white image.

'Your grandchild is due in October.' Udeni had remained standing. She had her arms crossed over her chest. Vidya could see the tension in her fingers as she gripped her elbows.

This was a clever ploy. A pregnancy was difficult, but a baby … a baby was harder to be angry about. From the stunned silence, and the way her parents were both staring at the image, it seemed to be working. Vidya was impressed.

The doorbell rang, making everyone jump.

'I'll get it,' Udeni said.

Who could that be?

'Leo,' said Udeni. 'Come in.'

Oh, God. Leo hadn't got her message in time. Vidya's blood ran cold. She wanted to introduce him to her parents, but not yet. Oh, shit. Oh no, no, no. Vidya turned around to see Leo step in. He was still in his work suit with a coat over it. He looked, like he always did, neat and handsome. Standing next to Udeni, here in the small living room, he seemed very tall. His eyes went to her face, a small smile flashed at the corner of his mouth.

Now both parents were staring at him instead. 'Who is this?' said Thatha.

Vidya's mind went blank.

Leo took a step forward. 'I'm Leo,' he said.

She had been hoping for a bit more time, but … oh, well. She stood up. 'Erm. Leo, meet my parents. Amma and Thatha, meet Leo. He's my boyfriend.'

Both parents turned to stare at her.

'I've heard a lot about you,' said Leo.

'I wish we could say the same about you,' said Amma.

As Thatha shook hands with Leo, Amma widened her eyes at her.

'Well, it hasn't been very long,' Vidya said.

Leo nodded. 'Only about a month. But we've known each other for longer. We work together.'

'Oh. You're a lawyer?' said Amma.

'One of the solicitors at the firm, yes.'

'Aaah.'

Udeni, who had retreated to stand behind their parents, rolled her eyes at the note of approval. Perhaps they should have led with Caleb being a lawyer. That might have helped.

'So, tell us about yourself, Leo,' said Amma. 'Sit down, sit down. Vidya, make the boy a cup of tea.'

'Actually,' Leo said. 'I was meant to be taking Vidya out to dinner tonight …' He looked at her, his eyes dancing. 'I guess since your parents are here …'

'Oh, you should go out,' said Udeni. 'I bet you've made a reservation somewhere nice and everything, knowing you.' She mouthed *run* to Vidya.

Leo pulled out his phone. 'I can cancel—'

'Oh. No, no. You should go,' said Amma. 'Don't mind us.'

Vidya looked at Udeni again, who mouthed, *Go!*

Fine. 'Okay. If you're sure. Just … let me brush my hair.' Vidya practically ran to her room and dragged a brush through her hair so that she could pull it into a hasty ponytail. Through the open door, she could hear Leo being quizzed by her parents. His answers were calm and measured. No charm offensive, no trying to impress. He was coming across as the serious and solemn person that he was. Her parents were going to love him. She smiled at herself in the mirror. He was everything she had never known she'd wanted.

When Vidya came back into the living room, the atmosphere was more relaxed. Leo was answering a question about his family by telling them about his sisters. When he saw her, he stood. His gaze travelled from her feet to her face and his eyes lit up. She felt a little flush of pleasure.

'I'm sorry to dash off like this,' Vidya said. She felt terrible, but she wasn't going to apologise for having her own life. Not anymore.

Both parents and Udeni said, 'Go, go.'

'It was lovely to meet you,' Leo said, politely. 'I'm sorry to leave so soon.'

'You must come round for lunch one weekend,' Amma said.

'I'd like that.' Leo's voice was entirely sincere.

'We will organise a date with Vidya.'

'Okay.' He held out his hand to her. 'Shall we?'

To her surprise, from behind their parents, Udeni gave Leo a wink and a thumbs-up.

'Oh,' said Leo. 'I nearly forgot.' He dug into the pocket of his coat. 'I was buying some stuff for my sister and she suggested I get this for you, Udeni.' He pulled out a small parcel wrapped in pastel-green-and-yellow paper. 'I know it's early, but …' He passed it to Udeni.

It seemed that Udeni had not been expecting this. Vidya glanced at him quizzically. He squeezed her hand.

Udeni ripped open the parcel and pulled out a tiny yellow-and-cream onesie. She let out a shaky breath. When she laid the onesie on the table, both parents stared at it, eyes wide. Udeni looked up, her eyes sparkling with tears. 'Aw. It's perfect. Thanks, Leo.'

'You're welcome,' he said.

He gave Vidya's hand a little tug, but she was too busy watching her parents. Amma was stroking the onesie with wonder. Thatha's eyes had filled with tears. If they were only seeing a pregnancy before. They were definitely seeing a baby now.

As they walked towards the underground, Vidya said, 'Did you not get my message?'

'I did,' said Leo. 'But I also got this.' He pulled out his phone and showed her the screen. It was a WhatsApp message forwarded from Caleb. From Udeni.

Caleb, pls forward on to Leo: Leo! Please come save Vidya. My parents have descended without warning and are making a fuss. I told V I would deal with them without hiding behind her and I will. I need you to come and take her away. Please. Udeni

'Oh.' Vidya didn't know what to make of that. Her baby sister had definitely grown up.

'Quite impressive, your sister,' Leo said.

She was just beginning to realise that this was true. All these years she'd been so busy viewing everything Udeni said or did through the lens of her being irresponsible, that she hadn't noticed how creative and brave Udeni was. Leo seemed to see things a lot more clearly than she did.

'That onesie was a great idea,' Vidya said.

'That was Caleb's suggestion,' Leo said. 'He told his mum last weekend and she's wild with joy about being a grandma. Keeps trying to buy things for the baby. He thought something like that would be a good way to move the focus on to the future.'

'And you just … came to meet my parents, just like that.' This was the part that baffled her the most. Surely, meeting a girlfriend's parents was a terrifying prospect. Especially for someone who thought people didn't warm to him easily. 'Weren't you nervous?'

'Terrified,' he said, a little bashfully. 'But they love you. And I love you. We have a lot in common. I figured the sooner we worked that out, the better.'

Vidya stopped walking. Leo stopped too, and turned to see why.

'You love me?' she said.

He gave her a patient look. 'I thought that was obvious.' When she didn't respond, he said, 'It's okay. You don't have to say it back. Just because I know doesn't mean—'

She threw her arms around his neck. 'I think,' she said. 'I think I love you too.'

He beamed at her and kissed her. When they pulled apart, he looked around above their heads.

'What?'

'I was just checking that there wasn't a seagull waiting to interrupt.'

Vidya laughed. 'Goddammit, Charlie,' she muttered against his cheek.

'We really should get to the restaurant,' he said, regretfully.

Hand in hand, they walked down the steps to the underground station. She was Vidya, the sensible one, who didn't take risks and didn't have adventures, but lived her life in her sensible groove. Now she found someone who was willing to be sensible with her … and she couldn't imagine anything better.

The End

A Letter from Jeevani Charika

Thank you so much for choosing to read HOW CAN I RESIST YOU? I hope you enjoyed it! If you did and would like to be the first to know about my new releases, sign up to my mailing list. You get a bonus 'six months(ish) later' scene as a thank you for signing up!

Sign up for my mailing list at https://rhodabaxter.com/jc-bonus/

My second favourite hobby (after reading) is watching Korean dramas. Leo was inspired by all of the buttoned-up but desperately romantic lawyers I've seen in K-dramas – especially Attorney Do in *Shooting Stars* and Attorney Kwon in *Touch Your Heart*; in my head, he looks a tiny bit like Lee Dong Wook. If you know, you know.

A long time ago, when I worked for the University of Hull, I used to spend the odd day in the Scarborough campus. It was a strange thrill to work in an office when the view outside (and the sound of the gulls) made you feel like you should be on holiday. I tried to capture some of that feeling in the book.

I hope you loved HOW CAN I RESIST YOU? and if you did I would be so grateful if you would leave a review. I always love to hear what readers thought, and it helps new readers discover my books too.

Thanks,
Jeevani

Knowing Me Knowing You

Five years ago, Alex met the man of her dreams on New Year's Eve – but he never called. Years later, she's given up on men and accepted that 'New Year's Eve Guy' will always be the one who got away.

Until the day he turns up at her office – a management consultant tasked with 'streamlining' the company. New Year's Eve Guy – Gihan – might shut down Alex's team!

As she gets to know the real Gihan, will sparks continue to fly – or will Alex have to accept that the man she knew as New Year's Eve Guy was never real to start with?

Picture Perfect

Niro is a photographer who's lost the joy of taking photos. Burned by a bad break-up, she's in desperate need of inspiration.

Vimal is determined to win back his ex-girlfriend. When he hears she's bringing her new boyfriend on a group holiday, he impulsively declares that he's bringing a plus one too.

Their mutual friends have the perfect solution: Niro can pretend to be Vimal's new girlfriend and join the holiday. Imagine the incredible photographs she could take in the Swiss alps …

She's not thinking about love. He's thinking about someone else. Can they fake a picture-perfect relationship – or will real feelings get in the way?

Don't miss this funny and uplifting fake-dating romance for fans of *The Kiss Quotient* and *The Love Hypothesis*!

Playing for Love

When Sam's not working on her fledgling business, she spends her time secretly video-gaming. Her crush is famous gamer Blaze, and she's thrilled when she's teamed up with him in a virtual tournament.

But what Sam doesn't know is that Blaze is the alter ego of Luke, her shy colleague – and he has a secret crush too.

Luke has a crush on Sam.

Sam has a crush on Blaze.

How will this game of love play out?

A fun, feel-good romance for fans of *You've Got Mail*, Helen Hoang, Jasmine Guillory and Lindsey Kelk!

Acknowledgements

There are so many people to thank. If I forget someone, blame menopause brain.

A huge thank you to awesome aunties Jill and Linda, who helped me out with descriptions of hotels in holiday towns and let me use their names for the two ladies staying at the hotel. Thanks for all the other stuff too, of course!

Thank you, Kate, Alison, Imogen, Sheila, Ruth and Janet – the magnificent ladies of the Naughty Kitchen, who keep me going when I want to give up. They also helped me find a name for Leo that wasn't Oberon.

Thanks especially to my husband and kids for putting up with my wittering on about seagulls and chips and generally being a bit vague about real life.

In October, the local novelists in my area run a book and book-related things auction to raise money for the local Foodbank. Thank you to Diane Askew, who won the chance to have her name in the book. I gave her name to a senior partner at the law firm because I've met her and I could totally see her running the place.

Thanks, as always, to my agent and to the team at HQ for letting me write a book with a convoluted set-up (again).

Most of all, thank you, my reader, for buying my books (or borrowing them from the library). I couldn't keep doing this without you.

Dear Reader,

We hope you enjoyed reading this book. If you did, we'd be so appreciative if you left a review. It really helps us and the author to bring more books like this to you.

Here at HQ Digital we are dedicated to publishing fiction that will keep you turning the pages into the early hours. Don't want to miss a thing? To find out more about our books, promotions, discover exclusive content and enter competitions you can keep in touch in the following ways:

JOIN OUR COMMUNITY:

Sign up to our new email newsletter: http://smarturl.it/SignUpHQ

Read our new blog www.hqstories.co.uk

𝕏: https://twitter.com/HQStories

: www.facebook.com/HQStories

BUDDING WRITER?

We're also looking for authors to join the HQ Digital family! Find out more here:

https://www.hqstories.co.uk/want-to-write-for-us/

Thanks for reading, from the HQ Digital team